BIRD OF PARADISE

C J Halton

Copyright © 2024 C J Halton

All rights reserved

The characters and events portrayed in this book are fictitious. Any similarity to real persons, living or dead, is coincidental and not intended by the author.

No part of this book may be reproduced, or stored in a retrieval system, or transmitted in any form or by any means, electronic, mechanical, photocopying, recording, or otherwise, without express written permission of the publisher.

ISBN-13: 9798336872965
ISBN-10: 1477123456

Cover design by: Art Painter
Library of Congress Control Number: 2018675309
Printed in the United States of America

For Mouse

Whatever is destined not to happen will not happen, try as you may. Whatever is destined to happen will happen, do what you may to prevent it. This is certain. The best course, therefore, is to remain silent.

RAMANA MAHARSHI

CONTENTS

Title Page
Copyright
Dedication
Epigraph
Birds 1
War 26
Mother 60
Chemistry 98
Restaurant 141
Cocaine 176
Appetite 214
Video 259
Car 299
Son 368

Birds

There were people in the village who found it odd when Mary Tierney called her daughter Marie. It was only a step away from calling her Mary, perhaps not even a full step.

'Oh here she is, *Mrs I-like-myself-who-do-you-like*?'

That's what Bet Cooper used to say when she caught sight of her coming down the lane pushing her pram; Bet Cooper, who liked herself better than anyone she'd ever known, with her tattered ermine coat and her glossy red lips and her heaving trunk, chock-full of bacon and eggs and cream slices.

Marie's mother was born of farming stock deep in the Lancashire countryside just after the First World War, and from the start Marie was taken back to the little hamlet of Eccleston enough that she knew it as well as her own back yard. Her mother remained always devoted to the place, homesick for it, pining openly for its ramshackle beauty, for the strange and rigid conformity it imposed.

Mary Tierney never had any desire to leave

that pretty village, but marriage forced her hand. She moved out in the autumn of 1945 and for as long as she lived, she never wanted anything but the familiar call of chaffinches from the garden and the tiny red-brick school-house and the cobbled high-street with its shop-fronts proffering tender bloodied flanks and Eccles cakes and silken hosiery.

Marie knew this.

She knew that as a child her mother had marched into the corner shop and asked, 'Have you got any broken biscuits?' and when the shopkeeper said, 'Yes, I think I do,' her mother - in her broad Lancashire accent - shouted, 'Well you'd better go and fix them,' and whooping in delight had streaked out into the road, her friends trailing behind her, their laughter shaking the birds from the trees.

One of Marie's earliest memories was of being pulled on a sled through soft cotton-like snow on the country lanes beneath cobalt skies and a canopy of black oaks.

She could still smell the twinkling wet freshness of diaphanous mornings in the fields, hear the velvet scud of her grandfather's voice along the walls of his crumbling cottage. It was all there, in the chaotic web of synapses linking heart and mind and senses, an indelible imprint running through her like the words in a stick of rock.

She was older now than her mother had been when she died and she woke every morning with the dull throb of life pressing at her abdomen. Marie found it hard to believe it was 2020. To her mind, this didn't even sound real - it sounded like something from a dystopian novel set in the future - and it made her feel like something had gone wrong somewhere, as though time had gone haywire and leapt ahead of itself.

She never rose quickly because she first had to square with herself the delicate grief of being alive another day, knowing what she knew; that she was old and alone, that nobody looked on her lovingly, that her skin no longer held to her bones like a glaze but hung loosely in spite of her thinness, in spite of her one meal a day and her long walks without destination.

She turned from her side on to her back and looked up. The morning was opaque and muted against the ceiling.

'Come on,' she said. 'Let's go.'

It seemed to her that if she spoke the words aloud they might be truer, so every morning she spoke them and in that way she split herself in two so she wasn't waking and rising and stretching alone.

Breakfast was a cigarette and a black coffee. It was an early ritual because she hadn't been able to sleep more than four or five hours for many years now.

She'd sit in the old wooden chair at her tiny kitchen table and unfurl her hair until it was halfway down her back, then comb it out with a cigarette in one hand and the brush in the other, her head bent slightly to one side, her eyes unfocused and staring, not at the fridge but beyond that to the edge of the world.

Sometimes he was there from the moment consciousness overtook her and other times she didn't think of him until she was out on the street with the wind blowing her silk scarf up over her mouth and across her eyes like a blind upon a screen. On those days, she'd berate herself for taking so long. A whole hour and she hadn't even considered him.

Unconscionable.

What's wrong with you? she'd think to herself, a shot of adrenaline radiating out through her chest.

On days like those she felt undone from that moment on, so she wouldn't venture beyond the near streets or let herself be drawn into conversation with one of the women in the post office. The last thing she'd do was walk into a coffee-shop or take a bus into town.

On days like those, she had to go home and wait and if the waiting grew too long she might have to pour herself a brandy and turn on the television.

Marie had once been beautiful – or at least striking – so had known what it was to draw surreptitious glances from strangers in the park and in the aisles of the supermarket. When the time came it surprised her that the fading of her looks should bother her as much as it did, or perhaps it'd be truer to say she wasn't so much surprised as ashamed, having never thought of herself as one of *those* women, but all that was behind her now.

*

Slowly she stood up and rested her hands upon the frosted pink surface of her little kitchen table, no longer remembering how lurid a pink it had once been, before a thousand sunny days had bleached away its brilliance. She only remembered Jamie wincing the day she brought it home all those summers ago, that he'd turned up to breakfast in his sunglasses the next morning.

She arrived at the surgery before nine - though her appointment wasn't for another twenty minutes - sat down in a scooped plastic chair and leafed through *The National Geographic*. Arid canyons and sub-Saharan tribes had little impact on her. Something about the far away-ness of those things was comforting, like the memory of clamping herself to her father's leg as a child.

She turned to a page with an advert for a Maltese holiday. The girl in the picture, the one sitting on a smiling man's shoulders, reminded her of a friend she'd once had, back when she was very young. This friend's name was Jean and she was one of six girls who lived in the house at the end of the street.

Jean was a boisterous child with raucous red hair that buzzed about her ears and hung over her eyes like a Hebridean bull's. She invariably had ketchup down her dress or mud on her chin and was forever poring over the mysteries of adulthood - the secret incantations that went on behind bedroom doors under a breathy chorus of moans - or plotting things, like how to catch a butterfly.

'Right, you stand there,' she'd say. 'Stand there and shut up and throw your jumper over it when I say.'

Jean's mother was sick. That's all Marie knew about it in the beginning because nobody ever saw her. She wanted to ask Jean what was wrong with her because secret mothers that never appeared from their houses were creatures of intense fascination to a child like Marie. She'd wanted to ask ever since she heard her mother and Mrs Dolan at the kitchen table parsing the facts over tea and shortbread.

'Well as far as I know, she hasn't seen the light of day for months,' her mother said. 'And that husband of hers is useless. I asked him how she was outside the butcher's the other week and he as good as told me to mind my own business.'

'Oh, he's a funny fella,' Mrs Dolan replied. 'And let's face it, it's him that's done her in. Six babies in nine years? It's a wonder she can stand up.'

'Well he wants a lad, doesn't he. I mean, fancy having six girls. She must be tearing her hair out. He'll be at her day and night, I tell you. When she's not cooking dinners and washing nappies she'll be flat on her back under him.'

'And he's nothing to look at, let's face it,' said Mrs Dolan.

'Well,' said Mary Tierney, 'neither's she.'

The two women laughed and Marie remained stock-still behind the door, hanging on their every word. She listened as they struck matches to light their cigarettes, her head resting against the parlour wall.

'No, but seriously,' said Mrs Dolan, 'do you think she's alright?'

'Listen, the only reason I haven't been over there myself is because the girls are running around the streets the same as ever.'

'Aye, and have you seen the state of them? I've seen less muck on a chimney-sweep.'

Marie was attuned enough that she could tell when she heard the soft intermittent hissing which of the two women was drawing from her cigarette.

'Well, she won't know what day it is, will she? Do you remember when she had that do outside church and they said it was a nervous breakdown.'

'Oh yeah,' said Mrs Dolan. 'What happened again?'

'Oh it was awful. She was hysterical. Going on about Jesus picking at her buttons. Crackers, she was.'

Mrs Dolan laughed again. 'God help her,' she said. 'Poor woman.'

'No, if you ask me, she's had another turn and he won't let her out because he doesn't want us all to see what's going on.'

'So when was the last time anyone saw her?' Mrs Dolan asked.

'Oh, not for ages. The only person I know who's seen her is Joyce from the paper shop. Apparently they hadn't paid their bill so she goes over, and isn't it Ivy that opens the door to her. She looked terrible apparently.'

'What, did Joyce say that?'

'Yeah. She said, "I asked if she were okay but before she could say owt her husband appeared and off she went like a scolded cat." Anyway, there must be something going on, the curtains are always closed, and I mean, *always.* Today's a perfect example. Bright sunny day and the house is shut up like a mausoleum.'

Marie would never usually interrupt her mother but that day her deference fell short of her curiosity.

'What's a mausoleum?' she said, inching her way through the doorway.

Mary Tierney put her cigarette to her lips, inhaled, and looked up at her daughter. 'It's where they put people when they've died.'

'Is Mrs Kirkby dying?'

'No, love,' said Mrs Dolan, smiling.

'So why is it like a mausoleum?'

'Because she's not well,' her mother said.

Marie fiddled with a loose stitch on her dress. 'What's wrong with her?' she said.

Mary Tierney put down her cigarette and looked at her the way she looked at the Braithwaite girl in the shop when she was pricing the items with quick dismissive fingers, too sullen to draw her lips into a smile.

'I'll tell you what's wrong with her,' she said. 'She's got the devil in her. Now that's enough, I don't want to hear another word on it.'

Marie's body tingled the way it always did when she was given a dressing down. She walked away and sat in the window of her bedroom and wondered what happened to a person when the devil got into them and whether their eyes glowed red and if they were locked into a violent battle or if they just disappeared so that only the devil was left.

'What are you looking at me like that for?' Jean said the next time they met.

Marie shrugged and said, 'Why doesn't your mum ever come outside?'

'She's too tired.'

Marie bit at her lip. It knotted her insides to know Jean's mother and the devil were one and the same.

*

Jean was nine when she disappeared.

She and Marie had been playing in the street outside Mrs Brogan's house and she tripped over a stray shoe and took the skin off her knees. It was a man's shoe and it didn't look worn or broken and Marie wondered how it had found its way to the gutter and where its twin was and what had happened to the man who owned this shoe.

Jean didn't care one way or the other. She went home and her eldest sister rubbed her knees with iodine and then she was sent out for a pound of butter and a tin of golden syrup and that was the last anyone ever saw of her.

In the beginning there was a large search operation and the police called at all the houses on the street to ask questions and take statements but after a couple of weeks, the effort was abandoned and people went back to their lives as though nothing had altered and Jean was never mentioned again.

Marie found this profoundly shocking, almost as shocking as Jean disappearing, and the two things merged into a single memory so that later her best friend became evanescent, a creature as capable of non-existence as she was sentience.

After they called off the investigation, Jean's family moved away and later Marie heard her mother telling Mrs Dolan that Mrs Kirkby had been put in an institution, God help her, and was it any wonder?

For a long time after the police capitulated, Marie felt compelled to continue the search herself, so when school finished each day she would seek out places she imagined Jean might have gone – the edge of the woods or the storm drains or the derelict houses near the train station. She carried on sifting through silent spaces for many months until one day she woke up and the urge to keep looking had vanished.

It was as though she'd been held by a clenched fist all that time and now it had relinquished its hold, it had dropped her.

After that she took up with another girl on the street and her friend Jean fell out of her consciousness altogether until she was much older, until an even more shocking thing happened.

*

The electronic bell sounded and her name appeared in red pixels on the digital display. When it slid from view there was a second of pure blackness and then it appeared again in the centre, flashing this time:

Marie Tierney. Room 3.

Dr Parker was sitting in his chair, his tortoiseshell glasses perched half-way up his nose. He was staring down at his computer screen, his shirt opened enough that his chest hair curled up over the lip of the fabric.

'Take a seat,' he said. 'I'm nearly with you.'

She sat down by his desk and laid her hands in her lap. Then he turned to her, his blue eyes catching in the sunlight.

'Marie, it's good to see you,' he said. 'Are you well?'

'Yes, I'm fine.'

'You know, Margot said to me just the other day how she hasn't seen you in months. We must check in on Marie, she said. I said, You're quite right, we must. And now you've saved me the trouble.'

Dr Parker smiled and Marie nodded, surrendering a thin smile of her own. She hoped he wouldn't carry on talking. She'd always known when to stop talking just by observing a person's face.

'Have you been looking after yourself?'

'Yes,' she said. 'I walk every day and I only smoke a cigarette at breakfast and one before bed now. I know you'll tell me that's still too many but it's better than I was.'

'No, you've done very well, Marie,' he said. 'You're an example to us all.'

She felt he didn't mean this, that his words appeared mechanically from the production line of his mind, burnishing themselves along the walls of his neural pathways and arriving smooth as butterscotch in the cleft of his tongue. She thanked him anyway.

'So what can I do for you?' he said. 'You know, we did call you for a check-up last year and you didn't come. I think perhaps it was more than once, Marie.'

The feeling that began in her throat and

descended down into her stomach reminded her of accidentally gulping down a hard, unsucked lozenge; a pebble of shame to macerate later. She said, 'I'm not one for the surgery I'm afraid.'

'Well, there's a few around here who could learn from your example,' he replied.

Marie blushed and for a few moments the room was quiet. It was so quiet she could hear the muted drone of a conversation in another room.

Dr Parker pinched at the tip of his nose, then turned his head slightly and surveyed her over the top of his spectacles. 'What is it, Marie?' he asked.

'It's back,' she said.

Dr Parker took off his glasses and laid them down so the arms straddled a glass of water. He said, 'What makes you think that?'

'I just know,' she said.

*

Her father had been a labourer.

He'd helped build the town hall and a wing of the hospital where she was born, though mostly he worked on commercial buildings and industrial sites. His name was Tom Tierney and he'd once been known as a jack-the-lad with a seditious streak and an eye for the ladies.

When he was twenty-three he fell from scaffolding, split his head open and broke his back. He would have swallowed his tongue but the foreman stuck his fingers down his throat and pulled it clear.

He was never the same after that, that's what everybody said. Marie had no idea one way or the other because she wasn't born until he was twenty-five, so the only Tom Tierney she ever knew was brooding and doleful-eyed by day and etherised with ale by night.

For many years he endured shooting pains up his spine, lightning-claps frying his nerves and disgorging themselves in his skull like firecrackers, but Marie never knew this either. She only knew he was having *one of his turns*. That's what her mother called them and when Marie asked what that meant she was told, 'It means he needs peace and quiet, so go out and play.'

Tom Tierney continued labouring for another twenty years, until the seizures sealed things. The doctors couldn't say if it was the head injury or the drink that started them but pretty soon he wasn't safe to be on site. That's how he dislocated his jaw and turned his nose into a boxer's snout. For a while the foreman turned a blind eye, but in the end he appeared at the house and told Tom he'd have to let him go.

'And how do you suppose we'll put food on the table?' asked his wife.

'I'm sorry, Mary,' came the reply. 'There's no way we can keep him. It's too risky.'

She saw there was no argument to be had, folded her arms against fate. 'Well that's that then.'

Marie's father died the day before his forty-seventh birthday in the yard outside his house. He'd been drinking in the The Black Bull and just as he put his hand in his pocket to fish out the latch-key he had another fit, only this one was the daddy, it spliced through his brain like a bullet.

'Your father's died,' said her mother down the phone.

Marie sighed and said nothing.

Thank God it's over, she thought. She felt a terrible guilt for that, it constricted around her like a noose and convinced her she'd set upon herself an immutable curse. All those years later, when that awful thing happened, she had the sense that finally she was paying for that thought, finally she was being undone – not by degrees, but all at once – as a bomb undoes the body standing in its wake.

*

It was at the reception after her father's

funeral that she noticed how gaunt and hollow her mother's face had grown. The woman was still working, gathering plates and scraping potted meat and bread crusts from their faces.

It wasn't obvious for a long while that she was crying, it was only when she stood before the sink and let her head drop for a second that the sunlight caught the skin of a tear as it moved over her cheek. Marie was going to say something, she was just thinking about what that should be when her mother dragged the backs of her hands across her eyes and turned to her.

'Whatever you do,' she said, 'don't get married.'

Marie looked at her. 'What?' she said. 'What do you mean?'

Her mother shook her head. 'I mean it. Just stay on your own,' she said, and she walked out of the kitchen and went upstairs to her room.

When she returned after half an hour, she acted as though nothing had happened. 'You've cleaned everything up,' she said, looking all around the space.

Marie said, 'It didn't take long.'

Her mother nodded vaguely and turned away. 'I suppose you'll be rushing off back to London tomorrow then.'

Mary Tierney didn't want her daughter to see her face when she said this. That's how it seemed anyway, because she was facing in the other direction, using her hand as a cloth to wipe down a surface that needed no wiping down.

'I'm not sure yet,' said Marie. 'Maybe Friday.'

After that it was silent in the room and her mother sat at the table and lay her hands neatly in front of her. Marie waited a while and then she sat down opposite her and slowly extended her arms until her hands bisected the invisible line at the centre of the table. Her mother reached out tentatively until the tips of their fingers met.

'Imagine what he'd say if he could see the pair of us,' she said.

'You two holding a seance are you?' said Marie, in a gruff silly monotone.

Her mother smiled, withdrew her hands and began to cry. Then just as quickly she cleared her throat, stood up and walked out of the room again. This time she didn't come back, and after that they never spoke of anything other than what to have for dinner and the price of nylons in London and how close the heat was.

*

She'd been terrified about going home that summer, the summer her father died. To her mind her abdomen was as swollen and distended as a spider's. She'd been sure her mother would notice the second she laid eyes on her, and her father's funeral wasn't the time for it, so she consulted her room-mate Linda, and Linda told her, 'You've nothing to worry about, there's no way you can tell,' and together they went shopping to pick out an outfit to disguise what to Linda's mind needed no disguising in the first place.

Her mother never caught on.

Five months later, in January 1969, when the baby was born, she didn't catch on to that either. Just as she'd never caught on to her daughter dropping out of secretarial college after a single term to become a model.

Marie was sad about all the things her mother didn't know about her, and she was even sadder that she hadn't come to know them by some preternatural instinct, because she still held on to the notion that if your mother really loved you, she'd just know.

The baby's father was a Welsh photographer who shot fashion spreads. He was much older, old enough that he already had children who'd come of age and left home. It happened after a shoot in a Mayfair hotel room.

'I can't blame him,' she said after she found out she was pregnant. 'I knew what I was doing.'

But a lie was a lie was a lie.

She named the baby Jamie after the butcher's son who'd gone into the Navy when he was eighteen. Back when she was a child, Jamie used to sneak sausages and black puddings to her in a handkerchief when his father's back was turned.

'How'd you manage that?' her mother would ask when she came home.

She'd shrug and her mother would smile and this made Marie happy inside in a way almost nothing else did.

As a teen she developed a crush on Jamie and when he left home and joined the Navy, she pined after his Grecian lips and quick, blood-wet hands, and marshalled by a lonesome cupidity she walked over to the butcher's shop one January morning and asked Mr Dean for his son's address so she could write to him. She was so embarrassed she could feel her cheeks burning as she spoke.

Mr Dean found the whole thing very funny and Marie was mortified enough that when she got home she ran up to her bedroom and cried. *You're pathetic,* she thought to herself, only it was her mother's voice that played in her head.

Later she sat down and wrote a letter.

Dear Jamie,

I know you probably didn't expect to hear from me but I thought you might get bored at sea or else sea-sick because of the waves, and I wanted to say hello and remind you that we haven't forgotten you. What's it like where you are? Nothing has changed at all here. For example, Miss Coulson is still a miserable old bag.

Yesterday I knocked on her door because my mother asked me to deliver a parcel that had come to us by mistake. Anyway, when she answered the door she said, 'And what do you want?' as though I was her worst enemy.

I told her I was dropping off her parcel and handed it to her and then she said, 'In future I'd thank you to put a comb through your hair before you show up on my doorstep,' and slammed the door.

My mother says she's sad from things that have happened to her but I'm starting to think she's just a miserable cow. Plus I don't see how she can talk about my hair when her own hair is like a wad of iron wool. And for her information, I did comb it. Can I help it if it's blowing a gale?

I don't know if I should say it but I miss seeing you around. The street's less fun without you. Actually it's as dull as ditchwater. Tell me it's better where you are!

Marie

After three weeks a letter addressed to her appeared on the mat. When she opened it and saw it was from Jamie Dean the feeling was like fireworks going off in her belly and spiralling up through her gullet to burst in her brain.

Eventually, after corresponding with him for a year, she worked up the courage to tell him she liked him. She knew by then she'd matured so she included a photo with the letter. After three weeks, he wrote back saying he'd be home the following spring and he couldn't think of another girl he'd rather take out.

Jamie was into his last month of active service when he drowned off the Bay of Biscay; a routine training exercise derailed by a freak storm rolling in from the Atlantic. Marie was seventeen and he was twenty-one and she'd spent the last three years thinking she'd marry him. This was something she'd never told anyone but it seemed to her as sure as the stars in the sky.

That it didn't materialise – that he went and died instead – was a thing that stunned her completely, because up until then she believed that if you wanted something that badly it would just happen.

*

She told her mother about the baby over the phone.

After she said the words there was a long silence before her mother said, 'I don't understand. How can you have a baby when you haven't got a fella?'

Marie explained that the father had come and gone very quickly.

'And what about your studies for God's sake?'

That's when she admitted she'd walked out on secretarial college two years earlier. 'I've been working as a model.'

'Model and prostitute by the sounds of it,' said the voice on the other end of the line.

*

Jamie was a serious child, he wore the expression of a person with the world on his back. He had a natural inclination to protect vulnerable things - to transmute the frail into the hardy - and a strange habit of stumbling across injured birds and bringing them home.

'Where do you find these things?' Marie would ask, her tongue a confluence of frustration and affection. Before Jamie, she'd scarcely come across an injured bird in her life.

They'd pad out a shoe-box with dish cloths and cotton wool and feed the bird with seed from a saucer and water from the lid of a jar. Finally, after a few days, they'd go to the park and Jamie would tell the creature to fly away. Then he'd lay the box on the ground and wait. He was very patient, inordinately patient for a child. Sometimes he'd wait an hour for those birds to crawl out, to re-acclimatise.

One day, when he was seven, they brought out a dove he'd nursed and watched as it tried to fly, but the bird couldn't fly, it could walk and it could nest and nothing else. So they took it to the vet and the vet said, 'The wing's broken, she won't fly again.'

'Can't you fix it?' said Jamie.

The vet looked at him, offered a sympathetic turn of the lip and shook his head. 'I'm afraid I can't.'

'So what do we do?'

The vet looked first at the mother and then the child. 'I think it'd be kindest to put him to sleep.'

Jamie fixed his eyes on the man. 'But what about when he wakes up?'

*

Father Gannon called on Marie almost every day in the beginning. He wanted her to start seeing people again, to come back to church. He knew the only way through it was God, and he wasn't going to give up on her, not on this woman who'd stood before him so many times with the prayer on her tongue.

She'd sit in her place at the little pink table in the kitchen and he'd sit down opposite her and together they'd pass an hour.

'God's the only solace,' he'd say.

'Please don't talk about God,' she'd reply.

*

Marie sat in Dr Parker's consulting room not saying anything. She looked into his eyes and he looked into hers. Soon the space between them seemed to dissolve and for the first time in many years she experienced a direct and undiluted communion with another person.

The feeling of this was like her body had fallen clean away and been replaced by pure white light.

War

As a young man, Dylan Hughes suffered from a strange affliction; the more he liked a girl, the more he stammered.

For a long time this made things impossible. The origin of the affliction he traced to childhood, to the time he caught his father in bed with a woman called Sheila Spark whilst his mother was in hospital recovering from scarlet fever. This was a long time ago in January of 1927, when Dylan was five years-old.

From his place in the shadow of the doorway, he'd been urged to come and get a proper look at the woman lying in his mother's bed. He'd been told not to be shy, nobody was going to bite him. Then Sheila Spark had thrown back the sheet to reveal her pink studded breasts.

This was a startling memory, a memory so thorny and hard to believe that Dylan wondered if he hadn't conjured it himself. He would have put it to one side had he not also remembered his father demanding – in that menacingly jocular way of his – that he tell this woman what *great tits* she had.

Here was the command that formed the axis upon which Dylan's neurosis began its rotation.

'Tell her. Say it. You've got great fucking tits, love.'

Dylan knew the f-word was a bad word, so bad it couldn't be spoken aloud. His mother had taught him that. So when his father goaded him to say it, the contradiction of it all nearly cut him in two.

He tried to do as he was told, to wrap his infant tongue around the syllables, but all that came out was a string of F's.

'You've got great f-f-f-f-f-f-f-f.'

He could still hear Sheila Spark's laughter, still see her mouth primed with red lipstick, a gelid black hole at the centre of her curse-ridden Medusa head.

*

Memories of his childhood in the damp green Rhondda Valley were fleeting and obfuscated, like reflections of passing cars in a window fogged up with condensation.

Outlines appeared to him at intervals, like the time he was standing with a girl on an underground platform at Euston and his mother appeared to him, dancing in the hallway with his baby sister in her arms.

Gwen had always been difficult to remember.

She ran from the edges of the view-finder whenever the camera began to roll, slipping imperceptibly into liquid, into dust. Sometimes he'd hear her voice – usually in the space between consciousness and sleep – saying things she'd once said. 'Dylan, go and see if there's any potatoes in the rack.' 'Come and watch your sister a minute.' 'No more kicking that ball inside.'

Other times she appeared to him laughing by the kitchen sink, cheeks as blush as apples, eyes flashing, tiny frozen pools brimming with love and sadness. *Was it me who made her laugh?* he asked himself.

His father was not hard to remember.

Dylan understood this was because he didn't wish to remember him, and the very act of wishing not to remember guaranteed the man's perpetual residency at the edge of his thoughts. His father never aged but remained lithe and fleet-footed, his inviolable eyes flashing in their sockets like black pearls. He appeared always smattered in coal dust and carried on him the smell of sweat and earth, and when he came through the door he stalked cat-like over to his wife and lifted her clean off the ground. Sometimes after a night in the pub he would put her to the wall and bite her neck.

What happened when Dylan entered

adolescence was that his mother began shrinking into herself, an ever-reducing Russian doll deleting itself shell by shell. Sometimes his father tried to coax her but this only subdued her further, and then he'd grow angry and ask her what had gotten into her, and sometimes he might toss a fork across the room or storm out.

Soon, he stopped coming home at all. He'd leave on a Monday morning and remain gone until Thursday. Sometimes Dylan would see him out on the streets with a woman with bottle-blonde hair, and his father would smirk and pass by him without speaking as though he was nothing, and after that a hatred began to crystallise in him like a tiny iridescent jewel in the pit of his belly.

At fourteen, Dylan walked into the library to shelter from a hail-storm and stumbled across a book about documentary photography. Inside were pictures of people sitting by the Seine in Paris and riding streetcars in San Francisco and wandering down Fifth Avenue draped in furs.

He'd never seen anything like it. He was so captivated by these images that he took that book and sat down in a corner to study them, and by the time he was done he knew this was it, this was the means by which he would escape his life.

At fourteen, he left school and began training to work in the local colliery. This was in the summer of 1936 and mining was the only option for a boy of Dylan's background living on the South Wales Coalfield. After seven months he used what he'd saved to buy his first camera and started photographing people on buses and in the high street as they carted their shopping bags and peered in shop windows.

One drizzly Saturday he jumped a train to Swansea and bought a book about focal lengths and aperture settings and by the following year he'd saved enough to leave Rhondda.

He was settled in London by the time his mother was diagnosed. He came home briefly when his sister Bethan wrote to tell him their father had left and now there was no money, no food. The house was icily damp and his mother lay on a bed shrouded in so many rags and blankets she looked like she was being swallowed.

'I'm not as bad as I look,' she said, her face blue with cold.

'I know, Mam,' Dylan said.

'I might make a pot of cawl later,' she said.

He waited for her to close her eyes and when her breathing grew dense he went out.

In the kitchen his sister picked at a scab on her arm and asked, 'What's gonna happen to me when she goes?'

'How should I know?' he said, arcing around her.

He stayed three days, woke up on the Monday morning, packed his bag and left again, this time for good.

'I have to be back at work tomorrow,' he told Gwen. Nobody had schooled him in the art of watching mothers die.

At the funeral he handed Bethan a little wad of cash and said, 'Don't do anything stupid with it,' and she looked at him dumbly, her eyes pregnant with grief.

He didn't hear from her until the following year, until she turned sixteen. She wrote to tell him she'd married a boy he'd worked with at the colliery, a hulking idiot by the name of Bryn, because she had no way of supporting herself. She wrote again when she had her first son the following autumn. Dylan replied only after many weeks had passed. It was his conscience that made him do it, something about being brought up good and Catholic. That's what his mother used to call it, as though the two went hand in hand.

A week after he sent that letter, the one telling his sister, *I'm sure the baby will be the making of you,* he moved out of his bedsit in Earl's Court and into a studio in Fitzrovia.

He didn't leave a forwarding address.

*

Dylan Hughes lost his virginity to a woman he wasn't attracted to at all.

Her name was Dora and she was the daughter of his landlord, a Jewish emigré from Poland with an eye for a business opportunity and a penchant for gold teeth.

Dora came into the world carrying her own burden. She was born with a condition that made her skin seethe and flay, and a cratored skull from where the doctor went in too hard with the forceps. When she was seventeen, her answer to this was to shut herself in the garden shed and drink weed-killer, only her mother walked in on her before she had the chance and stunned her back into the parentheses of life's dismal concourse.

Dora was a punctual rent collector, so consistent in her timings that Dylan would be ready with the brown envelope. When he handed it to her she'd say, 'Just a second, please,' and then she'd pull out the coins and count them from the palm of her hand.

He saw how she turned her head to her feet if he looked her in the eye so when she came over he'd direct his conversation at the chimney stacks and in that way he asked her how her day was going and how many calls she had to make and if she didn't mind tramping all over town week in, week out, to do the work her father considered himself too important for.

'Well,' she said, 'it's better than sitting at a typewriter all day.'

Dylan told her he was a freelance who shot fashion models. She didn't need to know he was merely a photographer's apprentice, just as she didn't need to know he was used mainly as a gofer and a thing to shout and scream at so this photographer didn't have to go home and shout and scream at his wife.

The night he bought a fish supper for them both was the night it happened.

'I thought you might be hungry,' he said as she counted out the money, and the way the rain glittered under the street-lamps made it look like fine white blades were falling from the sky around her.

He wasn't sure what made him do it but as they sat under a naked bulb eating fish and chips from newspaper, he said, 'You don't like your face much, do you?'

Dora looked clean into his eye for a second before the blood rushed into her head and began working at her skin.

'It's a nice face,' he said.

That's when he moved in and kissed her.

He could taste vinegar on her tongue and her

body began to tremble as he ran his hand over her thigh. The adrenaline moved through him and he could feel his breathing grow shallow as he stood and led her to the bedroom.

She was as placid as a doll, her feeble body limp in his hold. He manoeuvred her on to the bed and looked into her black marbled eye. There were no words, no admissions or reassurances then, just his thick hands yanking at her clothes, removing his own.

It was a strange sensation when it came, to be driving himself inside her, and something about her resistant energy made him feel like a person performing a recital to a hostile audience. There was also the compulsion to go harder, to make this dummy react, and once he'd allowed himself to detonate that incendiary thing in the cocoon of her slick wet flesh, the awareness that he'd been possessed by a force beyond himself.

Afterwards, he wanted the floor to open up and swallow him, because what was a man supposed to say after doing this to a woman?

Dora remained unmoving on the sheet and he didn't look at her but slowly eased his feet from the edge of the bed and sat up. He hung there without breathing for a second before pulling on his trousers. Then he walked to the doorway and waited for her to gather herself and put on her clothes.

Slowly came the sound of her moving on the mattress, her sharp breaths, the muted creak of springs beneath her. He could barely stand to hear her, to know she was thinking something, feeling something, reacting to this thing that had taken over him, this thing that had overpowered him and obliterated her.

It seemed to take her an age to reassemble herself, to place her feet on the ground and start walking towards him, and her fragility, her silent subservience, made him want to grab her and throw her on the floor. In that white hot silence he found himself turning to look at her face but her head was bowed and she came past him without saying a thing.

Dora never called on him for the rent money after that and he never saw or heard from her again. Inside him this was painful but he refused to look at it. He only told himself he was a man and he'd done what a man was made for doing and what else was there to think about any of it?

*

Soon he learned how to approach women at parties by smiling and complimenting them on some aspect of their presentation, and each time he did he found it was easy to get them talking, easy to make them laugh, and he felt proud of this trick of confidence he seemed to have mastered.

But he was composed only until some receptor in him sensed their interest transform itself into a sure attraction, and then the stammering would begin. The woman would inevitably ask if he was alright and the reply would hang there on his tongue like the ghost of a word, so he'd simply turn around and walk out as though he hadn't been saying anything at all.

Eventually he stopped trying with women altogether unless he wasn't attracted to them, and in this way he became the lover of the dispossessed, the unwanted. Each time he slept with one of these women it emboldened some inchoate thing inside him and in turn he treated each a little more carelessly than the last.

When he was much older, when he was already in his eighties and a whole new millennium had dawned, Dylan started to think about these women, these women who had been sitting patiently and obediently in the back of his mind all those years.

Who the hell do you go to about this stuff? he thought to himself.

He considered the question for a long time and then he batted it away but the pain of it wouldn't leave him, so he walked to a church near his home in Highgate. He walked into that cold, sacrosanct place and looked around. There was nobody there so he went to the vestry with his cane and his bad leg and knocked on the door. The priest who answered him was old, although younger than he, and he wore a cream cassock.

'Hello,' said the priest, his grey eyes widening within the borders of his glasses.

'Hello Father, I'm sorry to bother you. Are you about to go to mass?'

'No,' said the priest. 'I just haven't changed from the morning service.'

'I see,' said Dylan.

'Is there something I can help you with?'

'Father,' he said, 'can I talk to you?'

*

During the war, Dylan was injured in Southern Italy. He was treated for shrapnel wounds in 1943, and later he was sent home to a soldier's hospital in Hertfordshire.

One of the nurses there was tall and fair-haired with skin like honey, and her name was Julia. She had a glacial expression and a contoured jaw-line and immediately Dylan saw in her the opportunity to progress his photographic career.

In the beginning he complimented her on her bone structure and her figure and asked if she'd modelled before and when she said she had not he explained that he was a fashion photographer.

'You should sit for me,' he said.

'Me?' she said. 'Don't be silly.'

'I'm serious,' he replied.

'No,' she said, avoiding his gaze, 'I couldn't do that.'

Julia handed him a little plate of pills and pointed to a beaker of water she'd placed at his side.

He swallowed them, looked at her and thought, *What sort of a woman turns down the opportunity to be a model to slouch around doling out pills to a room full of invalids?*

The problem, he decided, was a moral one. *She must be religious and have the queer idea religious women have that modelling is by definition a debasement, equitable with escorting and all that goes along with that.*

So the following day after a desultory exchange, he said, 'And what about you? Are you religious?'

She motioned for him to raise his head, then placed a fresh pillow beneath it. 'Not now I'm not.'

'What do you mean?'

'Well I don't see how any God could let all this happen.' She scanned the men in the room with her eyes.

'So why don't you want to be a model?'

Julia began writing on a clipboard, then attached it to his bedstead. 'Back to this again, are we?'

'I just don't understand it. It's a lot more glamourous. And you could make a hell of a lot more money.' He tracked her as she moved around the bed, redressing it as she went.

'I trained hard to be a nurse. Why would I want to pack it in to sit around grinning at a camera?'

'Because I could turn you into a star.'

'Of course you could,' she said piquantly.

'I mean it,' he said. 'I promise you, I could do it.'

'I'm sure you could,' she said. 'Now take your pills.'

Julia handed him the tray and the beaker and he put them down at his bedside without shifting his gaze.

'I don't think you understand,' he said. 'I've worked with hundreds of girls. But never one like you.'

*

At first he photographed her in a small studio in Chelsea. He arranged outfits for her to wear and had her hair professionally styled, he paid for everything himself because it was an investment.

When he looked into her face, he saw a pristine still, a colourised photograph laid out in *Harper's Bazaar* or *Vogue*. Most importantly, underneath that photograph he saw a caption that read *Dylan Hughes*, and next to that a little symbol showing the image was copyrighted in his name.

From the start, Julia complained that she didn't like being pulled and prodded because it felt so disconcerting that she enjoyed being made into a version of herself she'd never imagined. Another thing that disconcerted her as she hung around in tailored dresses under searing lamps was when she began to fall in love with this man who offered her nothing but, 'Look towards the door,' and, 'Raise your chin'.

Eventually, she began to resent feeling like nothing but an image in a lens, so one day whilst leaning against a bureau in a ruched white gown, she asked, 'Are you blind or just stupid?'

'What?'

'Can't you see the only reason I sit here is for you?'

Dylan looked at her incredulously, and for once his tongue was a dead thing in his mouth.

That was the day Julia did something she never would have imagined herself capable of. She walked right up to this man and kissed him, and that was the first time Dylan had been kissed by a beautiful woman.

*

In the beginning, he saw only what he wanted to see, which was the pretty packaging of his new toy.

It was fine packaging and everyone told him what a lucky man he was to be wanted by a beautiful woman. But Dylan was stark and solitary, a black winter tree at the centre of a deserted piazza, while she was sociable and spry, prone to specious conversations and glib distractions.

'Want to hear something funny?' she'd say, and then she'd launch into a story about two people he didn't know, two people who said idiotic things, and he didn't find any of it even remotely funny.

Nobody should marry a person just because that person looks a certain way, just because that person doesn't cause you to stammer.

That's a thought he had about Julia afterwards, after he'd let things go too far. He first had that thought on the morning of their wedding, then again during their honeymoon whilst they were lying on a bed in a dreary Brighton hotel as it pelted with rain outside.

Julia had a persistent thought too which was, *Why is the woman the one who has to stay at home and cook and clean and run around after everyone while the man gets to have a life of his own?* But this thought didn't appear until she was was indentured by marriage and had two bug-eyed children staring into her face as though the world itself was unspooled from there.

*

'I'm a bad man,' he said.

'Come and sit down,' said the priest.

He led Dylan to a high-backed chair in a room off the hallway that was like a sort of holding room, a purgatory. It contained nothing but a series of chairs around the perimeter and a large Persian rug at the centre.

'I assure you,' he said, 'that whatever you've done, it's not as bad as you think.'

The priest paused and helped lower his guest into the chair, then sat down beside him.

Dylan wheezed and caught his breath. 'I've ruined everything I ever had, Father.'

'Did you hurt a child?'

'I hurt all my children.'

'Did you touch them?'

Dylan looked at him. 'Touch them? Of course not. Jesus, I'm not a child molester.'

'Then it's not as bad as you think,' said the priest.

'It is,' he said. 'I cheated on my wife, I cheated on her many times, hundreds of times. I couldn't be bothered with my children. I'd sooner be off with a woman or sleep in my studio than listen to them talk about school or interrupt me reading the paper. I used to say to them, Not now, Daddy's got a headache, go upstairs.

'I couldn't look at them because their faces would drop when I said that. And it made me angry, it made me want to hit them so hard they never got up. Imagine wanting to do that to your children. Imagine lying in bed wishing they'd never been born.

'I used to lie there next to my wife, my wife who didn't deserve any of this – and now I can't do anything because she's dead – I used to lie there and I knew she was crying – she used to cry so quietly you'd never know it, but I knew it because I could hear the gulping in her throat like she was swallowing it. Years that went on for, and I never said a thing. I just lay there.'

The priest placed a hand on his forearm and took a long slow breath to demonstrate he was considering things carefully. That's how it seemed to Dylan anyway, only that's not what was happening, because what was happening was that the priest was steadying himself against a memory that was pressing at his mind.

'Marriage is very tough,' he said. 'I've never

come across a couple who haven't gone through difficult times at some point or another.

'Once, many years ago, when I was at a parish in Liverpool, a woman came to me one day and said, Father, I need your help. I said, What is it, Kathleen? and she said, It's my husband, he beats me, he won't let me see my family, I don't know what to do, and then she broke down, so I sat with her and then when she'd calmed down I told her to go home, I reminded her of her duty to him, that she was still his wife.

'And that woman went home and do you know what she did? She put her head in the oven. And all she'd wanted was for me to say, Yes, you can leave.'

The only thing Dylan found more unpalatable than a crying woman was a crying man. To his mind it was completely unnatural, like a dog walking around on its hind legs. So when the priest's voice cracked, he simply focused his eyes on the far wall and pretended as though it wasn't happening.

*

There was a time when three shocking things happened to Dylan Hughes, one after the other, all within the space of two months. It began in the summer of 1958, when his children were ten and eight years old.

The first thing to happen was that his wife left

him for the man next door. This man's name was Frank Horner and he was also married, only his wife wasn't tall and beautiful like Julia. His wife was short and frog-mouthed and her name was Anne.

The way Dylan discovered his wife had left him was that he came home one afternoon to find a note on the kitchen table that began, *I've raised the children for the last decade, now it's your turn.*

Anne and Julia were ostensibly friends, but secretly – Dylan knew this, his wife had expressed this to him – Julia found Anne a dull and self-satisfied person, someone who was really only a half-person by virtue of the fact she'd been gifted every last thing in life by her rich, dead father.

She'd always been fascinated by why someone such as Frank, who'd flown Lancaster bombers during the war and could strip cars and build houses, why someone with so much nous, so much gumption, should marry such a static, dead thing as Anne.

Julia was a woman who'd learned to bury her questions, so it was an unusual thing for her to do, but one sultry August evening when both she and Frank were in their back gardens – while Dylan was splayed and recumbent in a hotel suite with a lambish model, and Anne was lying flat on her back in the bath – she cut short the innocuous conversation they were having and said, 'I know this is a funny thing to ask but, well, what was it about Anne?'

He squinted. 'I'm sorry?'

'I mean, what made you marry her?'

Frank's expression took on a startled quality. 'Actually, it's a funny story,' he said, rocking slightly on his toes.

'Oh?'

'Her father asked me to do it.'

'Why would he do that?' she said, using her hand as a visor to stave off the sun.

'Because he wanted to know she'd be alright,' he said, dropping his eyes. 'And I owed him a favour.'

Julia made an involuntary sound, a sibilant emission. 'Must have been a pretty big favour.'

'Well I suppose it was. He was very good to me during the war. And when he found out he was dying he was worried about what would happen to Anne. Her mother was already dead you see. The thing is, he never actually came out and asked. It was me, I offered.'

A shot of electricity buzzed through Julia.

She thought this was an astonishing thing to admit, that you'd only married your wife only out of duty to her father. She'd assumed that at one time Frank must have seen something – some glinting thing beneath what Anne demonstrated to the world – to make him love her.

To hear there had always been nothing made her want to reach out and tell him how what she thought had been love had been no more than a mirage and that her life was pure drudgery; that she fantasised about abandoning her family just so she wouldn't have to keep cooking dinners and washing clothes and telling her children to tidy away their toys.

Dylan came to know all this after she left because it was all in her note, and when he sat down to read it, he wasn't angry because how could he be? He was guilty of every charge she levelled at him. What surprised him was that he knew every last longing of hers already. This woman he'd neglected all this time had given away everything in what she'd omitted to say, in the silences that had slowly entombed her.

The second thing – and this happened only six weeks later – was that Frank Horner, this cretin of a man who'd run off with his wife, a man who'd never shown even the slightest glimmer of instability in all the years Dylan had known him, attached a lead to the exhaust pipe of his Jaguar, ran it through the driver's window and turned the ignition.

He left behind two notes.

One was for his frog-mouthed wife and one was for Julia. When Dylan asked what was in this note she wouldn't say, and she never did say, which made him seethe inside because it was an eternal thing in her he couldn't reach.

The final thing to happen to Dylan that summer was that his wife returned to the family home and acted as though not a single thing had happened. She came breezing through the front door with her bags one evening as though she was coming in with the weekly shop.

'What's going on?' he said.

'I thought you'd need someone to make your dinner and iron your shirts and raise your children.'

Dylan stared up at her from his old chesterfield.

'You'll catch a fly in a minute,' she said.

Julia didn't shy away from the marital bed. If anything, she seemed to sleep more soundly than before. It was Dylan who was disquieted because she went around with no shame at all, this woman who had cuckolded him and walked out on her children.

On the third evening, he watched her pushing the hoover around their bedroom, singing from the corner of her mouth, and it made him so mad he wanted to put his fist through the wall. When he crawled into bed that night it felt like a blood-eyed bat was flapping around his chest cavity.

At two in the morning he reached out and turned on the bedside lamp.

'Just what the fuck's going on here?' he said.

'What?' she replied, blinking through the glare.

'You leave me for that nutcase next door, five minutes later he kills himself, and then you waltz back in here as though nothing's happened. What the hell's wrong with you, woman?'

Julia pulled herself into a sitting position and drew the hair back behind her ear. 'I don't know, Dylan,' she said, 'what *is* wrong with me?'

He looked at her, at her unblinking eye, and she seemed to him as remote as a figure rendered in oil.

'I think you must have had some sort of breakdown,' he said. 'It's all I can think of.'

'Probably, that's probably true. And what about you? What's your excuse?'

He felt a cold lick in his chest, as though a large mammalian tongue was lapping at his insides. 'What the hell's that supposed to mean?'

'How many women have you slept with since

our wedding day?' she said. 'I've slept with one man. Frank. It wasn't very good, but to be honest I didn't care about that. I just wanted a friend. It's been a long time since I had a friend.'

'You have friends.'

'No I don't. You don't know because you don't know me. You haven't asked me a question in ten years. And before you start, *Where's my tie?* doesn't count.'

Julia took a breath. 'Do you know that one day a man came to this house and asked me if we were interested in leaded diamond windows, and I said yes, just because he was someone to talk to. He sat with me on the sofa and drank tea and ate biscuits and after an hour I told him I'd talk to you and if he came back the next week I'd give him an answer.

'So the next week he came back and he sat on the sofa again, and I fed him tea, only this time he called me a tease and started trying to touch me and I got scared and told him I hadn't intended to tease him, and do you know what he said?'

Dylan looked at her.

'He said, Yes you did. Why are you done up like a dog's dinner to sit around the house all day? And then he forced himself on me. So I tell a lie. I've had two men since our wedding day. But maybe I got what I deserved because I did dress up like that for him, he was right.'

All Dylan could think of when she'd finished talking was that awful woman, Sheila Spark. He could hear her heckling him from his mother's bed and the image of her seemed to fuse with his wife so that he couldn't separate the two.

For a second he had an impulse to put his hand over Julia's face and bang her head off the bedpost but he wasn't a violent man, so instead he got up and dressed and then he left the house and drove into town to do the only thing he could think to do to soothe himself.

In the morning he came home and said nothing, and neither did his wife. She'd already played her final hand.

*

Since when did priests start confessing things to complete strangers when they were supposed to be listening to them, when they were supposed to be offering counsel?

What the hell is this? Don't you realise I've been holding this in my whole life and now you're trampling right over everything I'm saying and turning it into nothing? It isn't nothing. This is my life you're walking over.

That's what Dylan wanted to say.

But after a minute a thought drifted into his mind, which was that he'd triggered something in the priest, and the man had been moved to tell him what he'd done all those years ago and how much shame he carried on account of that.

Dylan realised this was his opportunity not to recoil, that he could do a new thing in this moment, even if it felt awful, and it did feel awful. It felt like he was on fire, yet still he put his hand on the priest's shoulder and still he said, 'It's alright, it's fine.'

And the greatest thing he did was not to move from that place. He sat there in the full horror of the situation and agreed with himself not to move until it was over.

*

As a young father, it had felt to Dylan that if he took his crying child in his arms, he would collapse or have a brain haemorrhage or something. That's how physical it had been.

That's why he didn't acknowledge his children except from a safe distance, even when they were grown, even when they were men. It's why he let his wife run away to South Africa with a stranger and why he told that model she must be mistaken when she called him one day and announced she'd given birth to his son.

'You're mistaken,' he said, taking his glasses from the bridge of his nose. 'And don't call this number again.'

He said this and then he put the phone down.

But soon a ribbon of guilt began to move through him so he made some calls and within an hour he'd found out where this young model lived. He sat down at the desk in his studio and wrote her a cheque, and he sent it alongside a slip of paper upon which he wrote, *For the baby*.

The model's name was Marie and ten months earlier, in April of 1968, he'd photographed her for *Tatler* in a Mayfair hotel. He'd taken with him a hamper full of champagne and handed her a glass the moment she walked in the door.

'For you,' he'd said.

He didn't know it, but Marie didn't like champagne, and the fact she couldn't make herself like it seemed analogous with her inability to convince herself she belonged here. She was a half-educated Northern waif and everyone could see it.

That's how she felt anytime anyone in this eviscerating city looked into her face, and it made her want to disappear; not figuratively, but literally. She wished to dissolve into a small pile of ash and blow away on the wind.

Dylan understood instinctively that she didn't know how to say no, but this wasn't a conscious understanding. If it had been, he'd have recognised he liked girls like this because they'd been conditioned to be passive and compliant, to go through life being driven by other people. He'd have seen it was nothing to do with their charm or their sweetness or any of the other saccharine ideas he sold himself.

Marie took the glass and thanked him, and when she took a sip the tartness of the liquid made her wince, a reaction she concealed with a yawn.

After they'd used up the first roll of film, he reminded her not to forget that flute of champagne and she could see he was in some way perturbed that she hadn't poured it into herself so she gathered her resolve and drank it down in one.

'A girl after my own heart,' he said, peppering the walls with his trenchant laughter.

Marie felt the warm sense of relief she always felt when she knew she'd pleased a man, so when he poured her another glass she didn't tell him the truth, that she hated champagne. She said nothing and smiled, and the warm feeling inside her was replaced by something steeped in dread, because already she knew where this was heading.

Soon the shoot seemed to recede into a vacuum and before long he announced, 'I think we've got it,' as though he was a surgeon excising a malignancy from an organ.

He opened another bottle – *how many do*

you have? she wanted to yell – and poured her another glass. She drank it down in one again, only this time it made her gag, and the vomit pooled in her throat.

Dylan looked at this young woman who stumbled on her fawnish limbs, this creature who couldn't seem to focus her eyes and who flopped on to the bed with the merest of encouragement from his blunt hand. He looked at her dully, the way a man looks at a pretty young woman when his life is bursting with pretty young women.

Lowering himself on to her he began to kiss her unmoving lips and when he opened his mouth she let her jaw relax so he was able to slide his tongue inside. Before he could pull at her dress she put her arms around him and started to rotate so she could coax him on to his side. She was cognisant enough to know to remove this dress herself as she couldn't risk him tearing it or stretching the fabric.

She'd saved for three months to buy this dress.

They called it a babydoll dress but nothing about the price-tag was babydoll. She'd gone without meals for this dress, and even though she knew it was stupid to have spent all that money on it, she wanted to know what it felt like to own a dress girls like her were never supposed to own.

He wasn't as rough with her as she expected and as she made the sounds she knew he would want to hear, she decided it wasn't that bad. There was a thrill about knowing she would go back to her friends with a story. She liked having something to say that involved sex because it felt like currency, and when she told the other girls she knew she'd increase her capital somehow which made her feel pleased in advance, even if something else in her felt constricted and airless.

Dylan liked sex to go on for as long as possible because the moment he came, he knew he'd come plummeting back to earth again, back to his thoughts, which were so often tainted by regret now, like once pure rivulets marred by crude oil and effluence.

That's why he didn't rush and why at intervals he froze and contracted, refusing to allow nature to dictate a denouement. He'd honed his technique the way an athlete learns over years how to pace himself for a marathon. Several times he was about to climax and each time he withdrew and gripped Marie's shoulders tightly to contain himself, then finally he allowed himself to finish and dropped down on her so that his neck compressed her face.

He panted and whispered, 'Thank you'.

She could hear the sincerity in his voice, and a little of the warmth crept back into her belly because she'd made him pleased a second time.

After a few moments, he rolled over on his back and immediately she got up from the bed and began collecting her clothes from the floor.

Dylan watched her do this, he watched as she put on her underwear and pulled her dress over her head, he watched as she stepped into her shoes and collected her bag, and all he could think about was what it said about him that she did it all with such urgency, as though smoke was seeping in beneath the door.

'Can I go now?' she said.

'Of course,' he replied. 'You can do whatever you like.'

*

In the summer of 1987, when Dylan was already rooted in the autumn of life, a young man in blue jeans and a baseball cap appeared on his doorstep.

'Yes?' he said.

'Hi,' said the man. 'My name's Jamie.'

'Right,' he said. 'And?'

'Can I talk to you a minute?' he said.

Dylan understood the young man was nervous, it was clear from his darting eyes and the way he fiddled with his fingers.

'About what?'

'It'll only take a minute.'

'Okay,' he said. 'Come in.'

He walked back through the house and waited for the young man to follow.

'Do you know who I am?' asked the figure standing in the doorway of his studio.

'I do,' Dylan replied as he lowered himself into an armchair. He couldn't look at the man, so he gazed out of the window.

'I'm Jamie,' he said again.

'And your mother's name is Marie.'

Dylan continued to stare out of the window into the garden beyond with its panoply of jasmine flowers and fox-gloves in full bloom, to where starlings were taking seed from a feeder.

*

The priest gathered himself and clasped his hands together as if to escape the stranger's consoling hand.

'Please excuse me, I shouldn't have said that.'

You're damn right you shouldn't, Dylan wanted to say. *Years I waited to say this and now you've ruined it, you bastard.*

But then he looked at the man, saw the shame in his face, and something inside him softened.

'It's fine,' he said, 'don't worry.'

'Please continue with what you were saying.'

'No, it's alright,' said Dylan, 'I'm okay now.'

He gave a nod and slowly he began to hoist himself out of the chair.

'But you weren't finished,' said the priest, taking his arm and looking at him with imploring eyes.

'I was,' said Dylan, transferring his weight to his walking stick. 'I was.'

Mother

Marie made the comment everyone made when they met Anderson, the one about what an unusual name he had.

'My dad's fault,' he told her.

Then he explained that his parents were Michael Sylvester and Elizabeth Anderson, and after he was born they decided on Christopher Anderson Sylvester, only his father got himself very drunk somewhere between the baby's cot and the registry office and the rest was history.

Marie bought the flat next to Anderson's mother. This was in 1971, when she took all the money she had, coupled it with the money Jamie's father had sent her and bought a little place on the top floor of a five-storey tenement off Bethnal Green High Street.

She'd never set foot in East London before but she was terrified of mortgages, of debts and loans and interest rates - those things may as well have been written in hieroglyphics - so she'd bought outright. That's how she ended up in Bethnal Green, it was the only place she could afford without taking on a mortgage.

The tenement was on Tent Street and looked out over Weaver's Fields. From the back of the little flat she could see the City of London and St Paul's Cathedral. Sometimes, if it was a bright morning, she would stand with the baby in her arms and point out the Houses of Parliament and the Tower of London in the distance, and the baby would mimic her, arrowing his little finger at the sky and gurgling in her ear.

Anderson's mother didn't waste any time, she came knocking the morning Marie arrived. She stood on the threshold in a floral apron with a cigarette in her hand and white curlers in her hair. 'Hello sweetheart,' she said. 'I'm Lizzy.'

'Marie,' she replied. 'Pleased to meet you.'

Lizzy smiled. 'I can tell you're not from round here.'

'No, I'm from Lancashire.'

'Really? A northerner in the East End.'

Marie nodded. She felt shy and exposed, like a child pushed forwards by her mother.

'Where's your husband?'

'Oh no, it's just me and the baby.'

Lizzy grinned and drew on her cigarette. 'Boy or girl?'

'Boy.'

Marie went to fetch the baby from his cot and

turned him so Lizzy could stroke his head and coo for him.

'You need anything, just come and see me, alright darling?' she said, winking.

Marie didn't own a scrap of furniture when she moved into that flat. To begin with, the only thing she bought was a cheap mattress from a low-end department store. Then she found a second-hand shop and bought a bed-frame, a sofa, and a coffee table.

All this was new to her, she'd never spent a single minute imagining how she might furnish a home, she just wasn't that person. Marie was someone who wanted to walk into a room and for things to be in place already. She didn't care if the furniture was somebody else's taste, she didn't even know what her taste was.

What she learned from Lizzy was that the woman who owned the flat before her had been there since the thirties. To begin with it had been her and her husband and then in the coronation year he went into cardiac arrest half way through Sunday lunch.

Before that he'd run a flower stall on Bethnal Green High Street and when he died, Lily - that was the woman's name - took charge of it, she couldn't survive without the income. She used to bring Lizzy flowers every week.

'Here you go, darling,' she'd say. 'Lilies from

Lily.'

It unsettled Marie when Lizzy pointed out where she died. 'I was the one who found her,' she said, eyeing the mottled green carpet.

After that, Marie never stood in that corner of the living room. It made her feel like she was interfering with this dead woman, and that was a thing that never changed as long as she lived in that little flat with its alabaster walls discoloured by cigarette smoke and its gloomy architraved windows.

In the beginning, Marie knew people on the estate talked about her, that stories circulated about the type of girl she was. It was obvious from the way the other women stared at her, from the way they carried on staring at her even though they could see she knew what they were saying. That's why she went everywhere with her head bowed.

Lizzy brought her out of herself, she chaperoned her around and introduced her to people at the chemist and in the bustle of the open-air market. Those first few months in that strange new world she relied on Lizzy totally. That's why when her boiler broke down she didn't think twice.

'Don't worry,' the woman said, 'my boy fixes boilers for a living.'

Anderson came that evening, had the thing

firing again within an hour. 'It won't last long,' he told her, 'but it'll do till I can get the parts in.'

She made him tea while he worked at it and afterwards he showed her the scars on his hands from working with corniced metals and skewering tools and boiling water.

'What's that one?' she said, pointing to a scar by his left eye.

'Oh that's from when I rolled my motorbike,' he said, grinning. 'Slid under a truck and came straight out the other side.'

He returned the week after and replaced the worn-out parts and Marie made him sandwiches and poured him a glass of beer because he refused to take any money from her. She washed her hair in the kitchen sink while he worked and then after he'd finished, he offered to hold the baby while she used the hair-dryer.

'Are you sure?' she said.

'Yeah, we'll have a whale of a time, won't we?' he replied, and then he screwed his face up and made animal sounds until the baby squealed in his arms.

When she was finished, Marie took Jamie and held him on her hip, and Anderson told her she suited being a mother, she was a natural. He had no idea what that meant to her because nobody had said anything kind about her having a baby until then.

It had either been, *The damage is done, you'll just have to get on with it,* or, *Don't worry, it'll be alright in the end*, but nobody ever said anything about what a miraculous thing it was that her body had seeded and incubated this little person, nobody had told her what a good mother she'd be.

She stood there rocking the baby and gazing at Anderson, musing on the thoughts turning over in his brain. Ever since she was a child she'd been able to sense what people were thinking, as though she could peel back their scalps and peer into their minds. Usually it was the things they didn't want to say out loud. People leave so much out, that's what she'd learned. They circled around a thing without ever landing on it, it was to do with not wanting to get it wrong, not wanting to offend.

Her idea was that Anderson was too much of a gentleman to ask so she volunteered the information herself. 'He wasn't planned,' she said, kissing her son's head. 'His dad didn't want to know.'

'Prick,' said Anderson, shaking his head. 'Anyway, sod him. Geezers like that you're better off without.'

She was stunned by this.

She'd expected he would nod and say nothing

or give away his disapproval by some micro-movement, a curl of the lip or some glinting thing in his eye. She'd never met a man in her life who didn't have ideas about the person she was, and here was this stranger looking right at her without making a single judgement.

*

After the boiler incident, Anderson started to knock on her door whenever he came over to his mother's.

'Hello you,' he'd say. 'Just thought I'd make sure my work's holding up.'

Later, when he'd pushed the boiler angle enough he'd start on the baby. 'I've come to see how this little geezer's doing,' he'd whisper, reaching to grab Jamie's hand.

Marie didn't care that it was a ploy to get to her because she could see he liked her son, the same way she could see he liked her. It was a definite thing inside her that she didn't have to question.

At the start it was cups of tea, then cake, and finally he'd bring bacon and eggs and she'd make dinner while he rolled around on the carpet with Jamie.

'Don't tell my mother whatever you do,' he said. 'If she finds out I've been getting my dinner cooked ten yards from her front door she'll blow a gasket.'

Marie folded her arms. 'Doesn't she know you're here?'

'Course she don't,' he said. 'She thinks I've gone home.'

In the evening she put Jamie to bed and if he went off quickly, she'd sit down in the living room and Anderson would bring in tea and biscuits.

She didn't own a television so they'd sit with the radio on and talk and sometimes he'd stand up and sing along. Marie would shake her head and laugh and he'd reach for her hand and pull her up and after a minute she'd allow him to spin her around like a ballerina, even if she was embarrassed, even if she was so mortified to be seen dancing she couldn't bring herself to look him in the eye.

The first time they kissed it felt like signals were passing between them, as though electrical impulses were being transmitted to the furthest outposts of her body. She could feel him in the maw of her chest and the pulp of her thighs, a searing flash through her arteries and bone marrow. A kiss before this had ended with her tongue, but this continued on through her bloodstream like a virus, blossoming in her abdomen like a cornucopia of bright flowers.

When it was over and Anderson pulled back she didn't know what to do, it was like waking up on a spotlit stage with a lectern before her and an expectant audience waiting for her to begin. His eyes glistened under the ceiling light and he swept her hair behind her ear, put his lips to her cheek. For a few moments he did nothing but look at her and then he laughed, a gravelled mewl from the corner of his mouth.

'Don't laugh at me,' she said.

'I'm not laughing at you.'

'But you are,' she said, the blood cleaving to her cheeks.

He said, 'I just can't believe all this is happening.'

'All what?'

'You,' he said. 'You're so…'

She couldn't listen to whatever it was he was about to say, she'd never been able to negotiate a compliment, so she broke away from him and walked to the bathroom, her little heart snapping at her ribcage as she went. She stood in front of the mirror, held on to the faucet and pushed out the air until the dull ache behind her eyes subsided, the one that made it feel like her head had been loaded with concrete. She looked into her pale face and waited for something to make sense.

Afterwards she splashed herself with cold water and checked to make sure there was nothing stuck in her teeth. When she returned he was sitting on the couch in his underwear, and when she sat down he put an arm around her and pulled her into his chest. Then Leonard Cohen came on the radio and in some vague and abstract way it felt to Marie like all the backstories of the world had conspired to place her here with this man's arm around her and that pretty song in her ear and the setting sun fading to nothing beyond the glass.

*

It amazed her that Anderson could just as easily be found servicing a boiler in a sprawling Belgravia townhouse as a tiny basement flat in Holloway.

She'd always been fascinated by money, by people with wealth and status and power. As a model she'd found herself at parties with these types of people and had always been terrified by them, it was to do with the way they moved through life with the conviction that other people were there primarily to fulfil their desires, their whims, their expectations.

'Imagine being one of those people in those houses,' she said to him one day.

'What do you mean?'

'To have a nice house and nice clothes and to know you never had to worry.' She cast a wistful eye at the ceiling and he looked at her and shook his head.

'I wouldn't be one of those bastards for all the money in the world,' he said. 'They're idiots.'

'Why?'

'If I go down the Nag's Head estate and fix a boiler, I get tea, I get cake, I get bacon sandwiches. Those bastards in their fancy houses never give you anything. They don't even smile, they just stand there watching you, making sure you don't nick anything.'

'Really?'

'Yeah. If you were like any of them lot, I wouldn't touch you with a barge-pole.'

Marie laughed when he said this. So much of what Anderson said made her laugh, it was to do with his simplicity. What surprised her was the other side of him, the side she learned about the day she asked about the last girl he went out with.

That's when he told her about the barmaid from The Queen Adelaide whose name was Sharon. He'd liked Sharon from the moment he met her so he'd given her the treatment. That's what he called it, *giving her the treatment.* Then he'd invited her to the races. Go on then, she'd said, and that had been that.

It felt odd to Marie, listening to him speak about another woman, about someone who sounded so much more vital and alluring and beautiful than she, even though he hadn't said a single thing about her appearance.

'So what happened?' she said.

He smiled and raised his eyebrows. 'Cheated on me.'

Marie hadn't expected this. She said nothing.

'Best thing about it, it was Terry from the estate. Pinocchio we used to call him he had such a fucking hooter on him.'

Anderson laughed when he said this, though she could see it still stung. The thing that shocked her was when he told her it was four years since all this had happened.

'And you haven't been out with anyone since?' she said.

'Nope.'

'Why?'

He pawed at his face with a calloused hand. 'I just wanted a break.'

Marie understood he'd expected Sharon would be his wife, that they'd have children and build a life together. It made her feel strange somehow, like she couldn't compete with the woman who'd gone before. She nodded and they were both silent and after a few moments he excused himself and went to the bathroom. Afterwards she didn't mention Sharon again, not ever, and neither did he.

*

One day she asked if he'd do her a favour and watch Jamie so she could have a bath – it had been so long since she'd been able to relax in the bath – and as she lay there in the hot scented water with the steam curling over her face she was startled by the unassailable trust she apparently had in this man who until a few months ago she had never even set eyes on.

When she'd towelled off and returned in her dressing-gown he was on his knees on the carpet with the baby in one hand and a cloth in the other.

'What happened?' she said.

Anderson looked up at her. 'He was sick, weren't you, buddy?'

He kissed Jamie's forehead and continued scrubbing at the carpet. Then he walked over and handed her the baby and it was clear he had no idea what was going on inside her, he simply smiled and went off to the kitchen with the cloth. She was undone by that, by the way he did everything without any sense of what it meant to her.

It took a long time for her to let him sleep with her. Having a child had made her into a different person. She couldn't let a man in her bed until her son trusted him completely, until she trusted him completely. Anderson didn't push her either, he just said, 'When you're ready.'

Marie found the whole experience paralysing in the beginning, she'd never slept with a man before. Sex had always been followed by standing and dressing and leaving, or waiting while the other person stood and dressed and left. To actually lie there unmoving in the dark with the sensation of skin on skin and the sound of a lion-chested man breathing, that was a revelation.

It was so alarming to her that she wondered how anyone ever did it. *How do they sleep through this?* she wondered, and she was glad when she had to get up for the baby. But soon she grew accustomed to it and after a while she missed Anderson's warm body and the low rattle of his snoring when he didn't come around.

*

He was the one to say it first.

'I love you too,' she replied, the words trickling out in a whisper. She could feel one leg trembling as she spoke, it petrified her to say this, and as if to move past the moment she added, 'but you know we can't carry on like this. We have to tell your mum.'

'I know,' he said. And the smile fell from his lips.

It was a humid September evening when he took himself off to his mother's to have the talk.

'It's gonna be fine,' he told her, and then he kissed her and walked out.

Anderson's idea was that he'd lay the groundwork and then he'd come back for her, and after that the three of them would sit down together and thrash it out.

She understood it wasn't going well when he'd been gone an hour. Some time after ten he appeared again and that was when she knew for sure, it was written all over his face.

'What did she say?'

He stood stiffly in the doorway of the kitchen, like a person who'd wandered into in a stranger's house. 'She was a bit surprised. It's not you, it's just-

'It's because of Jamie, isn't it?'

Anderson plugged his eye-sockets with his thumb and forefinger. 'She's old-fashioned,' he said. 'She don't understand.'

No-one should treat you any different.

That's what Lizzy told her when she confided how difficult she found it to be a single mother and absorb everyone's judgements about it, as though she'd crossed an invisible line and was now a person who belonged in the dirt.

'Anyone gives you any trouble on account of that baby, you send them to me,' she said.

Marie had been so grateful for that, for the woman's kindness and her willingness to back her. But Lizzy's compassion had its limits.

She was used to it by then, to people contradicting themselves as soon as a problem got too close to home. Her own mother had done the same thing.

'He's my grandson before anything,' she said, the first year after Jamie was born.

But how many times had she invited them home?

'No, Marie,' she'd say, 'I'll come to you. I'm not having Molly Farrell and the rest of them poking their noses in.'

*

Anderson thought the smartest approach would be to do things on neutral ground. It shouldn't be at hers and it shouldn't be at his mother's. They should all meet and have dinner somewhere where nobody felt at a disadvantage. That's what he told her. Marie didn't bother to mention that it made no odds whether they ate on a park bench or at Claridge's, she would always be the one at a disadvantage.

It goes without saying, she thought. *That's how it is with mothers and sons.*

San Remo was the name of the place. Anderson knew the owner there, a man called Lorenzo. Lorenzo had a black moustache and a beach-ball stomach and he spoke in a sonorous baritone, as though he was addressing a crowd on the opposing bank of a river.

'Ciao ragazza,' he said to Marie, and then he said it again to Anderson's mother, bowing each time.

'What the hell's he going on about?' said Lizzy, as though he wasn't standing right behind her, waiting for her to sit so he could hand her a menu.

Marie was relieved to have Jamie with her because he gave her the opportunity to remove herself from the situation, to tend to him or placate him, to offer any single thing he needed. What disorientated her was that Lizzy took charge of the baby almost immediately and insisted on feeding him morsels of pizza and mollifying him when he started whining and writhing in his high-chair.

Marie wondered what made a person act this way, like a prima-donna for all occasions. Apart from anything, Lizzy didn't know how he liked things, she didn't know the right way to soothe him.

'I've raised four kids, just leave him to me,' Marie was told when she got up to intervene. The woman could say one thing and mean another so squarely. It was like her own mother all over again.

Anderson asked Lizzy what she wanted to eat and she said she didn't know and did it matter, wasn't this foreign muck all the same?

'Come on,' he said, 'you like spaghetti, you like lasagne.'

'All I want is a few chips and a fried egg.'

'Fine,' he told her. 'I'm sure that's fine.'

Marie could feel something in her stomach curdling, a premonitory sensation laying out the course of the evening. Anderson pumped her hand with his own beneath the table, and she attempted a smile. When he went to the toilet, she took a stuttering breath and looked at the impenetrable woman sitting across from her.

'Is there anything you want to say?' she asked.

'About what?'

'About me and Anderson.'

Lizzy shrugged. 'When he gets an idea in his head it's easier to let him get on with it.'

The whole time she spoke, the woman was looking at Jamie, wiping marinara sauce from his mouth, pushing melted cheese over his lips.

Marie wanted to go around the table and take her son, she wanted to tell Lizzy to leave him alone and to look at her when she spoke, but she didn't do that. Instead she asked, 'Do you hate me now?' She could feel the sweat gathering beneath her arms as the words came out.

'I don't care about you,' said Lizzy. 'I care about my son.'

Marie watched the woman's face as she said this, she watched her shrunken lips and her sharp glaucous eyes. She let the words hit her and allowed her body to absorb them, to bruise under their weight. She could sit back then, she could sit back without eating another thing and wait for the evening to wilt to nothing.

In a way she was relieved, it was to do with knowing where she stood, with understanding there was no need even to defend herself.

Afterwards, when his mother was back in her own flat and he was splayed out on Marie's couch, Anderson smiled and brushed the whole thing off as though he was shucking sawdust from his overalls. 'She'll come around,' he said, 'it's just gonna take time.'

He wrapped an arm around her and kissed her forehead, but somehow this made her angry. She didn't understand what was going on with him, if he actually believed this or if he couldn't come out and say what to her was so obvious.

She didn't sleep that night, she just lay there like a cadaver cut with shadows and streetlight.

Eventually she got up, went to the living room, sat down on the sofa and began to sift through things. She wondered whether she should be the one to end it or if she should wait until it unravelled of its own accord. Then she wondered if she was being too pessimistic, if there was a way to navigate the situation and how she should go about it.

Every minute this was going on she was aware of the woman living and breathing just beyond the wall, this woman who had once liked her, who had protected her and coddled her with her own cloying brand of compassion and who now wanted her to disappear.

In the very early morning, when the sun was still straddling the horizon, Anderson came through and asked her what was wrong and how long she'd been sat here like this and if she'd managed to get any sleep.

Marie shook her head. 'What are we going to do?'

He sat down and placed an ursine arm around her. 'It'll be okay. I promise.'

'How?' she said. 'Your mother's not going to change her mind about me.'

He squeezed her shoulder and raked his hair with his free hand. 'Course she will. It's just gonna take time.'

Marie turned and looked into his face. 'Do you really believe that?'

Anderson looked back at her for a moment and then dropped his gaze. 'Come back to bed,' he said.

'You go,' she replied. 'Jamie will be up soon anyway.'

*

At the beginning of the following week she decided on something. When Anderson left for work she sat with Jamie in the living room and pushed toy cars over the rug with him, and as she did she considered the dilemma from every angle. It was just after eleven on a Monday morning when she went over to his mother's and knocked on the door.

'Can I come in a minute?' she said when Lizzy appeared, still in her nightgown and curlers.

'What for?' the woman replied.

'It'll only take a minute.'

'I've got an appointment and I need to do my hair so it'll have to be quick.' Lizzy widened her eyes, then turned and said, 'Hello sweetheart,' to Jamie and stroked his head.

They sat down at her formica-topped kitchen table. It was a place Marie had sat many times before and now here she was in that same chair in the same room, knowing she was viewed not with affection but with suspicion and hostility, as though she'd been manipulating the situation all these months just to get to the woman's son.

She delivered the first line as she'd delivered it to herself ten times or more already that morning.

'I know you don't want to talk to me,' she said, 'but I can't just carry on as though nothing's happened. And I understand I'm not the person you'd have chosen for Anderson, but isn't there a way we can work this out?'

Lizzy looked at her blankly. 'Not as far as I'm concerned.'

Marie could feel the colour drain from her cheeks, she could feel her eyes growing teary. 'I don't know what you want me to say. Do you think I'm a bad person?'

'Come and talk to me when your son brings home some woman who's lumbered herself with another man's child,' she said. 'Then come and talk to me.'

Lizzy pulled a cigarette from a packet and struck a match.

'What do you think I'm going to do? Do you think I want his money?'

Lizzy pushed her tongue against the lining of her cheek. 'Yes, I think you want his money. I think you're taking him for a ride. I think you want to know you can sit back and do nothing and you won't have to worry.'

'That isn't true,' said Marie, the barbs reverberating in her chest. Jamie began pulling at her necklace and she took his little fingers and held them. 'No, not mummy's necklace.'

'I suppose my son bought you that.'

Marie sighed. 'I love him.'

Lizzy released a plume of smoke and it caught in the sunlight. 'If you loved him, you'd do the decent thing and let him go.'

'Why would I let him go? He'd be heartbroken if I let him go.'

'For a week or two maybe. And then he'd move on and find someone to have his own family with.'

'But Jamie and I are his family.' She heard herself say this and thought about how hollow it sounded, like a sentence she would never say, not ever.

'Don't make me laugh. You've only known each other five minutes. I don't know who that child's father is but it's not my son, and that's all there is to it.'

Lizzy straightened in her chair and pushed a finger towards Marie. 'You get one shot in life. You meet a fella, get married, have kids. You decided to drop your knickers for any Tom, Dick or Harry and now you have to live with it. You can't turn around and decide to start playing happy families as though it never happened. You made your bed.'

She didn't want to cry in front of this woman, she didn't want to give Lizzy the satisfaction of asking her to pass the violin. So she stood and hitched the baby on to her shoulder, and then she left.

*

You can say what you like, the fact is you can't have a relationship with a man who's given up his mother for you. It sits there in the background like cancer. That's what Marie came to see.

Anderson had done everything he could to avoid this. There'd been a series of discussions or arguments, give them any name you like, they amounted to the same thing. No amount of reasoning with Lizzy made a difference.

'Enough's enough,' he said one evening, after another attempt to talk the woman round. 'Come and live with me,' he said. 'Move into mine and we won't have to see her anymore.'

Marie lay on the bed listening to him. Then she listened to herself, to the ideas that were ricocheting around inside her like pinballs. One idea was that she should do as he said, but along with this idea came the feeling she'd be doing something she wasn't ready to do just to avoid the woman. Another idea was that she should call the whole thing off and put the flat up for sale and get out of that God-awful place. She let her head sink into the pillow and waited.

'I don't know,' she said. 'I need to think about it.'

She could see he was hurt when she said this, that he'd been confident of a different response. He dropped his head and said he had to go, he'd agreed to meet a friend for a beer, a line she understood was a fiction. When he'd gone she remained frozen and dazed on the bed like a cartoon character mown down by a steam-train with a ring of bright stars circling her head.

Later she found herself wanting to do something she could never have predicted, not after everything that had been said when the baby came.

She swung her legs around and sat on the edge of the mattress looking at her son in his cot. She watched him sleeping, listened to the breath rolling in and out of him. Finally, she walked to the living-room, sat down and picked up the phone. She raised the receiver to her ear and the butterflies began roiling around inside her.

She dialled a number and waited.

'Hello,' said the voice on the other end of the line.

'Hello,' she said.

'Is that you, Marie?'

'Yes, Mum.'

'I thought so. How are you?'

'I'm fine.'

'And how's the baby?'

'Oh he's fine. He's asleep at the moment, he's giving me a bit of peace for once. You'll have to come and see him soon.'

'I will,' she said. 'He must be getting big now.'

'Yeah, he is. How are you, Mum?' Marie coiled the lead from the phone around her finger.

'Oh, you know, the boiler's broken down, so that'll be another small fortune down the drain.'

'Mum, don't worry, I have a friend who fixes boilers. He'll come and fix it, don't worry.'

The woman said, 'Who do you know that fixes boilers?'

'Oh, just a man I know. It's him I want to speak to you about actually.'

Marie felt the adrenaline rising in her chest.

'Oh yeah? Sounds like trouble.'

'I don't know what to do.'

Her mother sighed into the mouthpiece. 'Why, what's happened?'

'Nothing. I met someone. Actually it's my neighbour's son, only she doesn't approve because of the baby. She's stopped speaking to us.'

Her mother was silent, and then there was a faint hiss and Marie could tell she was drawing from a cigarette.

'Well, what did you expect, that she'd be laying out the red carpet?'

'She used to like me. She was really good to me when I came here, but since all this she won't even talk to me. Anderson wants us to move into his house.'

'Anderson? Has he no first name, this fella?'

'It's a long story. That is his first name.'

'Anderson?'

'Yes.'

'Well she must be a crackpot to begin with, calling him that.'

Marie sighed. 'Please don't start.'

'Well what do you want me to say?' her mother said. 'What can I say? I'm still amazed you got yourself pregnant in the first place.'

'Mum, will you let it go. I made one mistake. Do I have to pay for it for the rest of my life?'

'Listen Marie, you'll not find many mothers who'll be jumping for joy when their lad comes home with a woman who has a kiddie in tow.'

'No,' she said.

'Honestly, I wish you'd never moved to that city, it's caused nothing but trouble.'

Marie could feel the hairs on her neck stand up, it was as though a jet of cold water was sluicing her spine. 'So what are you saying? That now I have to spend the rest of my life on my own?'

'Just think about that little one. How long have you known this fella?'

'About six months,' she said.

'Right, so you don't really know him at all. But you're set to move in with him and drag that little lad along for the ride, is that what you're saying?'

'I don't know Mum, that's why I wanted to speak to you.'

'Well I think you're mad. What do you think'll happen when you've had a fight and he goes running to his mother? Or when she rings up and announces she's ill? You won't win, love, not in the end.'

Marie knew there was no answer to this. 'Maybe,' she said. 'Maybe you're right.'

'Listen, I was married to your father for twenty-five years and I'll tell you now, it was hard work. And his mother was the least of my problems.'

Marie could feel herself wilting, a sick rose drooping towards the soil. 'But what about me? I want a family. I want a normal life.'

'And you think this is the best way to go about it, do you?'

'I don't know. Why not?'

'Marie, if you don't know, I can't help you.'

'What's that supposed to mean?'

'It means that whatever you do she'll be there, hanging over you. She'll become bigger than you are, than either of you are, and eventually you won't be able to ignore it. And then one day he'll meet some dolly-bird and he'll see how much easier his life could be and that'll be that.'

She pictured things happening as her mother described, she pictured herself sitting alone in this room with the woman sitting on the end of a phone-line telling her, I told you so. 'I don't know,' she said. 'I just don't know anymore.'

Her mother's voice softened. 'Look love, things have changed now. It's Jamie that's got to come first.'

'I know that. But what do I do? What if we break up and she still hates me? She knows everyone around here. They'll all hate me.'

'Don't be daft. Once it's over she won't bother. She's just throwing her weight around. Listen, if she gives you any trouble, I'll come down there and set her straight myself.'

Marie sighed and pushed the air from her nostrils.

'I mean it,' said the woman. 'I'm still your mother.'

After she ended the call, Marie stared out across the canvas of the city with its streetlight-studded arteries and its brutal towers illuminated at intervals so their windows twinkled like constellations stitched into the night.

Inside her she could feel her heart breaking, it was a real thing. What she understood was that she'd never experienced this type of pain before. Now a fissure ran through her and stung in a way that made her curl up like a sick animal on the sofa.

*

For a few seconds Anderson squinted his eyes and stared at her and said nothing at all.

When he did speak, he said, 'What?' as though the meaning of her words had been obliterated somewhere between her lips and his ear, and then when he was done turning them over on his tongue and had swallowed them down he said,

'You're breaking up with me? '

He was wearing a white t-shirt with a hole just below the neckline and flared blue jeans. He pulled a hand through his hair and a clump of it stood up almost vertically, and she would remember this always, this image of him standing there with the dangling bulb from the kitchen ceiling bathing him in an opalescent wash, his mouth hanging open, that tangle of hair reaching branch-like towards the stars.

'I'm sorry,' she said, her voice quavering. 'I have to put Jamie first. I can't just move into your house and act like nothing's happened. She's your mother.'

'Just give it a year. She'll come round in the end.' He moved closer and put a hand on her shoulder.

'She won't.'

Anderson dropped his arm and looked at her. 'I thought you loved me.'

'I do love you. But I have to put Jamie first. I can't be a good mum with all this going on. And I'm not ready to move in with you.'

The words passed over her lips like needles.

He stood motionless in the doorway as though someone was tamping at his skull with a revolver. 'So don't,' he said. 'It doesn't mean we have to break up.'

'It does if I want to walk around the estate with my head up.'

'And that's more important than you and me is it?'

Marie sighed and drew her fingers over the ridge of her forehead.

'So that's it, is it?' he said. Suddenly his hands were on his hips and his eyes were glittering with tears.

The baby began to cry and Marie looked towards the bedroom. Her chest was hot and a blunt pain was starting up in the front of her head. 'I have to go and see to him.'

'I can't believe you're doing this.'

She turned to him and he looked at her like a person he didn't recognise. 'I'm sorry,' she said, and she walked past him and went to the bedroom.

She flicked on the lamp, reached down and took Jamie from his cot and then she sat on the bed and began to soothe him, and that was the moment she left her body and was floated into a capsule behind herself, to watch like a dull holidaymaker with her face pressed up against the glass of a tour bus as her life began to dislocate and fragment.

*

Within a week, Lizzy was smiling again and

greeting her with, 'Hello darling,' as though nothing had happened. The first time Marie saw her out on the stairwell, she said, 'Give him to me, I can hold him while you take the shopping in.'

But she understood who the woman was now. Under no circumstances would she let Lizzy touch her son, not even in passing.

The way she found out Anderson was marrying someone else was that she overheard a woman in the playground telling a neighbour he was engaged to her niece. She marvelled at how he could replace her so quickly, it had been five months. By the end of that awful day she knew she couldn't bear to be in his orbit now, she had to sell the flat and go.

She'd seen him only once in the intervening weeks, on Bethnal Green High Street, about two months after they broke up. She looked up one morning and there he was, stalking towards her, his hands in his pockets, his hair cropped closer to his scalp than before. Her body was flooded with anxiety, with guilt, with feelings she had no name for. She didn't know whether to stop and say hello or what she ought to do. Nobody teaches a person how to behave in these situations.

'Hello,' he said, coming to a stop in front of her.

'How are you?' she replied.

She thought he looked well in spite of what was going on beneath the surface.

'You know,' he said, 'I'm okay.'

She felt terrible when he said that, so terrible she couldn't look him in the eye. Obviously he was lying, she'd broken his heart. All she'd been able to think about since the break-up was Sharon, the woman who'd gone before, and now she'd done the same thing to him, or almost the same thing.

'It's nice to see you,' she said. 'You look well.'

'You too.'

He smiled and told her he'd better get on his way, his mother was waiting.

She thought about that now, about his mother sitting in her flat licking her lips, knowing some puckered childless woman was going to be her daughter-in-law, knowing her grandchildren would be hers by blood. She thought about how Anderson would be brimming with relief knowing he could have both his wife and his mother and he wouldn't have to take on someone else's son. It had all worked out perfectly for them.

She felt such shame about that, about knowing they'd got what they wanted while she sat in her tiny flat, poor and insensate and dogged by the notion she was getting what she deserved.

Marie couldn't stay in that place and be forced to make small-talk with Anderson and his bride out on the walkway, to watch as the woman's pregnant belly came on, to listen to Lizzy carping and laughing beyond the wall.

She put the flat up for sale towards the end of 1972 and it sold quickly, to a man who was middle-aged and drab and wore his weariness squarely, like someone who'd tried and failed and was no longer ashamed about any of it.

The week before she left she ran into Anderson again, only this time he was with his fiancée. They were coming out of the newsagents on Dunbridge Street, a couple like any other. The girl was young, she looked like someone who'd been nowhere and seen nothing, like a person who was still waiting for the shock of life to hit her. Her big eyes were alert and wary, and though she was holding Anderson's hand, she hung back behind his shoulder like a child.

Right away it was clear to Marie that Lizzy would walk all over her.

'Hello,' he said.

'Hi,' she said.

He let go of his fiancée's hand and crouched to stroke Jamie's head. 'Hey buster.'

Jamie cocked his head and clamped himself to

his mother's leg, he didn't know what to make of this man anymore. Anderson smiled at him and stood back up.

'He's gone shy on me.'

'Oh it's just a phase, he's like that with everyone.'

Anderson put his hand to his fiancée's back and drew her forward. 'This is Joanne,' he said.

The girl was wearing a bomber jacket and Doc Marten boots and her lips were coloured pink.

'Hi Joanne. I'm Marie.' She reached out and took the girl's hand, a damp little fish in her palm. She could see the girl knew already who she was.

'Nice to meet you,' she said.

Joanne's voice was meek and apologetic and something about it made Marie pity her, even if another part of her wanted to push her into the road.

'You too,' she said, smiling. She looked from one to the other and understood neither had any idea how to deal with the situation. She realised she could make it hard for them, she could ask a lot of questions about weddings and honeymoons and baby names, but what would be the point? It was over now, what difference did it make that he was marrying an adolescent?

She settled her eyes on Anderson and smiled.

'All the best,' she said.

'All the best, Marie,' he replied.

When she walked away, it struck her that there wouldn't be another man like him, not ever, and the sadness of this was hard and sudden like a blow from a fist.

*

On the morning she was due to leave, Lizzy appeared at her door, a conciliatory smile on her lips. 'Is this it then?' she said.

Marie nodded and the woman handed her a white envelope.

'Don't open it now. Save it till you get in your new flat.'

'I can't take this,' Marie said, and she tried to hand the envelope back.

'Please,' Lizzy said. 'Take it.'

Marie sighed and let her arm fall limp.

In the evening she pulled the envelope from her bag and discovered inside a hundred pounds in crisp five-pound notes. Everything hit her then, it was like a wave breaking over her. She sat down on the arm of the sofa and let it spill out and soon Jamie came over and said, 'Mummy,' and then he began to cry and she lifted him on to her lap and kissed his forehead.

'Look,' she said, holding out the money in

front of him. 'We're rich.'

Chemistry

It was hard to believe Inez had been married four times, she just didn't seem like that type of woman. She wasn't that type of woman either, not at all.

When she was very young, her father would say, 'Inez, you're one in a million.' He meant it too, because out of all his children, out of all the children he'd ever known, she was the calmest, the most placid, the most congenial.

Her father, an ecumenical man, believed Inez to be an earthly expression of the Almighty, a prototype without the baggage of ancestral hurt or hereditary defect. What's true is she was born without greed or malice, without the drive to sublimate anyone else.

Even as a young child she required no distractions to keep her happy. It didn't matter if she was with other kids or alone, whether she had a book or a toy to hand, she'd just sit and let the day wash over her like sunlight washes over a houseplant, and no matter what circumstances arose she met them with equanimity.

Her mother had wanted to call her Emmeline – after Mrs Pankhurst – but her husband objected on the grounds that it sounded too similar to her own name, Emilia.

'Every time I call for one of you, the other one will come running,' he said.

So instead they named the child Inez, after another suffragette, an American called Inez Milholland, who'd been educated at the same school as Emilia – Kensington Secondary School – and had marched with Pankhurst at demonstrations in London before returning to the States to champion women's rights. Milholland was exactly the sort of woman Emilia wanted her daughter to become; pioneering, recalcitrant, unapologetic.

Inez was raised near the village of Little Missenden in Buckinghamshire. Her parents wanted a simpler life away from the city, so they packed up their London home and moved to the country in the spring of 1934.

They chose the Edwardian red-brick house with its ornately carved wooden porch and gabled roof because it was surrounded by fields and gently rolling hills, which to Emilia's mind made it the perfect house to raise a family. Inez came first, in 1935, then Fergus the following year, and finally, Rose, in the autumn of 1938.

Inez loved this house.

She loved its sash windows and its parquet floors and most of all she loved the way the morning sun drenched the pinewood dining table with its pewter jugs of daffodils and wild tulips lined up along the centre.

She loved also the peat-smelling earth of the forest to the east, and the sly crackle of twigs beneath her feet as they melded with the sweet cacophony of the birds above. Sometimes, if she stayed long enough she felt as though she wasn't a person in the world at all anymore but a part of the forest itself, indivisible from the soaring silver birches and the velvet moss and the fluting serenade of all those skittering birds.

As a student, she was conscientious without demonstrating any innate gift of creativity, learning and repeating what was taught in rote fashion, an imprecise machine regurgitating the curriculum as best she could.

When she was ten, Mrs Bronson - her English teacher - told her mother, 'Inez's compositions are coherent enough, but she lacks imagination. They read like shopping lists, Mrs Drake, which as I'm sure you're aware, will take her nowhere at all as a writer.'

Her mother paid no attention because Inez had no desire to be a writer. She had no desire to be anything. Emilia would say that her eldest daughter was like a fine reed that bent to the will of whichever wind blew in her direction, always letting herself be blown yet never breaking no matter how strong the gusts. She enjoyed making these trite analogies about her children. She had the idea they made them sound bohemian and ethereal, and the raised eyebrows of the other mothers did nothing to dissuade her.

It was only later, when she began at high school, that Emilia began to grow concerned about the girl. That Inez was never selfish or spiteful was offset by her apparent lack of passion or drive or ambition. With each passing year, she seemed to become more and more an empty vessel, content to drift around like the softly scuttling dust on the porch step, unfazed either by circumstance or situation and completely unconcerned about her future.

Her siblings loved this about her as they could manipulate her in whatever direction they wished, and in this way, she found herself forever doing Fergus's homework or tidying Rose's room. Not once did she feel hard done by or used either, for the simple reason that she found pleasure in these tasks.

To Inez's mind, all work contained within it a kernel of satisfaction, if only you knew how to approach it. This wasn't an intellectual conclusion she'd arrived at, for Inez spent very little time intellectualising. She simply enjoyed lounging in silence as much as hearing the piano, and she enjoyed both as much as she enjoyed sweeping the tiled kitchen floor. To Inez, one situation was only different from and neither greater nor lesser than the next, and she invited them all with a serenity disarming in one so young.

*

Emilia's concerns at the time of her daughter's early adolescence grew primarily from her ambivalence about forming bonds with other people.

Inez never brought classmates home the way her siblings did or asked to go out in the evenings. She never spoke about her friends or gave the impression she had even superficial ties, and as time went on the situation began to play on her mother's mind.

'Darling, what's going on at school?' she asked her daughter one Saturday as they prepared tea. This was towards the end of 1948, when Inez was thirteen.

'Oh, just the usual,' came the reply.

Her mother poured steaming water into the huge teapot and clicked the porcelain lid into place.

'Darling, you're such a good girl,' she said. 'And you've always been so easy to get along with...' She twisted on the spot, unsure of how to continue. 'Well, it's just... you never mention any friends or bring anyone to the house and, well...' She ran a hand through her unruly hair and offered an awkward smile.

'I know,' said Inez. 'I never invite anyone to the house.' Then she walked to the fridge and took out the milk jug, unaware that this was not a satisfactory end to the conversation.

'But why, darling?' asked Emilia, her voice rising the way it did when she was struck by anxiety, *nerves* being the word she used to describe this condition.

'It never occurred to me,' said Inez. 'We see each other all day at school.'

She began setting down the cups on the kitchen table.

'But you *do* have friends, don't you darling?' said Emilia, covering her throat with a hand to conceal a burgeoning rash.

'Of course. I'm friends with everyone.'

And though her daughter smiled, a disquieting feeling snaked through Emilia and within an hour she was in bed with one of her migraines, and there she would stay for the remainder of the day.

In truth, Inez didn't have any friends at that time, and for the most part the other children in her class considered her an anomaly. While huddles of girls sat gossiping and speculating before class began, Inez could almost always be found staring vacantly through a window or studying the backs of her hands or gazing abstractedly at the looping patterns in the grain of her wooden desk.

This was precisely the scene when Vanessa Morrison called out to her from her seat at the back of the classroom one morning. 'Are you a witch?' she said.

'No,' said Inez, having taken the question at face value.

'So why are you so weird then?'

Vanessa Morrison was tall and feline with hooded eyes and ragged blonde hair, and for the last two years her father had been climbing into her bed in the middle of the night. She didn't have the vocabulary for the places he took her, she only knew that by night she was terrified and by day she seethed with rage, an emotion that had to find its landing place somewhere.

The first time she hit Inez was after a gymnastics class.

'Who do you think you're looking at?' she said, and then she closed her fingers into a fist and punched Inez in the mouth. 'If you tell anyone, I'll kill you,' she said. 'You tripped and fell, bitch.'

Inez didn't hate Vanessa for what she'd done, she wasn't even angry. She simply felt shaken and disorientated, and later, after she'd gone home and told her mother she'd fallen from the hobby-horse, she uncovered a feeling she'd experienced only fleetingly before. Inez had never really been afraid of anything, and here she was, scared to go to school.

*

That first assault had been like a gateway drug, and now her tormentor was hooked. One day she might trip her in the playground, the next she might douse her in water from the stagnant pond.

What Inez learned was that the worst thing wasn't the event itself but the anticipation of this new malediction. *Will it be now?* she would think each time the bell sounded at the end of class.

On a still, overcast day in May, Vanessa followed her to the bus-stop flanked by a coterie of her disciples. As Inez reached the bridge crossing the stream, one of the girls called her name, and when she turned around the whole group ran at her, scooped her up and held her aloft like an offering. The sudden fear that bloomed in her was like a cool hand pushing up through her organs.

'I think it's time you went for a swim,' said Vanessa.

'No don't,' Inez said, her voice fluttering. 'You'll kill me.'

'Three, two, one,' said the voice.

What she heard as she fell was laughter, as though something funny was happening, and then a muffled slamming sound.

Almost immediately there was a man standing over her, pulling her on to the bank of the stream. She could see the curious horror in his eyes when he crouched and looked into her face and she wanted to tell him it was alright, but her jaw was locked in place.

After that she fell asleep and when she regained consciousness and asked where this man had gone, the woman standing over her in a starched white pinafore told her, 'I'm sorry, I don't know who you're talking about.'

'But he was there by the stream,' Inez mumbled.

'Just rest,' said the nurse. 'Don't try to talk.'

Fine, she thought. *I'll find him myself.* And just like that, the first lick of a desire was born in her.

Inez suffered a fractured skull, broken collarbone, broken wrist and three displaced vertebrae in her lower back. She was bound in so much plaster she looked like a mummy.

Emilia did what she felt she had to do when she first saw her daughter's eyelids flutter into life that evening, which was to act as though nothing terrible had happened and show her with her lips, with her eyes, that everything was fine.

Inez said, 'What's happened to my face?'

Her mother leant over and stroked her hairline with the backs of her fingers.

'Don't worry darling, it's nothing that won't heal.'

Inez raised a hand to her cheek. 'What's happened to me? I can hardly open my eyes.'

'They're just a little swollen, darling.'

Inez said, 'Can you pass me a mirror?'

Emilia held her daughter's gaze. 'No darling,' she said. 'Not now.'

*

It was almost nine months after she was thrown from a bridge that Inez walked into the police station to inquire about the man who pulled her from the stream. By then, the only visible signs of the trauma were the small scars on her cheekbone and her forehead. All the rest were hidden beneath her clothes.

The officer on the desk that afternoon was a bald middle-aged man with a bright sanguine face.

'There's a man I'm trying to find,' she began.

'Is there indeed?' he said, looking up from his newspaper.

'I'd be dead if it wasn't for him.'

The officer, whose name was George, had a granddaughter of eleven, and for a moment he saw the girl, whose hair was raven and whose eyes flashed like beacons, lying broken in the pebbled stream with the clear water moving over her.

When Inez finished talking he flicked through a log-book under a table-lamp until he came to the entry he was looking for. Then he took a pen and made a note on a scrap of paper.

'Right,' he said. 'Let's go.'

She turned his name over on her tongue as the car rattled through the lanes. 'Leonard,' she whispered. 'Leonard Rosenthal.' She could still see his green eyes swimming in their sockets.

'Yes?' he said when he opened the door.

'Hello,' she replied.

He squinted, tried to place her.

'Can I help you?'

'I just came to thank you,' she said.

A woman from deep within the house shouted his name.

'Is that your wife?' she said.

'No,' he said in a hushed tone. 'My mother.'

'Oh. You don't recognise me, do you?'

'Sorry,' he said.

Leonard wore slacks and a knitted vest and his dark hair fell in coils like a doll's.

'I'm Inez. The girl you pulled out of the stream.'

'That was you?' he said.

'Yes,' she said, biting at her lip. 'I wanted to thank you. I would have come sooner, but it's taken ages for my back to heal.'

'Of course,' he said. The man began fidgeting with his collar. 'I'd invite you inside but she's ill.'

'Your mother?'

He nodded and said, 'Yes.'

Inez paused and looked past him into the cloistered hallway of the house. 'What about your wife?'

'What wife?' he said.

She sensed a deep and impermeable sadness in this man, and though she was only fifteen, she decided to take responsibility for him as he'd taken responsibility for her. She'd erase the sadness that seemed to orbit him like a planet, she'd replace it with something pure and vital. She believed she could do this just by being next to him, as though love emanated from her in waves like radiation from a sawn-off hunk of uranium.

To her mind, marriage to a person was not about chemistry or falling in love – not that she knew anything about love – but about meeting the person where they stood and allowing the love that flowed out from you naturally to direct itself towards them.

She understood she was too young to marry but she wanted to make her intention plain which is why she wrote a letter to Leonard explaining that she'd return when she was seventeen and if he was still unmarried then she was willing to be his wife. She wrote this note matter of factly, from the perspective of a person without emotional investment in the recipient's acquiescence.

*

Inez was someone whose word was sacred.

That's why she took a bus deep into the Buckinghamshire countryside, walked a mile, map in hand, then arrived on Leonard's doorstep shortly before two in the afternoon. This was three days after she turned seventeen, only now she had a woman's body, a body that belied its inexperience.

'Yes?' he said when he opened the door.

Inez waited and her waiting was rewarded with a sudden flash of recognition. It was clear from the man's expression he'd never expected to see her again.

'How are you?' she said.

'Yes, I'm alright,' he replied. 'How are you?'

'I'm well, thank you.'

'Cold, isn't it?' he said, his cowlick swirling in the breeze.

'Yes,' she said.

Inez shivered and snapped her teeth together but Leonard only looked at her, and she understood he wasn't going to invite her inside.

'Do you remember the note I wrote you?' she said.

'Yes,' he said, 'but I never took it seriously.'

Inez wished she could push back the hands on a clock and reverse herself back to the early morning, to her warm, fettered bed. She would remain there and let the whole day sink beneath her.

'Are you married?' she asked. *Please say yes*, she thought.

Two years had elapsed and she wasn't keen to marry, not now. She'd rather stay at home with her mother and the cat.

'No,' he said. 'But don't worry. I don't expect a young girl like you to marry me. I wouldn't do it to you.' At first he laughed briefly and then a melancholy settled over him, or that's how it seemed to Inez.

'Leonard,' she said, 'how old are you?'

He squinted and said, 'Thirty-six.'

Perhaps it isn't such a great difference as it seems, she thought. *After all, men mature so much more slowly than women.*

Her mother had taught her this.

'Okay,' she said.

*

Emilia was sitting at the dining table, a pot of tea in front of her. 'Darling, you don't owe this man anything,' she said. 'It just isn't a good reason to marry.'

Inez was over by the sink, and she didn't turn from arranging her lilacs in the tall pewter jug. 'It isn't that,' she said.

'Well, what is it?' said her mother. She stood and walked over to her daughter, teacup in hand, arriving next to her by the draining board. 'Put the flowers down a minute, please.'

Inez laid them down and turned square on to this woman, this creature who was so much shorter than her now. 'I just know it's the right thing to do.'

Emilia put down her cup and pressed her daughter's arm. 'But darling, you're talking about the rest of your life.'

'I know,' Inez said, and returned to her lilacs.

'You say it as though it's nothing,' said Emilia.

'I don't think it's nothing. I just think it's the right thing to do.' Inez began sifting the flowers with long delicate fingers.

'Inez, you're seventeen years-old. How can it be the right thing to do?'

'Because it's God's will, what Daddy calls God's will. I can feel it.'

Emilia shook her head. 'And that's all you have to say on the matter is it?'

'Yes,' she said, and she turned to face her mother. 'But thank you for asking.'

Emilia looked at her daughter for a moment, at her lambent smile and limpid eyes, and then she poured her Earl Grey into the sink and walked away.

*

In the beginning, Inez moved into the house Leonard shared with his mother, and it was a shock because the woman was troubled, deeply so. Her name was Pearl and her husband had been killed in the First World War, he'd been shelled in a trench and buried on foreign soil. Her feeling was that Pearl had never recovered from this and it had turned her into a different person, but this was only her feeling, she didn't really know.

What she did know was that the woman was

an alcoholic. Inez had never been around alcohol before, and suddenly she found herself living side by side with a person who drank gin as though it was tea.

Pearl had only agreed to the marriage on the basis that Leonard would remain in the house and from the start she warned his new bride, 'Don't think I don't know your game. You'll not get him out from under me.'

Inez bore the woman's stupors with grace and absorbed her taunts and remonstrations without comeback. Leonard was mortified by it all and sometimes he would apologise in the dead of night as they lay side by side in the marital bed, the same bed in which they read and slept and attempted no physical affection for fear of being heard by the woman on the other side of the wall.

'It doesn't matter,' she told him. 'Don't worry.'

After four months an extraordinary thing happened. Pearl got up and walked into the bathroom one Sunday morning and never walked out again. One of the tributaries from her heart blew a leak and she died right there on the throne.

Inez found her. She didn't panic or call for an ambulance, she just held the woman and something emanated from her and enveloped that cooling body like a glove envelops a hand. It was her instinct to stay very still, and when her husband appeared and asked what the matter was she replied, 'She's gone.'

'She's dead?' he said.

'Yes,' she replied. 'She was dead when I found her.'

When the house had been sold, they moved to a small flat on the outskirts of Amersham where Leonard was closer to work and Inez was closer to her family.

She loved this flat. She loved its strange angles and its slanting floorboards. She loved also that this is where she found out who she was married to; that her husband had once fallen from an open window and knocked out his front teeth, that he'd been bullied not only by his mother, that he was allergic to pineapple.

He wouldn't talk about the war except to say he was one of only six of his squadron to come home. She would never hear about the time his nose was broken by another soldier's rifle after it was blown clean out of his hand, or about the day he used the body of a friend as a shield to protect himself from gunfire. These were the truths she would never know, yet she knew the torments they caused, she felt them just as a woman almost ready to burst open feels the wax and wane of her nascent child.

Without his mother, Leonard began to bloom.

The blood travelled up through his neck and traversed the plains of his face and gradually his pale skin grew florid.

'It sounds like a fairytale that a person can change colour because he's been set free, but it's true.'

This is something Inez would say.

'If something sounds hard to believe it's almost certainly not true, and if it sounds impossible to believe it almost certainly is.'

She would also say this, because she'd heard a woman with a low honeyed voice say it on the wireless one day, and now she understood the woman had been right.

Leonard was a chemical engineer and all Inez knew about his job was that he was involved in designing plastics which could be sold as commercial products, either as constituent parts or as packaging. Sometimes he conducted experiments to test the stability of different materials in his lab and one day, after altering the chemical composition of a new type of plastic, he heated the substance beyond a certain point and there was an explosion.

Two men dressed in grey flannel suits came to the house to tell her. These men were scientists also and they said that accidents of this nature were extremely rare. They used technical language to explain the chemical reaction, but she could barely understand what they were talking about. She wondered if they knew she had no knowledge of polymers and combustibles.

'I'm sorry,' she said, 'I don't understand. Is Leonard alright?'

The first man became flustered and cleared his throat while the second said, 'Leonard's dead.'

Inez hadn't expected to be a wife at seventeen or a widow at eighteen, but life had its own way. She sold her home to a young couple – although not as young as she – and it made her happy that this flat with its strange asymmetry and long shadows that rippled on the varnished floor like flowing water would go to these newlyweds. She knew they were newlyweds because they told her often.

'The thing is, we're married now,' one or the other would say, as though they were children playing at being grown-ups, and Inez did not tell them they were talking to a widow.

All the furniture she had chosen and Leonard had paid for she decided to offer them to help them get started.

'You can have everything in here if you want it,' she said.

'Are you sure?' asked the young woman, clutching at her necklace.

'Of course.'

'But let us pay you something,' said the young man.

'This chiffonier, this looks expensive,' said the young woman, and she stretched out a slender hand towards a chest of drawers.

Inez had never heard this word before. Chiffonier. 'Don't worry,' she said, and batted away their offers. 'You can have it all.'

The young woman smiled at her and took her hand. 'Thank you. That's so kind of you.'

'You're welcome.'

'Where's your husband?' asked the young woman, because Inez still wore her wedding ring.

'Oh, he's waiting for me in America.'

She had no idea what induced her to say this. She'd known she would lie about him when they brought him up because she wanted to spare them the discomfort, but she had no idea she'd bring America into it.

*

'You'll move back in here with us,' said her mother.

'No, Mother. Once the flat's sold I think I'll go abroad for a while.'

Emilia almost dropped the azalea she was

carrying. 'Abroad? What on earth are you talking about?'

Inez felt such warmth towards her mother, towards this woman who worried about her so deeply, that she almost walked right over and embraced her. 'I think I might go to America,' she said.

Emilia set the plant down. 'America? Darling, have you taken leave of your senses?'

Inez didn't attempt to answer this.

She'd never been on an aeroplane, and the thought of sitting in a metal tube being catapulted through the clouds made her feel like a curtain of icy water was drawing itself across her chest. She booked herself a seat on a liner to New York instead.

Inez imagined lounging on the deck and drinking cool lemonade and looking out across mile upon mile of lustrous blue water with the breeze running over her skin, and the idea seemed like a small slice of paradise. For the rest of her life she would wonder whether travelling on a liner was really how she'd envisaged it, with the rolling water and the sky and the sweet astringency of lemonade curling over her tongue.

*

'Is this seat taken?' asked the man.

He was halfway to sitting down by the time she had the chance to answer. It was the week before she was due to set sail and Inez was on her way to London to buy some clothes for the trip. She shifted her feet and tucked them beneath her seat, and the man stretched out his legs. He was very tall and broad-backed and his body took up both his own seat and a section of the seat next to him.

'God, it's hot,' he said, and he ran the back of his hand across his forehead.

'Yes, it's lovely,' said Inez.

'Well it's too hot for me,' he said, and he put his head back against the rest.

Inez looked at his face and saw he had one blue eye and one brown eye.

'Yes, they're different colours,' he said.

'I'm sorry, what?'

'My eyes,' he said. 'One's blue and one's brown.'

He moved his index finger from one eye to the other as he spoke, only he pointed to the brown one when he said the word *blue* and to the blue one when he said the word *brown.*

'That's unusual.'

'Yes. Do you have a tissue?'

The man was sweating and the beads had gathered on his forehead and were beginning to streak down over his temples.

'Oh,' said Inez. She picked up her bag from the seat beside her and began to root around. 'Yes, here you are. Don't worry, it's clean.'

She passed him a crinkled handkerchief and in the process realised his hand was almost twice the size of her own. He used his thick fingers to dab his forehead with the delicate square of white cotton and then he folded the handkerchief and reached out to hand it back to her.

'No, you keep it,' she said.

The man looked embarrassed and he turned and peered out into the fields beyond the glass. Inez understood he must have the impression she was perturbed by the idea of touching the handkerchief after he'd mopped his forehead with it. This made something in her chest fly and when she looked at him, his head remained pointing into the fields beyond the glass.

'Are you going into London?' she asked.

'Yes, I'm going back to the office,' he said, looking back at her. 'I've just been at a viewing.'

The man was wearing a royal blue suit and had placed a black leather briefcase on the seat next to him.

'What is it you do?'

'I sell houses.'

'I see. Do you like selling houses?'

'It's a job,' he said, shrugging. 'What are you doing in London?'

'I'm going shopping.' Inez smiled and the man smiled back, and for a few seconds nobody said anything and then she felt suddenly very self-conscious because she realised they were still grinning at each other, so she said, 'I'm sailing to America next week.'

'Really?' he said. 'To New York?'

'Yes, that's right.'

'How long are you going for?'

Inez bit at her lip. 'It's a one-way ticket.'

'I see,' he said. 'A little adventure.'

His one blue eye and his one brown eye twinkled.

'Yes, I'm excited,' she said, and she raised her shoulders and grinned again.

'And who are you going with?'

Inez turned and looked out at a row of scattershot houses. 'I'm going on my own,' she said.

She expected the man to react with incredulity or disapproval, this was how everyone reacted when she told them of her plans, but instead he said, 'That's a brave thing to do.'

She turned to face him again. 'Why do you say that?'

'Because it is brave. To just take off and not know what will happen.'

'But would you not do something like that?'

The man made a *hmmm*-ing sound and said, 'No, I'm not very brave.' Then he paused and looked out of the window again. 'I like things as they are anyway.'

Something inside her sensed this wasn't true.

For a while nobody spoke and then as the train drew into the city, she said, 'I haven't even told you my name. I'm Inez.' She reached forward and allowed the man's hand to swallow hers.

'Pleased to meet you, Inez,' he said. 'I'm Adam.'

He withdrew his hand and reached into the inside pocket of his blazer, then handed her a crisp white rectangular card. The card said, *Imperial Properties*, and beneath that it said, *Adam Everlast – Property Sales Agent*.

The letters were ornately drawn in calligraphy she associated with aristocracy and prestige. She turned the card over with her fingers and then she read the words again and reached out to hand it back to him.

'No,' he said, 'that's for you.'

Inez wondered what use she would have for a

company that sold expensive houses but placed the card in her purse as she didn't want to offend him a second time.

Soon the city closed in around them and suddenly everywhere were buildings and people and industrial chimneys with slanting grey towers of smoke rising from their dark mouths.

'Do you live in London?' she said.

'Yes, in Chelsea.'

'That's a nice area, isn't it?'

'I suppose it is,' he said. 'I only live there because it's close to the office.'

They looked at each other for a moment and then each grew shy and turned to the window, and the atmosphere seemed to Inez to change then so that something in her began to feel constricted, as though she was wearing a corset that had been bound too tightly.

It was only a few seconds after the announcer's voice began issuing from the tannoy, saying, 'We are now arriving in Marylebone,' that Adam cleared his throat several times. Neither one looked back at the other, and he started to speak whilst still blinking into his lap.

'I understand this is a very odd thing to do,' he began, 'particularly given you're leaving the country next week, but would... well, would you have dinner with me?'

They each blushed and avoided the other's gaze and as the passengers began to congregate in the aisle beside them, she said, 'When?'

'Erm, today I expect.'

'Yes, that's probably easiest,' she replied, and both were embarrassed because they had each been stricken by the sense that their ability to communicate sensibly had been pulled away like a rug from beneath their feet. When the train came to rest, the other passengers moved down the aisle and left the carriage.

'I suppose we should get off,' he said.

'Yes,' she replied, smiling. 'I suppose we should.'

They stood up and Inez led them from the train. Adam Everlast inhaled and exhaled deliberately and they walked stiffly along the platform like two wooden things on strings. At the entrance to the station, he said, 'I'll come and get you at five. Where will you be?'

Inez gazed into the steel corniches above and began to deliberate. 'Well I'm going to Regents Street,' she said, 'and then I'll walk down to the park.'

'Which park?'

'Green Park.'

'How about we meet at the entrance to the park then? On Piccadilly.'

For a moment she looked at him and in response he gazed off into the middle-distance to where a carriage was pulling away.

'Yes okay,' she said. 'That should be fine.'

*

Inez felt it was undignified to begin with another man so soon after her husband's passing and Adam Everlast agreed, so for six months they met once a week and had dinner at her mother's table in the umbra of familial propriety.

'Well I can't say I'm happy about it,' her father told Adam. 'But at least you stopped her getting on that damn boat.'

'Francis, that's no way to talk to him,' said Emilia. 'Adam's a gentleman, anyone can see that.' Then she let out a strange high giggle, one her husband hadn't heard in twenty years.

Inez married Adam in June of 1956, when she was twenty-one and he was twenty-six. They moved to London and bought a house in Kensington, a white townhouse with vivid pink bougainvillea that clung to the walls and snaked around the front door.

Inez loved this house. From the start she said it would be a wonderful house to raise children, and for the next five years they tried in vain to conceive. Finally, they went to the doctor and then to a series of specialists but none could determine the problem.

'It could be the accident,' said one.

'You mean when I fell from the bridge?' she said.

'That's the one,' he replied, his aquiline face already pointing in another direction.

She wanted to adopt but Adam didn't like the idea. He'd once listened to a radio programme about a couple who adopted a child, and the child was very difficult to manage, and this couple stuck with him even though he started to get into trouble with the police and become violent.

One day, the mother – the adopted mother – lost her temper with the child because he'd stolen from her – this is what the police said had happened – and he picked up a fire-iron and hit her across the head with it. He kept on hitting her with it until she was dead. Then when the adopted father came home, the child hit him with this same implement and he continued hitting him until the man was also dead.

Adam was not scared for himself, but he was scared for Inez. He'd listened to this radio programme when he was still a child and it had altered him in a way he could no longer unpick. He understood that if something happened to him as a man he could open that part of himself up and fix what had been damaged, but the traumas of his childhood were elusive and implacable, metastasising in the shadows like tumours.

As it turned out, it was a tumour that undid it all.

This was in 1967, when they'd been married for eleven years. It started one day when they were at breakfast. Inez had made them their morning porridge, and they'd just begun to eat it when her husband sneezed four times in quick succession. Adam Everlast's sneezes were geyser-like expulsions and Inez had always found them as endearing as they were startling, only on this particular morning, as he released the last of his quartet, a sudden repellence descended on her and impelled her to stand and walk to the window.

At exactly that moment a blue-feathered bird was touching down on the high brick wall enclosing the garden.

'Look,' she said, tipping her head. 'Isn't that a swallow?'

'Isn't what a swallow?'

'That bird,' she said, pointing. 'What else would I be talking about?'

Adam shifted in his seat and looked out. 'I don't know, darling. I don't know anything about birds.'

'It's fine,' she said. 'Forget it.'

Inez walked out of the room with a strange knot in her chest. She couldn't remember ever telling her husband to forget anything, it just wasn't a thing she said.

Something inside her was shifting so that soon enough she began to smoulder when she looked into Adam's face, or when he made one of his facile jokes about what the girl said to the soldier, or when he bundled her up in his muscular embrace.

'Oh, get off,' she said to him one evening, right after he tossed his newspaper down on the kitchen table and took hold of her, planting a kiss on her neck, in her very favourite spot. She yanked an arm free and drew back her head and for a moment he froze before stepping back and regarding her open-mouthed, a wounded expression on his face.

'What's wrong?' he said.

'Nothing' she said. 'But why do you have to be grabbing at me all the time?'

'What's going on, Inez?' he said, this huge man who appeared suddenly diminished, his shoulders down.

'What do you mean?' she said, turning away to flip bacon on the griddle.

'I don't know what I'm supposed to have done.'

'Don't be a baby,' she said. 'Just sit down and I'll bring your dinner.'

Things progressed steadily in this direction until Adam knew better than to touch his wife, until he took his meals alone at the kitchen table while she sat watching the television or went out to play bingo, until they rose separately and didn't ask one another how their days had been, until their affections were nothing but memorials seared on his mind.

After six months of this, Inez opened her wardrobe one day and noticed a red silk blouse. She studied it a moment and then reached out and touched it, running her fingertips over the fabric. Her breath caught in her throat and she pulled the blouse from the hanger and held it up to the sun. She sniffed at the neckline and suddenly a fire caught in her belly. Inez took the blouse and walked to the kitchen, to where Adam was pouring water from the kettle.

'What's this?' she said.

Her husband turned to look at her. 'A blouse by the look of it.'

'I know what it is, Adam. Who does it belong to?'

'I've no idea. Where did you get it?'

'It was hanging in the wardrobe.'

He shrugged his shoulders. 'Then I'd imagine it's yours.'

'It is *not* mine,' she said. 'How the hell did it get in my wardrobe?'

Adam shrugged again. 'I've no idea. I can assure you it isn't mine.'

'This isn't funny. Who have you had up there?'

'I'm not going to entertain this, Inez,' he said. He lowered his cup and began moving towards the doorway.

'Don't you dare walk out,' she said. 'Is this that girl from the post office?'

Inez was furious. She'd seen how that stupid girl looked at him, how she giggled whenever her husband said the slightest thing.

'I don't know who you are anymore,' he said, shaking his head at her.

Adam Everlast turned away and walked to the front door, and then when he arrived he pulled it open and walked out, and the things she shouted after him he didn't hear.

The red silk blouse did belong to Inez. She'd bought it a year earlier, worn it once and decided it wasn't for her. It had made her feel like she was playing a part, the part of a woman she didn't understand, and she didn't like that feeling. It was the sort of blouse she could imagine very well on somebody else, but on her it was wrong and she could feel its wrongness all over her when she wore it, even when her eyes were trained on the sky or the person opposite.

The whole experience had made her wonder what she'd been thinking when she took it to the cash register and willingly handed over money for it. For that reason alone the garment had been memorable, but memory was failing her now. Like so many aspects of Inez's psychology, it was beginning to unravel.

*

When Adam said, 'I don't know who you are anymore,' right after his wife accused him of sleeping with the girl from the post office, he didn't realise it was because she was no longer his wife.

Inez didn't realise this when she filed for divorce after twelve years of marriage either. Nor did she realise it when she married a man nine years her junior without a second thought, but it was a sort of madness that had come over her, and this madness had been caused by a mass that was pressing on her pituitary gland. It wasn't until she began drinking and left her new husband that all this came to light.

Inez was admitted to Charing Cross hospital with a head injury after falling on the steps outside Marylebone Library in the autumn of 1969. That morning she'd walked out of her dingey bedsit on Greek Street carrying a brown paper bag concealing a quart of single malt whiskey.

She'd walked up through Soho Square and on to Oxford Street, raising the bag to her mouth at intervals to drink from the bottle, and the sting in her throat as it went down felt redolent of medicine. Inez had walked slowly, a cipher against the backdrop of old London, so that the people swept past her in shoals like mindless fish chattering to one another and gulping down air and staring into shop windows as though that were enough to make a life.

The sky was daubed with grey like the sky of a sad painting, and the only sounds on the high street were the endless chugging buses and the dreary lilt of women's voices crooning to each other as they went by.

On the corner of Cavendish Square, she passed a lady with a stoop and a little dog, and she said, 'Good morning,' and the lady stared at her for a moment and then she drew her dog closer and continued on.

For a while Inez walked aimlessly, but it occurred to her as she rounded the bend on to Marylebone High Street that she could chance her arm in the library. Sometimes they would leave her be with a book and other times they would ask her to go, it depended who was on duty. Last time it had been the awful woman with the black curls and the cold white mouth saying, 'Excuse me, I'm afraid you'll have to go.' And for what?

Inez knew to keep things in her pockets when she entered the library, so that's where her hands were firmly planted when she tripped on the cool stone step, and that's why her forehead broke her fall and redefined her whole day, her whole life.

In the hospital, a nurse circled around her and took her bloods and wrote on a clipboard that hung from the end of her bed. Inez was not awake, she hadn't regained consciousness after the fall. Scans had been taken and a hairline fracture to the skull had been identified. Beneath that was a cloudy sphere nestling at the base of her brain.

'Jesus Christ,' hissed the consultant, staring at the amorphous white blur on the scan. 'I'm going for a cigarette.'

The junior doctor shadowing him nodded, then leaned in to see for himself.

There was no choice but to operate.

The consultant took her parents to a room with six chairs and a low table and once they'd sat down he said, 'Inez has a tumour on the brain.'

They looked at him blankly.

'It's located just beneath the pituitary gland,' he said. 'Which is here.'

The consultant showed them a diagram of a human brain and pointed with a fountain pen.

'If we don't remove it, it'll kill her.'

Tears began to form in the corners of Francis's eyes. The consultant did not like for people to cry, so he didn't look at him again.

'Unfortunately, the operation is very risky,' he said. 'I'd say it was seventy-thirty against. But it could be that the odds are worse than that.'

The consultant focused his attention on Emilia. 'Is there anything you want to ask?'

She ran her thumb over her lips. 'This tumour,' she said. 'How long has she had it? Is there any way of knowing?'

The consultant tilted his head to one side. 'It's difficult to say. I suspect it's been growing for several years.'

She nodded. 'And is it possible it could have caused changes in her personality? You see, Inez went from being the sweetest girl you ever met to someone we didn't recognise. She stopped having anything to do with us.'

'I see,' he said. 'It's a possibility.'

'Doctor?' she said. 'If the operation works, does that mean there's a chance the old Inez will come back?'

The consultant tilted his head again. 'It's impossible to say. And I don't think we should get our hopes up.' He nodded to them, and then he excused himself and went out.

*

Inez did wake up, and when she did the first thing she asked was, 'What happened?'

Just as she'd done all those years before, Emilia said, 'Don't worry darling, it's nothing that won't heal.'

Inez shifted her eyes to her father. 'Where's Adam?'

'I don't know,' said Francis. 'At home I expect.'

A crestfallen expression coloured her face. 'But why isn't he here?' she said.

Francis turned to his wife and she took her daughter's hand. 'I don't think he knows you're in hospital, darling.'

Inez shifted in the bed. 'Why not?'

Emilia smiled because she didn't want her daughter to panic.

'Will you call him?' said Inez.

'Yes,' she said, 'but first we need to talk to the doctor.'

*

When Adam arrived at her bedside, Inez smiled and said, 'There you are,' and it was clear to him she'd been asleep for a very long time and was only now waking up.

'Hello Inez,' he said.

'What's wrong?' she whispered.

Adam considered things for a moment. 'Nothing,' he said finally, and he took hold of her hand and held it, and then he sat down by her side.

*

Inez was married for the fourth time at the age of thirty-six. Her fourth husband was also her second husband, and in another way, her third. His name was Adam Everlast.

Theirs was a small service at the Marylebone registry office. Inez wore a simple lace dress she found in a tiny boutique on the Portobello Road and pinned her hair with a clip embroidered in white flowers. It was September of 1971.

The house in Chelsea with the bougainvillea had long since been sold. Adam had walked out on his life and his career and for a year he'd travelled because he thought, *If you can turn into a different person overnight then so can I.*

He'd even taken a liner to New York.

When he told Inez this, she told him about how she'd always imagined it must be to travel on a ship. 'Is it like that?' she asked.

He paused and considered what she'd described and then he said, 'No, not really.'

In a way this made her pleased.

After they remarried, they decided to start afresh in North London. They found a handsome townhouse in Angel that had been split into three units and bought the ground floor flat.

Adam took a job at a local estate agents, and the houses he showed were modest and the people he took to see these houses wore clothes from inexpensive department stores and worried about whether the second bedroom would be big enough for two children to share. He liked these people better and he was happier then, and he didn't miss the money he'd earned before.

Inez loved this flat because it had a large bay window at the front and french doors on to a small rose-garden in the back. She loved that in the morning the light would stream in from the front and in the late afternoon it would stream in from the back. Sometimes she would stand in that throw of sunlight and the feeling was like a great light being switched on in her chest and illuminating her from the inside.

One Saturday, the year after they arrived, Adam came home from buying his morning paper and said, 'There's a woman moving in upstairs, she's on her own with a boy. I'm going to give her a hand with her boxes.'

Inez made tea and invited the woman in. 'I'm Inez,' she said. 'It's lovely to meet you.'

The woman was pale and shy and when she said, 'I'm Marie,' it was hard to make out the words.

'And who's this?'

'Oh, this is Jamie,' the woman said, patting his head. 'Say hello, Jamie.'

But the boy didn't say anything.

Inez ruffled his hair and crouched down to him. 'Hello sweetheart,' she said. 'I have some biscuits in the kitchen. If Mummy says it's okay, you can come and choose one.'

She looked up and Marie smiled.

'Go on,' she said. 'Go with the nice lady, I'm here.'

Inez took his little hand and they walked into the kitchen, and then she opened a cupboard and pulled out a box and placed it on the counter. 'Now this one's chocolate, this one's wafer, and I bet you know what this one is, don't you?'

Inez held up a pale round biscuit with a fleshy scarlet centre. The little boy nodded and lowered his head.

'What is it, sweetheart?'

'Jammy dodger,' he whispered.

'Yes, jammy dodger. Which one would you like?'

Jamie pointed to the jammy dodger and Inez handed it to him.

'Take another,' she said. 'Anything you like.'

The little boy considered things for a second and then he picked out another one just the same.

Afterwards, when the young woman and her son had gone upstairs and Adam had gone out to watch the rugby, Inez sat down at the dining table and gazed absently through the french windows. After all that had gone on, and here she was in this flat she loved with this man who had forgiven her everything without a single thing pressing at her brain. And if that weren't enough, now this mother and her beautiful – *because that's the only word for him,* she thought – her beautiful child, had landed in her lap.

She could still see him standing in front of her, his little head bowed, the hair tumbling over his eyes.

'Oh Inez,' she said.

Restaurant

Henry Fletcher unlocked the door to his car, slung his briefcase on the passenger seat and stepped inside.

He didn't drive in the direction of the school but instead directed his mustard Volvo towards Holborn. His destination was Hatton Cross, and when he arrived he pulled up to the kerb, cut the ignition and flicked the remains of his Marlboro from the window.

The sun was sharply white and made the diamond necklaces in the jeweller's window glitter. Inside, the shop smelled of vetiver and old money and the glass-topped cabinets formed a wide corridor leading to the counter where the proprietor was standing with his eyes fixed on Mr Fletcher.

Mr Fletcher regarded the man. He was tall and lean and his hair was slicked with oil. He wore a tailored blue suit and an inscrutable expression and his hands were laid out on the vitreous counter like claws.

'Good morning, sir,' he said.

'Good morning. I'm here to collect a ring.'

The man nodded and asked for Mr Fletcher's name. He gave it and the man said, 'Bear with me a moment,' and then he disappeared into a dimly lit room behind a white door. Above this door was an elegant clock with a black face and gold hands.

No sooner had Mr Fletcher turned and surveyed the shop than the man was returning, holding a crimson box. 'Here we are,' he said.

'Can I see?'

The jeweller handed him the box and he opened it and held the ring up to his eye. The little nest of diamonds flashed as the light passed over them, and a thread of adrenaline moved through him. After a moment, he snapped the box shut and thanked the man and the man nodded and looked at him with cool blank eyes, like two pebbles in a stream.

*

He was five minutes late for his first class of the day, and when he entered the room a boy with dark hair was sitting on top of a pile of clothes on the floor in front of the blackboard and ten or twelve other children were stood around him jeering. When they saw Mr Fletcher the children froze, and after a moment they dispersed, creeping back to their desks in silence.

'What's going on here?' he said.

The boy sitting on the pile of clothes lowered his eyes.

'Well?'

The boy did not look up, and Mr Fletcher realised then that the pile of clothes beneath him was a child.

The first boy stood, and the one who'd been curled up foetus-style unfurled himself and sat up. Mr Fletcher took this child's arm and hoisted him to his feet.

He turned to the first boy. 'I'm waiting,' he said.

'He started it.'

'What did he do?'

'What's the point?' said the boy. 'No-one believes me anyway.'

'That won't wash with me. Go and stand against the wall. The rest of you, shut up and stay in your seats, I'm going to be right outside the door. If I hear one voice, you're all spending lunchtime with me.'

Mr Fletcher took the other child outside. He closed the door behind him. 'Jamie,' he said, 'what happened?'

'Nothing.'

'If you don't tell me what happened, I can't help,' he said. 'I can see what's going on here, I know this isn't a one-off.'

The caretaker was wheeling a metal bucket along the floor and the boy turned and looked at this man – a man who looked too old to be working – and carried on looking at him as he passed by them.

'There are things we can do,' said Mr Fletcher. 'But only if you let us help.'

The boy put a finger in his mouth and bit at the skin around the nail. His fingers were raw from doing this, they were bloody along the edges of the cuticles. Mr Fletcher had noticed this before. It wasn't something he wanted to see, it made his stomach turn. 'Would you like me to help you?' he said.

Jamie took his finger from his mouth and shook his head.

'Why not?'

The boy said, 'I'm fine.'

At lunch time, he thought about calling the boy's mother. He knew she was a mess, that she didn't work, that she'd been involved with social services. He knew there was no sign of a father, that her son parented himself. Perhaps this was a projection, perhaps he didn't know this. What he knew was that he didn't know what to do. He decided to do nothing.

He thought about Kathy, about what she'd be

doing right at this moment. *Chances are, she'll be eating lunch. A salmon sandwich or a salad, something small.* Kathy only ever ate small meals. That's how she was so slim.

'Kathy knows more about the Second World War than any woman I know. Or man for that matter.' This he told his friend Tony when he first started seeing her.

'And that's what you look for in a woman is it?' Tony said. 'Jesus Christ, Henry, no wonder you're single at fifty.'

'Forty-eight,' Mr Fletcher said. 'I'm forty-eight.'

He met Kathy through a lonely hearts column. He never imagined he'd post a lonely hearts ad, or want to meet anyone desperate enough to post an ad of their own, but there it was.

'How shall we pretend we met?' he asked her. This was during their third date. Kathy was pushing a fork through a mound of arborio rice when he said this.

'Let's say we met at a train station,' she said. 'On a platform.'

'Why?'

She smiled. 'I don't know, I just think that'd be a nice way to meet.'

'Because of *Brief Encounter*?'

Her face dropped. 'No,' she said, 'it's nothing to do with that.'

Kathy didn't want to be seen as romantic or emotional or any of the things that would mark her out as feminine, as someone not to be taken seriously, as *only a woman*.

She was an academic, and just to get a seat at the table she'd had to know more than the men (but make them feel they knew more than she), get better results from her students (but assure her male colleagues it was thanks to their tutelage) and publish papers that were at least as respected as the rest of the faculty (whilst giving the impression it was on account of the proximity to the testosterone-fuelled rigour under which they'd been conceived).

In the early days of her career, she'd experimented with cropped hair and stark make-up, but it turned out this didn't align her with her male colleagues. Then they saw her not only as a woman, but as an unattractive woman - she'd overheard the word *dyke* being bandied around the department - so for a while she explored masculinity's counterpoint and donned short skirts, showcased clamouring semi-exposed breasts.

Then they leered and made remarks but they didn't respect her, so in the end she concluded there was no answer if you were female, and after that she learned to accept she would be measured primarily by her appearance until such time as her body of work could no longer be treated as incidental.

She had a PhD in Political Theory and ran classes on International Relations and Conflict Resolution. Mr Fletcher had never met a woman he'd been so in awe of. Neither of his first two wives had known anything about the political climate beyond their own back yards. In bed, he and Kathy would coil their limbs around each other, light cigarettes and discuss the Israel situation or the revolution in Iran, and it felt to him like life was finally unfurling itself. But that was always succeeded by the notion that it could end in the blink of an eye.

What if she's hit by a car or gets cancer or something? he'd think. *Because that's possible. Anything's possible.*

Kathy would have been a man if she'd had the choice in the beginning, and by beginning, you could go right through to her mid-twenties. But having made of her life what she had she felt differently now, and if someone offered her the switch she wouldn't have to consider it.

She'd married at twenty-eight, and by then she wouldn't have traded being a wife for being a man. The falling in love thing had done that to her. That's what it was about in the beginning, and later it was the genuine appreciation of her own womanhood, but this was a late-flowering realisation.

Her husband's name was Richard but Mr Fletcher didn't come to know about him until one Sunday in June of 1980 – four months after they met – when he took a copy of Tolstoy's *Anna Karenina* from Kathy's bookshelf and a photo of the man fell out.

'Who's this?' he said. He could see the shock in her expression when she angled his hand towards her and looked into that creaseless plaintive face.

She snatched the photo away, then immediately composed herself and handed it back to him. Richard had a wide jaw, black hair and dark shining eyes. He wore a polo shirt and slacks and it was evident that beneath his clothes his body was hard and sculpted. Mr Fletcher had assumed he'd be scrawny or skewed in the face, that he'd be an awkward academic type. A beautiful man he'd never imagined, not for a second.

'What happened with Richard?' he said that night.

Kathy gave him a look.

I see, he thought. Only Mr Fletcher didn't know what he saw.

Later they went to bed in silence and did not make love. He couldn't sleep and in the end he raised his head and peered over at Kathy. He could make out the whites of her eyes under the fractured light from the street. 'How long have you been awake?' he said.

'I don't know. All night I suppose.' She sat up and brought her legs around so they dangled from the side of the bed.

'He died,' she said.

'Richard?' said Mr Fletcher.

'Yes.'

Mr Fletcher could feel his heart pumping. 'What happened?'

'He was in Scotland on a field trip… he got into a helicopter one day and it crashed.'

He was stunned by this, the idea made the hairs on his arms rise up. 'I'm sorry,' he said, and he placed a hand on her shoulder.

Kathy let her hair fall over her cheeks. She told him it was fine and then she stood and walked to the bathroom. She didn't return for a long time and they didn't speak of Richard again, but afterwards Mr Fletcher felt like he was always in the room with them, that when they kissed he was watching from just beyond his shoulder, that when they made love he was right there with them in the bed.

*

Am I really going to do this? he thought as he sipped his tea, as he looked absently into the moving branches beyond the glass.

He could feel the edge of the box against his chest. Mr Fletcher didn't eat that day. He avoided the staff-room and went instead to his car at lunch-time, and once he'd closed himself inside, he turned the engine over and drove out of the gates. He followed the traffic for a mile or so and then turned into a side-street and pulled up behind a row of parked cars.

He took a cigarette from the packet and lit it and then he wound down his window and sat back with his head pressing at the rest. The smoke ribboned around his face and caught in his throat so he put his arm outside the window and held the cigarette against the door. Then he looked down at the protrusion in his blazer, and switching the cigarette to his other hand, he fished out the box. Something about the feel of it made him shiver when he tracked a course along the satin-edged ridge.

He held the cigarette in his mouth and let it hang there between his lips while he opened the box and looked inside. The cluster of diamonds winked at him and he drew from the cigarette and let the smoke roil from his nostrils so that it passed through the mouth of the ring. Mr

Fletcher closed the box and put it back inside his blazer. He opened the door and stepped out into the day and then he stood with his back against the wall of a terraced house and imagined delivering the words.

Am I supposed to speak first or kneel? Will that embarrass her? Maybe I should do it at home where she can't be embarrassed, he thought.

A woman came out from the neighbouring house and looked at Mr Fletcher and then she locked her door and set off down the street. After walking twenty yards she turned back and stared at him, and something about her expression troubled him - as though she was an omen - and he returned to his car and drove away.

*

He yawned, dragged the sleep from his eyes and took from his briefcase a thin pile of essays.

'Go away and write an essay titled, *The Room*,' he told them. 'It doesn't have to be long. Two sides of A4. The aim of the exercise is to write an original composition based on an ambiguous concept.'

'What's ambiguous, sir?' a child asked.

'In this case it means obscure or indistinct.'

'What's ambiguous about a room, sir?'

'Well, you could write about the style of a room or something that happened in a room or even a metaphorical room. Anything.'

'Sir, what's *metaphorical?*'

'No,' he said, 'I'm not telling you again. Look it up.'

Mr Fletcher laid the pile of essays out in front of him, their edges dog-eared and curling. The first one he picked up was written by a girl with a habit of chewing on her split-ends. The girl's name was Yasmin.

He began to read.

The room was paynted yelow and Rachel liked it becoz it was huge and brite from all the sun becoz ther was a masive window. Rachel was doin her nails and her mum come in an said what nail polish is it I love it and Rachel said none of your buzniss get out and then her mum went mentel.

Mr Fletcher smiled. He thought about Kathy and how she laughed when he showed her the essays the younger kids wrote. Sometimes she'd laugh so much that tears would form in the corners of her eyes. Kathy loved the innocence of those kids, their imperfectness, their willingness to get it wrong.

'They won't always be like this,' she'd say.

He pulled out the next essay, which had been written by Jamie Tierney, the boy who was being bullied. He wasn't a remarkable student, he almost never volunteered an opinion or asked a question, but Mr Fletcher wasn't a teacher who ignored kids like this. He knew they wanted to be invisible, to remain perpetually beneath the radar. He knew all about that, he'd been one of those kids. That's how he knew that deep down, what they wanted was for someone to tell them they were good, they were worth something.

He understood this, and he also knew that merely understanding a thing didn't change it. That's why he would ask Jamie questions and try to praise him when he gave an answer, even if his answer lacked cohesion or completion. He could find an element of truth in what the boy said, and that was enough to offer some affirmation.

'What Jamie's done there is to demonstrate that what a person says and what they mean are sometimes different. Well done, Jamie.' This was something he'd said in class recently.

When Jamie's mother sat down in front of him on parent's evening, Mr Fletcher told her, 'He's a good pupil. He listens well, he concentrates in class and his general understanding is sound. His compositions can be slightly unfocused but I think he has the potential to be a good writer.'

'Oh,' the woman replied, 'that's wonderful.'

Mr Fletcher could see she really did think that. He'd been struck by Jamie's mother, by her emaciated body and her strangely cut hair, but also by her devotion. It was obvious to him she was unwell and it was also obvious that she was devoted to her son. She made the fact patently clear when she said, 'He's such a good boy, he's so far beyond what I could have imagined.'

Mr Fletcher didn't know how to respond to that, whether he should ask what she meant or if he should say nothing and nod, but in the end he said, 'Yes, I can see that.'

It was apparent in the way the boy hung back, in the fade of his school shirts and his threadbare trousers that ended at the ankle that his mother didn't have any money. Here was another thing Mr Fletcher knew all about.

That night, the night his mother came in for parent's evening, he asked her if Jamie was happy in her opinion. He said this in place of stating a view he considered undeniable. The woman looked at him without responding and it made him wonder if he'd miscalculated by asking the question. She wasn't upset though, she was simply trying to locate the truth.

'I don't know,' she said. 'I hope so.'

'You know,' he said, 'we have a drama club. It's an after-school thing. We work on plays and at the end of term the kids perform them. I'd like Jamie to join, I think it would help to build his confidence. And I think he'd be very good.'

The boy's mother nodded. 'Have you asked him?'

'Yes,' he said, 'But he's quite shy, I think perhaps if you had a word it might help.'

'Okay,' she said, 'I'll speak to him about it. I mean, at the end of the day it's his choice.'

Mr Fletcher nodded.

He'd been hoping she'd assent with more enthusiasm. They didn't talk much more after that, and when the woman stood up and shook his hand he was struck by a sudden sadness, it was to do with the weightlessness of her fingers.

The following week he held Jamie back after class and asked him if he'd thought any more about joining the drama club. 'I think you'd enjoy it,' he told him.

The boy looked down at the floor and fidgeted for a few seconds. 'Maybe next year,' he replied.

Mr Fletcher nodded and let him go.

Afterwards he had the idea he should have pushed a little harder, done more to show Jamie he was wanted in the club. What was it about not being able to express these things, things he really meant but felt unable to say, except in his thoughts? It always felt so asphyxiating in the moment, anything to do with feelings, with praise, with love.

Perhaps all men are like this, he thought. *Perhaps we're born this way or perhaps we're conditioned to be like this.* Mr Fletcher had interrogated himself on the subject. He'd sat in his office-chair with a glass of scotch and really tried to get at the truth.

He blinked and looked down at the paper in front of him. Jamie's handwriting was disjointed and tiny, and he had to push his reading glasses back up his nose to see the letters. He raised the paper with his hands, angled it towards his face and began to read.

The Room

Last night I heard my mother crying through the wall and after that I couldn't sleep so I opened my eyes and every time a car passed, headlights ran across the ceiling.

Sometimes I wish she had a husband so she would have someone else in the room with her to talk to when she's upset but I don't know who that should be. The best thing would be if it was a vet or a conservationist because if a person treats animals well then it's more likely they will treat people well.

Sometimes when my mother goes out (like when she goes downstairs to see her friend Inez or if she goes to church) I go into her room and look around.

My mother's room is very empty. I don't know where she keeps her things because apart from all the clothes she has in the wardrobe, there is hardly anything there. She has drawers but these are just for socks and things. In front of the window, there is a white table with small drawers and a mirror on top. She keeps her make-up and hair brushes and things like that there.

When I was little, my mother used to sit me on her bed and I would watch her put on her make-up. She said I liked watching her do this but I don't remember.

My mother doesn't have any photographs in her room and there are no paintings on the walls except for one of a girl sat in a chair looking out of a window. This is a painting my mother had as a child.

Sometimes I wrote stories when I was little and gave them to her but I don't know where she put them because I can't see them anywhere in her room. I can't see any letters from other people either or drawings that I made. Hopefully she has hidden that stuff because at least then it means she hasn't thrown it away. I would like to ask her why none of it is here but then she will know I've been snooping around.

It makes me feel bad to go through my mother's stuff and maybe it means I am bad, I don't know. I don't think I'm bad because if ever she's upset I will say 'What's wrong mum?' and then I will talk to her a bit and say 'It will be okay,' and 'Soon it will get better,' but I don't know if that's true.

The last time I was in her room with her was when she decided she was going to go through her old clothes. Some of her clothes are over ten years old.

My mother showed me some of the things she used to wear when she was a model before I was born. Some of these clothes were crazy, like the bright yellow dress that had pom-poms hanging off it. I thought it was so funny that I made her try it on, and then she danced around in it and we laughed for ages because it looked so silly.

Sometimes, when she's like this, my mother is the best person in the world. And then other times she gets sad and then it's like a different person has crawled under her skin and taken her over (this is just a metaphor, I don't mean it).

My mother's room is next to my room, and this means I can hear what she's doing in there, like last night when I could hear she was playing a Beatles record. The Beatles are her favourite. She told me that one day before I was born she was walking down the street and she dropped her keys and George Harrison picked them up for her. At first she said this was the best thing that ever happened to her, but then she said 'No, the second best'.

If I could change anything about my mother's room, I would make it brighter. I would paint it orange or blue and then I would put some paintings of animals in there and some photographs. Also, I think it would be good if my mother took some books out of the living room and put them in her bedroom. This is just an idea though. I don't know if she would like it because she doesn't read much.

Probably the best thing would be if my mother got married. If she didn't have me she would be married already, but she's not because men don't want to marry a woman with a child. I know this because I've heard my mother say it on the phone. I can hear everything through the wall. That's why I don't do anything loud in my room.

My room is better than my mother's room because I have books in there and posters and model cars and other stuff like an old space-hopper, which I don't use, but sometimes I sit on it anyway.

What would be amazing is if I got a computer. I have asked my mum but she says we can't afford one. It doesn't matter because one day I will earn my own money and then I'll buy my own computer and I'll buy a house for her with a garden and her room will be ten times better than the one she has now. That's the plan anyway.

*

The sun had slipped through an opening in the clouds and was bleeding into the evening.

In the bedroom, Kathy was getting ready and in the living-room, Mr Fletcher was standing by the window peering out into the street. He could hear the whirring of her hair-dryer beyond the wall. She had her own flat on the other side of the river, but many of her things had migrated here now, or else she'd bought auxiliary versions to keep at his house so she wouldn't have to alter her routines or forego her ablutions.

He went over to the drinks cabinet, pulled out the scotch and poured himself a glass. Then he went back to the window and stood watching a young couple as they walked down the street hand in hand. Mr Fletcher looked first at the woman and then at the man, who was broad-shouldered and lean. He considered this man for a minute, he wondered what would happen if a man like this - someone young and handsome - were to make a play for Kathy and if she'd be persuaded to go off with him.

He walked over to the mirror, took a breath and let out the warm air. Something in his chest felt heavy and steeped in dread. He moved away from the mirror, picked up his cologne and splashed some on his wrists and neck. Then he replaced the bottle on the table, the same table where he and Kathy ate breakfast and read the papers and debated communism and autocratic states, the same table where they skewered green olives with cocktail sticks and sluiced down cognac at midnight. He picked up his cigarettes and lit one. He began to pace and think things over again.

After a minute, he stubbed out his cigarette in the ash-tray, a heavy ash-tray carved from marble. Two cherubs sat on opposing sides facing each other, heralding love's bugle-call to the Gods. This had been his mother's ash-tray, it had been in the family since before he was born. He surveyed the edges, the chip on the rim from when he knocked it from the mantelpiece as a child. He could still see his mother's face as she rushed into the room.

Kathy appeared in the doorway, a softly deific apparition. 'Shall we go?' she said. She was wearing a shimmering green dress, a dress he hadn't seen before.

He said, 'Is that new?'

'Yes,' she replied, running a hand over the fabric.

'It's nice. You look lovely.' Mr Fletcher came towards her and reached out to touch her shoulder.

Kathy turned away and made for the front door. 'I'm not sure I like the fit,' she said.

He followed the line of the dress as it travelled over the contours of her hips.

'It looks good to me,' he said.

As they walked down the front path he tapped at his chest to make sure it was still there. He could feel the sweat beneath his arms. In the car, Kathy was silent and it seemed to Mr Fletcher like another omen.

'You're quiet today,' he said, but apparently she wasn't in the mood to look at him because all she did was stare from the passenger window.

'I'm tired,' she said.

'Bad day at the office?'

'No, it was fine.'

'Well I've had better days,' he said. 'I have this kid, he's being bullied. Jamie, his name is. It's been going on for months, years for all I know, but he won't let me do anything.'

Mr Fletcher paused, shook his head. 'What do you do with a kid like that? The mother's a mess, she's sick or on drugs or something, I don't know. That's the thing I can't stand about it. I can't stand watching it. What are you supposed to do about stuff like this? I'm a teacher, not a social worker.'

Mr Fletcher kept talking because he wanted Kathy to interject or advise him or maybe just lay a hand down on his. He left his hand there on the gear-stick to give her the chance but all she did was carry on staring out of the window the whole time, as though he wasn't saying a thing. *What the hell's going on with you?* he wanted to ask, but he knew better than that by now.

'Actually, he's written an essay I want to show you,' he continued. 'I swear to God, you wouldn't believe it. I've spent the last year thinking he was totally average and then he hands me this. He's written this piece about his mother, and it's… well it's a great piece of writing, that's all. He has no idea what he's done. Twelve, he is.'

Kathy turned to him finally. 'What did you say his name was?'

'Jamie,' said Mr Fletcher. 'Jamie Tierney.'

'And how do you know this Jamie character wrote it?'

He turned to her and she looked at him briefly, then went back to staring out of the window.

'What do you mean?' he said.

'Well if you've spent the whole year thinking he's totally average and then out of nowhere he writes this wonderful essay, how do you know he's the one who wrote it?'

He pulled into the little car-park and found a space.

'Oh no, he wrote it. It's not that it's written in sophisticated prose or anything, it's quite naive. But there's a simplicity to it, a complete absence of sentimentality. It's something you have to see for yourself. I'll bring it for you.'

'I'll look forward to it,' she said.

Kathy drew her hair back behind her ear and he looked at the amber light from the streetlight on her cheek. He wondered how he had ended up with someone like her.

They stepped out of the car and he locked the doors while Kathy walked towards the restaurant alone. It was an Italian restaurant called *Ferrari's,* a favourite of theirs. She didn't enter but waited for Mr Fletcher at the entrance. When he arrived he pulled open the glass door and she slipped past him and went inside.

They were met by a young Italian waiter, one they hadn't seen before. This waiter had dark eyes and coarse black hair and he smiled broadly at Kathy. Mr Fletcher noticed this. The waiter wore a shirt which was unbuttoned enough that the topography of his chest was visible. He began to lead them to a table and Mr Fletcher saw the man was wearing trousers that clung to his buttocks. He thought about how Kathy would have noticed this also, about how she would go on noticing it. He wondered where they'd found this waiter with his muscles and his tawdry chest.

The waiter pulled out a chair for Kathy and she sat down. Then he leant right into her and grinned, and Kathy grinned back. Mr Fletcher thought it was quite a scene, he thought the waiter may as well stick his tongue in her mouth and be done with it. *Can't you see we're together?* he wanted to say.

He suddenly felt very hot and when the waiter came around the table to pull a chair out for him he batted him away. The waiter handed them each a menu and bowed and Mr Fletcher wanted to shoo him away but he all he did was nod. *This isn't how it's supposed to go,* he thought.

He had the sense this wasn't going to end well, he had an instinct for these things. He began to scan the menu, wishing all at once he'd never had the idea to propose, to frequent that jewellery shop, to bring her to this stupid restaurant. Kathy didn't need to look at the menu. She'd have a bowl of pitted olives and the mushroom risotto. He already knew this.

From the top of his eye-line he could see her scanning the room while he looked at the menu. He watched her gaze find its mark, and he knew where she was looking.

Mr Fletcher's eyes moved over the dishes and he realised at that moment he had no appetite. He couldn't think of a single thing he wanted to do less than eat. Perhaps propose marriage, perhaps this he wanted to do less.

'I'm not very hungry,' he said, looking up at her. 'Actually, I don't know if I want anything.'

Kathy narrowed her eyes. 'What? You're always hungry.'

'Not tonight it seems.'

She sighed. 'Are you ill?'

Mr Fletcher shook his head. 'No, I can't say I am.'

'Well you'll have to order something, we can't just sit here. Just order a pizza or something. I'll get some olives to share.'

He nodded. She wasn't in the mood for him tonight, this much was clear.

When the waiter came back to the table, he was beaming again, his eyes fixed on Kathy. This obviously pleased her as she smiled back brightly, a smile she reserved for dark oily strangers. She made her order and turned to Mr Fletcher.

'I'll have the cannelloni,' he said. 'And bring me a bottle of Gavi.' He looked at the waiter and the man bowed to him again.

Stop doing that, he wanted to say. *This isn't a pantomime we're making here.*

The waiter took their menus, thanked them, and grinned stupidly at Kathy, an expression she returned.

Mr Fletcher couldn't help himself. 'What the hell's wrong with him?' he said.

Kathy made a face. 'What do you mean?'

'Why does he keep bowing and grinning? Idiot.'

She was taken aback. 'He's just being polite.'

'Is that what you call it?'

'Yes,' she said. 'Henry, what's wrong with you?'

Kathy angled her head to one side. Mr Fletcher hated when she did this, it reminded him of when a teacher bent over a child and asked him what he thought he was doing.

'Forget it. It's just a little galling that you can barely look at me, yet it's all smiles with Casanova over there.'

Kathy drew back in her seat. 'Great, so this is how it's going to be, is it?'

'How what's going to be?'

'This evening, tonight. Do you realise I never wanted to come out in the first place? I wanted to eat beans on toast and go to bed.'

Mr Fletcher shrugged. 'So why didn't you?'

'Because I thought you wanted to come here.'

He shook his head. 'If I'd known the mood you'd be in, I'd never have suggested it.'

The waiter appeared again with the wine. 'Would you like to try?' he said to Mr Fletcher as he pushed the corkscrew into the cork.

Mr Fletcher raised a hand and flicked his wrist. 'Let the lady try.'

'Very good,' said the waiter. He pulled out the cork and smiled at Kathy. She frowned and turned away and the smile disappeared from the waiter's face.

He looked off into the body of the room as he poured and as she tasted the wine, and when she said 'It's fine,' he nodded without smiling at her and filled her glass with his attention directed at another table altogether.

'Was that better?' she said.

Mr Fletcher didn't feel like an argument. He raised his glass and drank a mouthful of the clear liquid. 'I'm sorry,' he said.

Kathy shook her head without fixing her eyes on him. He felt something black and leaden settle in his stomach. He'd planned to order champagne without her knowing and have it arrive with dessert, that was the moment he was going to go down on one knee and say it.

Ferrari's had seemed like the obvious place to do it. They'd come here on their third date, the date that cemented things for him. After that they'd come back often, perhaps six or seven times over the course of a year. It was a bad sign that their waiter, Marco, had gone. Perhaps he hadn't gone, but he wasn't here now. It was the first time he hadn't been here.

Mr Fletcher couldn't say what made him do it. It was as though an imposter's brain had supplanted his own and started firing off little electrical impulses that caused his arm to bend towards his chest, compelling the hand at its end to reach into the silk lining of his blazer. He pulled out the red satin box and held it in his closed fist on the table. He knew this wasn't only a yes or no to marriage, it was a no to all of it that awaited him, that was his feeling now.

'What's that?' Kathy said.

Mr Fletcher laughed briefly. He lifted his glass and drank. 'It's a ring. It's an engagement ring. I was going to propose, but you'll be pleased to hear I've come to my senses.'

It was clear she didn't understand what was happening. The waiter delivered a bowl of olives without smiling at either of them and disappeared back into the haze of the dusky room.

'Don't worry,' said Mr Fletcher, 'I don't expect you to say anything. I just wanted to take it out, it was digging into my chest.'

Kathy drank what remained in her glass and then she poured out more wine for them both.

'I had no idea,' she said. She pulled back a strand of her hair and tucked it behind her ear. 'I don't know what to say.'

He made a sound from behind his teeth. 'That's because there isn't anything *to* say. What would you have said if I'd seen it through, if I'd gone down on one knee and done the whole shebang?'

Kathy's mouth was open. He could feel her discomfort as though it was radiating out of her body in waves.

'I suppose I would have had to say no.'

'I thought as much. Should we stay to eat or

leave now?'

Kathy's mouth was still open.

'Let's stay to eat,' he said. 'I don't much feel like leaving this wine.'

The waiter appeared again, this time with a bowl of risotto and a plate of cannelloni. He set down their meals and asked if they wanted parmesan, black pepper. Kathy said the word *please* and the waiter ground the pepper and teased from his silver spoon the pale dust-like cheese. Then Mr Fletcher asked him to bring another bottle of Gavi and the man nodded impassively and receded into the labyrinth of lights and tables and bodies.

Kathy seemed reluctant to begin, she skirted around the perimeter of her plate with her fork, then laid it down and sipped at her wine instead.

'Go ahead,' said Mr Fletcher. 'You can start.'

He finished what remained in his glass and sat back in his chair. The steam from his cannelloni caught in the throw of candle-light on the table and he watched as Kathy slid a fork into her risotto and then over her tongue. He'd always been impressed by her movements, by the way she did everything so effortlessly. Even the way she carried food to her mouth was elegant and without fuss.

How can one person be so much? That's what he

wondered as he watched her. He'd always figured that if a woman was attractive, she must also be self-absorbed or superior or have an obtuse nature. That had been his experience. But Kathy, she was smart, she was good-looking, she knew how to laugh at herself. Hell, she was everything all at once.

The waiter brought and opened another bottle of wine and then when he'd gone, Mr Fletcher said, 'Why won't you marry me? What is it specifically?'

She lay down her fork. 'Henry, don't -

'No, come on,' he said. 'I'm ready to hear it.'

Kathy pulled her chair closer to the table and straightened her spine so she was sitting upright. She extended her neck and ran her tongue over her lower lip.

'It isn't specific to you,' she said. 'I can't marry anyone, I swore my life to Richard. That still stands, he's still my husband.'

He hadn't expected this. Something inside him softened. 'Is this a religious thing?'

'No, you know I'm not religious,' she said. 'It's just the way I feel. The thing is, Richard isn't dead. I mean, yes he's dead, but that's just his body. He's still with me. I know you'll think I'm crazy but he still talks to me, he still comes to me. Sometimes when I'm confused I'll ask him for help and he'll give me the answer. He'll show me.'

Mr Fletcher didn't know what to make of this. The most intelligent woman he'd ever met and here she was talking about conversing with her dead husband. It was about the last thing he'd expected. *What next?* he thought. *Should I ask if Richard wants to pull up a seat and join us?*

'Okay,' he said. 'But when you say he gives you the answer, do you mean he actually tells you?'

Kathy's tongue was working silently behind her lips.

'No,' she said. 'Look, for example, when I met you through the newspaper, well that was Richard's idea. Never in a million years would I have put an ad in a lonely hearts column. But one day I was at home and I said, Richard, help me. I don't want to be alone for the rest of my life. What should I do? Tell me what to do.

'Anyway, the next day I got on a train and a woman got off and offered me the paper she'd been reading. I took it and it was open on the lonely hearts page. I didn't think anything of it, I just turned over. That evening I came home and another copy of that same newspaper had been left on the gate-post outside my flat. Opened to the exact same page. I thought it was strange, but I immediately forgot about it.

'Then the next morning, someone left a note on my windscreen asking if I could leave that parking-space free that evening because they needed to put a removal van there. They'd written this note on a page of a newspaper. Anyway, I was about to start the car and something made me turn that page over. And guess what was on the other side?'

Kathy paused.

'That's how Richard speaks to me,' she said. 'It happens all the time. I know you probably think I'm crazy, but there it is.'

Mr Fletcher didn't know what to say. He didn't know what to think either, but slowly it came to him.

'So why don't you ask Richard if he's okay with you marrying me? If that's how this thing works.'

He knew Kathy wouldn't have expected this. She'd have been waiting for him to ask how someone with a brain such as hers could believe in all this, how someone who valued empirical evidence could settle for ghost stories or whatever she called this junk.

She put down her glass and looked at him. 'I don't know,' she said.

'Look, set Richard aside for a second. If he wasn't in the picture, would you marry me?'

She raised a hand to her face and ran a thumb and forefinger over her eyelids. 'I don't know,' she said. 'When I married Richard I was in love. It was different. I just knew it was what I wanted. I'm not in love with you, not like that.'

Mr Fletcher nodded and poured more wine into his glass. 'Well I'm not the man Richard was, that's for sure.' He thought about the sepia-toned photograph, about Richard's billboard face.

'Don't say that. You're a good man. I think you're a wonderful man.'

He laughed. 'I know, I know, but I can't compete with Richard.'

They both drank more wine. The waiter approached and then withdrew upon seeing their faces. Mr Fletcher took a minute and thought things over.

'You know,' he said. 'I don't mind about Richard. I know you still love him, I know he'll always be your husband, it doesn't matter to me. I just want to be with you. I just want to sit in this restaurant with you and eat and drink and talk about things. And then when we're done, I want to take you home and be with you there. That's all.'

Kathy lowered her gaze and pushed a fork through scattered mounds of rice.

'I do care about you, Henry,' she said. 'You're the nicest man I've met in a long time, you really are. I can't tell you how flattered I am that you'd want to marry me in the first place.'

She finished her wine and rested her face in her palm. Mr Fletcher looked at her, at the murmuring shadows resting on her cheek. He was quiet for a few seconds and then he smiled.

'Don't look so sad,' he said. 'Nobody died.'

They were silent on the journey home. Her face flashed amber each time they passed beneath a street lamp and at intervals he turned to look at her. At the traffic lights, he switched on the radio and tuned it with his index finger until he happened upon on a Nat King Cole number. He knew how she loved those old crooners.

The night air came in through the window and Kathy opened her eyes. She held her left hand in front of her face and looked at it. After a moment, the lights changed and Mr Fletcher worked the clutch, the accelerator.

Cocaine

When Diego Lopez Vega disembarked at Heathrow, he hauled his cases from the carousel, had his passport stamped, took a tube to Green Park and lay down on the grass.

It was so hot he couldn't understand what everyone had been talking about when they warned him about cold wet England and its endless grey skies. He couldn't understand it then and he couldn't understand it in the days that followed, but soon enough it hit him, and when it did he thought to himself, *What a shitty place London is.* But like so many immigrants to this city, he came to see that what was good here amounted to more than what was not.

'People think no-one turns up in a country with nothing, that these things only happen in movies, but they're wrong. When I arrived here, I had two bags and that was it. No job, no money, no friends.'

'No money at all?'

That's what Marie asked him, this man who'd started out in a sun-drenched Spanish metropolis and was now sitting on her couch, legs splayed, punctuating his sentences with huge olive-skinned hands, like the outsized paws of a lion-cub before his body has grown to meet them.

'Enough for a week maybe, but that's it. I came with nothing.'

Marie shook her head absently. 'And how old were you when you arrived?'

'Thirty-three.'

'Really?' she replied. 'That's quite old to come to a new country.'

He shrugged. 'Maybe, but I had to get out.'

She studied Diego's face. His eyes were so deeply brown they looked black. He had a square jaw and dark weathered skin - the skin of an older man - and when he smiled she could imagine a riot of camera-flashes strobing his face, as though he was commanding a red carpet somewhere.

Diego had no idea he was the sort of man she could imagine kissing, the sort of man she could imagine being cradled by in the dead of night. He had no idea she would be propelled to offer him the spare room in her flat purely because of the sensations his attention induced in her, but if someone had whispered this in his ear it wouldn't have surprised him.

What did surprise him was the sensation

induced in him when the woman's teenage son appeared in the doorway. It was like a blade threshed against flint when he caught sight of the boy's lazy blue eyes and pink carnal lips, and a flame shivved its way into life right there in his husk of a belly.

'Jamie,' she began, 'this is Diego, he's come to see the room.'

And the boy nodded and went away.

Diego moved into Marie's flat in Angel on a cold still day in February of 1986. He unloaded his possessions from the back of a cab and the woman sent her son out to help him carry them.

He had by then acquired more clothes and a television and a box full of books. In truth, the books were for show because Diego hated reading. Page after page of arcane words and blandly architected characters saying things nobody in real-life ever said. What was the point of them anyway, when there was television and sex and cocaine?

From the start he had no intention of disclosing his sexuality to Marie. He had no idea how she'd react and he was tired of being made to feel like he'd been sliced open at birth and implanted with a brand of perversion he couldn't absolve himself of. He'd never made any decision about it, it had been handed to him the way ginger hair and peanut allergies had been handed to other kids.

I can either hide away and do nothing or live how I like and fuck who I like and get on with it.

Here was something Diego said to himself a long time ago, when his life had already come off the tracks.

*

He was born in 1951, to a politician father and a socialite mother, a woman who had at one time been infamous amongst the elite of Madrid for her decadent sweatbox parties and avant-garde fashion statements, a woman so potent and charismatic she'd transcended the need of a surname. If you went back twenty years and asked anyone in Madrid worth their salt who Angelita was, they'd be able to tell you.

'Look at me,' she used to say to him, holding his chin between thumb and forefinger. 'Remember, you can have whatever you want in this world. If anyone says no to you, you say... Come on, what do you say?'

'I say, Who are you to say no to me? Do you know who I am?'

'Venga! You say, I am Diego, son of Angelita.' She threw up a manicured hand and snapped her fingers.

'Yes Mama.'

'And then you tell them what you want, and

they give it.'

Angelita really spoke like this, like a matriarch from a gangster movie. It was to do with where she started out.

Her father, Luis, a modernist who'd intended to follow in the footsteps of Picasso and Van Gogh and study in Paris, instead fell in love with a Segovian peasant girl, so when she fell pregnant at seventeen he assented to legitimise her with marriage and forestall his plans for the sake of their unborn child.

Then the civil war happened and Luis became a guerrilla fighter for the resistance. He and his compatriots attempted to ambush a fascist motorcade in 1937 but were captured and murdered in the forests outside Madrid, after which Angelita's mother was left to raise her alone.

To begin with, they lived off bread and oil and slept in basement rooms in the slum neighbourhoods of Vallecas, then later went about peripatetically doing whatever they could to make money. Serendipitously for her mother, Angelita turned out to be a hustler, a precocious naïf with a gilded larynx, and at twelve she began busking on the street.

Soon she was earning more money in an hour than her mother did in a week. By fourteen she'd negotiated a job singing in a bar. After a year she demanded more money, more outré costumes, a band. She did this without knowing what would happen, she was like a card-sharp with a bad hand bluffing her way through.

What she learned was that if a person exudes confidence and acts as if a thing is rightfully theirs, they can make all sorts of demands. *The world gives what you ask of it* became her maxim, her epitaph.

Eventually she was done playing the showgirl, she had another ambition in mind; infiltrating high society, something they said was impossible. At twenty-one, Angelita hung up her peacock feathers and retired to focus on the one thing that could secure her access to Madrid's elite; marriage to a powerful man.

She taught Diego that marriage was a contract that bought a woman luxury and a man respectability. The woman only had to be faithful and attractive and give birth and in return she could buy clothes and shoes, arrange parties and holidays, go to lunch with her friends, make the familial decisions. The man could do whatever he wanted, he could drink, he could sleep with other women – discreetly – he could have as little to do with his children as he wished, the only caveat being that he had to keep pumping money into her life, the way a red-blooded prospector pumped oil from the bowels of the earth.

'That's what a marriage is,' she told her little charge. 'A compromise.'

Diego had wondered about that at the age of ten, when his mother explained to him what a marriage was. 'But what about falling in love?' he said.

He'd spent his whole childhood being fed stories about handsome princes and sleeping beauties and now he was being offered a very different confection, one that was hard-boiled and mercenary and came dripping in avarice.

Angelita looked up from her monogrammed black compact and stroked his cheek with the backs of her fingers.

'Maybe in the beginning you fall in love, but that's like being drunk. In the morning you wake up and you have the reality.'

Diego looked at her. 'What do you mean?' he said.

She'd already turned back to her reflection to paint her eyelashes. 'Being in love is temporary. It comes and it goes. And what are you left with? You have to be smart. Especially a woman, a woman has to be smart. You don't have to worry, men don't have to worry unless they're poor.'

She was wrong about that though.

Diego had come to see that for a man who wasn't interested in women, there was always something to worry about.

*

He rarely crossed paths with Marie's son in the beginning. By the time he got home from work, Jamie was either asleep or hiding in his room studying for his E-Levels or whatever they were called. Diego had asked the boy about his studies when he first arrived, the same way he'd asked the mother about her leisure pursuits, he'd learned that these tedious excursions were a necessary social preliminary.

'What are you studying?' he'd asked, his big fingers drumming on the kitchen counter.

'English, art, and psychology,' Jamie replied.

It surprised Diego that a person could study psychology at seventeen in this country. It certainly hadn't been an option when he was at school. 'What will you do after?' he asked.

Jamie gave a staccato and meandering response, one that hadn't compelled him to listen. The only thing he'd been able to think about as he watched those lips move was unzipping himself and easing the boy down on to his knees.

On a hazy Monday morning in May, Diego decided to conduct an experiment. The mother had already gone out to work, he'd heard the floorboards creaking as she walked past his room.

Lately he'd been getting a feeling about the boy, a feeling that primed his body and made his blood run hot, so he went to the bathroom, took a shower and brushed his teeth. Then he went back to his room and once he'd climbed into his underwear, dropped to the ground and started doing push-ups. It had been a while and he had to call it a day at sixteen. It didn't matter. Between his job at the restaurant and his habit of replacing meals with cocaine, Diego had assumed a lean sinewy body without weight-lifting and circuit-training and all the rest of it.

He rose to his feet and surveyed himself in the mirror and then he daubed his neck and wrists with *Eau Sauvage*. His father had always worn Dior, and while the man was stupefyingly wrong about most things in life, when it came to matters of a sartorial nature he'd always been on point.

Diego had as good as stolen his father's entire template when it came to clothes, shoes, accessories, eau de parfum. That's why he wore Ralph Lauren polo-shirts and slacks, Italian hand-stitched loafers, Ray-Ban aviator sunglasses – even though he worked in a restaurant and made a quarter of the money a man servicing these tastes required.

He poured out a little hair oil, rubbed it

in his palms and drew his hair into a black cresting wave. He surveyed himself, walked out of his room and set off down the stairs. In truth it was too cold to be wandering around in his underwear but an experiment was an experiment, he couldn't turn up without a test-tube, without a flame.

The boy was in the kitchen fixing himself a coffee when he sidled up behind him and whispered, 'I thought you were at school.'

Jamie turned, a nullifying shock passing over his face. Diego said nothing. He watched as the boy assumed the mask of composure, as his eyes began to traverse the surface of his body, travelling first down, then up, then to another part of the room altogether. He could tell the boy was embarrassed, it was clear from the way he spun around and began fiddling with the coffee jar.

'No, I'm not in today,' he said. 'I mean, I am, but not until this afternoon.'

'Oh,' said Diego, a serpentine smile licking at his lips. 'So what are you doing this morning?'

Still the boy wouldn't turn around so Diego stepped forward, stood next to him and opened a cupboard from which he took a cup.

'Just sorting my shit out really,' Jamie mumbled, peering into his coffee. 'Are you not cold?' he said.

'No,' said Diego, 'I just showered.'

The boy nodded, took his coffee, went over to the little pink table and sat down. Diego turned and rested his back against the lip of the counter. He regarded the boy silently for a moment, a predatory bird keeping reconnaissance from an alpine ledge. 'Can I ask a question?' he said.

Jamie nodded. He looked briefly at Diego, then down into his cup again.

'Do you think my body's okay? I know it's weird to ask, but I'm not twenty-one anymore.'

Jamie looked up and scanned him for a second. Diego watched the boy's darting eyes and as if by some trick of transference, experienced the buzz of adrenaline flooding his chest. It sparked something inside him, a vertiginous sensation like the after-shock from an orgasm.

'Yeah,' said the boy. 'You look, you know, I mean, you're pretty toned.' He said all this while staring down at the frosted pink table-top, while picking at his fingertips and sweating from his forehead.

'Thanks,' said Diego, and he smiled and walked out.

*

In the beginning he did nothing to follow up on this experiment. He wasn't a man who rushed things, who had to see results the moment he decided on a course of action. He would rather wait for the right time, which in this case turned out to be early summer, because suddenly the boy was done with college, suddenly he was home, mooching around the flat, orbiting from couch to fridge to bed in an eternal adolescent loop.

'Are you enjoying the holidays?' Diego said to him one bright July morning.

'Yeah, they're alright,' said Jamie, turning from his position on the couch. 'How come you're not at work?'

'I decided to take a few days off, get some sun.'

He sat down opposite the boy in the armchair where Marie always sat. He looked at the discoloured arms and wondered what sort of person kept sitting in a chair like this, night after night, without doing a single thing about it. His mother would have taken one look at this chair and thrown it out. She'd have called for Gloria and said, *Gloria, get rid of this. By the time I come back in this room I want it gone.*

Jamie nodded and pulled a hand through his hair. He was wearing cut-off denim shorts and a white t-shirt.

'You don't like the sun?'

'No, I do,' he said. 'I'll probably go out in a bit.'

'We can go to the park together if you like.' He

smiled at Jamie. 'Do you fancy a beer?'

'Now?'

Diego nodded, got up and went to the kitchen, then returned with two bottles. 'Shit,' he said, 'I forgot the bottle opener.'

Jamie put out a hand. 'It's okay,' he said. 'Pass them here.'

Diego walked over and handed them to the boy, then watched him raise them to his mouth, first one and then the other. 'You shouldn't do that,' he said. 'You'll break your teeth.'

Jamie shrugged as he passed him a beer, and Diego laughed and put out a hand so they could clink bottles. Then he sat down next to the boy on the couch. 'So, what's happening?' he said.

The boy twirled a lock of hair around his forefinger. 'What do you mean?'

'Well, how's life?'

Jamie bit his lip and shrugged again. 'Erm, fine I guess.'

'Do you have a girlfriend?'

'No.'

'Nobody you're interested in?'

'No. Well, sort of. Not really. What about you?'

Diego smiled. 'Me? No, I don't have a girlfriend. I don't care about girls.'

'How come?' said Jamie, and again he began fiddling with his hair.

'Because I'm not into girls,' he said, and his face took on an austere quality, like the stuccoed bust of a Roman Emperor.

He watched the boy look at him. 'Have I shocked you?'

Jamie turned away. 'No, it's just… you don't seem-'

'Gay? I don't seem gay? No, that's true.'

'I just wasn't expecting…' His voice petered to nothing and Diego leant into him. It was only the slightest of movements, just enough for the boy to sense something, to feel it there in his chest.

'There's something I wanted to say actually,' said Diego. Immediately he shook his head and leaned back in his seat. 'No forget it, forget I said that.'

Jamie turned to him. 'No, go on. You can say it.'

'No, it's fine, don't worry.' Diego blew out a stream of air and peered off into the middle distance.

'Go on,' said Jamie. 'I'm curious now.'

'Okay, fine. But don't say I didn't warn you.' Diego straightened his back and made his eyes large. 'I know I shouldn't and I'm sorry, but I like you. I think you're very handsome.'

He leaned in again, allowing his face to drift towards Jamie's. For a long time he hovered there and then he leaned in further and their lips touched. At first this is how it went. It began with locked mouths and as the seconds fell away, the boy's lips opened and Diego was able to kiss him fully, like a hummingbird sucking up nectar from the pool of a virgin flower.

He wanted to do everything very gently because he knew how boys could be. They scare easily, that's one thing he knew. He wanted to ease Jamie into it, to let him feel like a man. That's why he let the kissing go on like that for a long time. It's why, when they were done with that, he invited the boy to take off his t-shirt, it's why he asked him, 'Can I touch you there?' before he placed his hand.

It's why he had condoms ready by his bed and it's why he let the boy take him instead of the other way around. As he saw it, it had to be this way in the beginning. It had to be this way because he knew Jamie would be terrified about AIDS. Everyone was terrified about it. That's why Diego had never been to get himself tested, he didn't want to know. What was the point when they couldn't do anything to treat it?

After he'd finished the boy off, he cleaned him up with a hand-towel and then he lay down next to him and told him he was the most beautiful thing in the world.

'Yeah right,' Jamie replied.

'You are. One day you'll see. But only when it's too late.'

He stroked the boy's hair, he kissed his nose, his forehead, his lips. He could see he was in shock, that he couldn't believe any of this was happening. Diego lay there a while without speaking and then he stood up and went to his dresser. 'Do you like feeling good?' he said.

'What?' Jamie replied, looking back at him.

'Do you like to feel good?'

The boy shrugged. 'Yeah.'

'Me too. That's why I have this.' From a drawer he pulled out a clear plastic bag of white powder and held it up to the light.

Jamie said, 'What is it?'

'Coke,' he replied.

Then he tipped the bag and poured a little out on to his dresser before using a credit card to till the powder, building first one line, then a second. When he was done he winked at the boy, then turned and used a rolled-up banknote to snort the first line.

Diego knew that if you wrong-footed a person, if you made them think something that was a big deal was really nothing, they went along with you. They might be conflicted or confused about it, but almost always they'd fall into line and do what you suggested was so easy, so natural. Jamie was no different. He was fresh out of childhood, he didn't know anything about life, about the world. He didn't know anything about cocaine either, except what the papers said, except what other seventeen year-olds with no clue about anything said.

The boy did as he was told, he went to the dresser, put the banknote into his nostril and breathed sharply. Then, when he'd watched Diego do a second line, he said, 'Can I have another?'

'Sure,' he said, smiling. 'But only if I get a kiss first.'

The boy kissed him, and after a couple of seconds Diego pulled away and began to fix the line. He said, 'Where did you learn to kiss like that?'

Jamie bit his lip. 'Why? Do you think I'm a good kisser?'

'I do. You kiss like someone who's had practice.'

The boy looked down and shook his head. 'Not really.'

'Well,' he shrugged, 'you're a natural.'

After he'd handed him the banknote, Diego took a step back and watched him vacuum up the powder. It turned him on to see this, to watch the boy opening up like a lotus under his influence. He took his hand and pulled him close into his body, and it felt in a way like he was drowning the boy, like he was pushing him down below the surface of a cold black lake.

'Come on,' he said. 'Fuck me again.'

*

When he was very young, when he was sat by his mother's side at the vanity table in her dressing room one morning, Diego turned to her and said, 'Mama, what happens after you die?'

His mother finished applying her eyeliner and said, '*Madre mía*! Where do you get these questions?'

At first she gave him a look, said nothing and began with her lipstick, but Diego wouldn't be deterred. So finally she set the lipstick down and eyed him in the mirror.

'Well,' she said, 'it depends on whether you're good or bad. You're a good boy so you'll go to heaven.'

'How do you know?'

'Because you're an angel. And that's where the angels live.'

'But what do angels do?'

'An angel,' said his mother, 'doesn't do

anything. If you're an angel, it's other people's job to do things for you.'

'But how do you know I'm an angel?' he said.

'Look in the mirror. Of course you are, you're perfect.'

Diego was pleased by her vehemence. 'You're an angel too, Mama,' he said, and the woman leant in and kissed his forehead.

What she taught him was that for a boy like him, the world was a place of absolutes, of guarantees, of diamond clarity.

He held this view without question for the next nine years, until he was sixteen, until the morning Gloria lurched into his bedroom, went down on her knees at his bedside, the mascara radiating out from her eyes like a black mist, and told him his mother was dead.

What happened then was that his father appeared, casting himself as a lead player in his life. Before this, his mother had acted as a barrier, intercepting any attempts the man made to influence Diego's trajectory. It hadn't been difficult as he was always at work and if he wasn't at work, he was either travelling or 'entertaining one of his concubines'.

Diego had been taught to view his father with suspicion, to defer always to the aegis of his mother, regardless of the situation. For as long as he could recall, his father had been of the mind that he was too pampered, too insular and lacking in all the attributes that made a man, a man. His parents had fought about this many times over the years.

'Can't you see you're turning him into a fairy?' his father would yell.

'I don't want him running around in the dirt kicking balls, he's not a fucking idiot,' his mother would reply.

His father always lost these battles, these attempts to ferry the boy off to boarding school and to football camps for the summer.

'Over my dead body,' Angelita would say.

His step-brother, Javier, he could do what he wanted, he could run around in the gutter and come home covered in blood and dirt, he was a *shit-for-brains.* Diego was a different proposition entirely. But all that was finished now.

The first thing his father did after the funeral was to sit him down at his mahogany desk with its ivory telephone and crystalline decanter and onyx ash-tray, and tell him, 'It's going to be alright.'

Diego knew this wasn't true, he knew this absolutely wasn't true, but he said nothing.

'You'll carry on at school and if you need anything, just ask.' When he received no response he looked at the boy and added, 'I'm still your father.'

Diego had never heard him speak like this, with emotion in his voice, saying words a parent ought to say to a child, yet which sounded so odd coming out of this man who was to him a stranger.

His loyalty was to his mother, it would always be to his mother whether she was here or not. He knew already that his father would be rubbing his hands together at the prospect of hacking him to pieces and restitching him according to his own polluted ideas about what a man ought to be. As his mother had told him a thousand times, 'You'd be at military school faster than you could blink if it wasn't for me.'

He was frightened by this, by what the man would do now the reins had been handed over, but his fears were soon allayed because his father didn't know how to parent and he didn't want to know. What he knew was how to buy things. Angelita had taught him this.

'Don't be stupid,' she'd told him when that woman threatened to go to the paper about their liaison. 'Give her what she wants.'

The first thing Diego asked for was a car, so his father bought him an Alfa Romeo, a Spider in cherry red. He took that car and he drove it into a wall. First he sank a bottle of bourbon and then he drove the Spider into a wall.

Next he asked for an apartment of his own, so his father bought him an apartment overlooking Retiro Park. Diego loved this apartment. He loved it so much he brought people to see it in the middle of the night, people he met in clubs, people who pissed on the walls and puked on the rugs, people who fucked on tables and bled into carpets.

One night a fire broke out and the apartment was gutted. Later his father sold it off because Diego's neighbours demanded it, one of them threatened to kill him if his *little son of a bitch* came back.

At twenty-three, he asked his father to buy him a bar, he wanted his own business. So his father bought him a bar and three weeks later Diego secured a loan from the bank using the bar as collateral. He used the money to buy coke and party and holiday in Paris and St Tropez, and the following year the bar was repossessed.

Diego spent the late seventies and early eighties in dive bars where men had sex and got high and danced until they could barely stand. He'd invite these men into his father's house when the man was at work, when he was travelling on diplomatic business, when he was attending conferences at the UN. Gloria knew all about it.

'If Angelita could see you now,' she'd say, her occlusive tongue sheer and inimical, a microcosm of his motherless world.

In spite of his discomfiture, Diego's father never said anything to his son about his sexual proclivities or the miasma of broken boys he trailed in his wake.

Once, when the man was abroad, his son held a party on the top floor of his house, only a political emergency curtailed his trip and the scene he arrived home to involved four naked men lying unconscious on the floor of his entrance hall, garlanded in murky fluid and circumscribed by their blackly shining paraphernalia. When Diego came down the stairs his father said nothing besides, 'Your friends have gone home.'

It was only later, when he learned about Diego's cocaine habit, when the boy came to him one night and said, 'I need your help, I can't pay my debts,' that his father lost his patience.

'You little fuck,' he said, slamming down a hand. 'All that money on drugs.'

That was the day he froze his son's accounts and severed his allowance. It was the day he handed him one last cheque and ejected him from his life for good.

*

He liked to listen to Jamie and his mother talking. The feeling it evoked in him was soothing and hypnotic, like the feeling he'd derived from watching Gloria iron the family's clothes before folding them into neatly pressed piles.

Diego understood they would never talk this naturally if they knew he was in earshot, so he always listened to their conversations surreptitiously, perching at the top of the stairs with his knees pulled up to his chin, his arms drawn around his shins.

'Have you seen this?' the mother would say.

'What is it?' Jamie would reply.

'Sarah Ferguson. Look at her. What *is* she wearing?'

Diego could hear the sound of a newspaper changing hands.

'I'd love to have seen the Queen's face when she waltzed in dressed like that,' the mother said.

'Like Little Bo Peep,' the boy joked, and the mother laughed.

'Can you believe,' she said, 'that she's about to be a Princess or a Duchess or something?'

'Why doesn't someone advise her about this stuff?' he said.

'God knows. The only person you'd advise to

wear that's a pantomime dame.'

'To be fair,' said the boy, 'some of your old outfits aren't much better.'

'Hey,' she replied, 'those are couture.'

Jamie said, 'Is that what you call that yellow thing with all the pom-poms hanging off it?'

'Don't,' she said. 'There's a hat to match that one, it has all these feathers pointing up at the front. They wanted to give the impression I was flying - the article was called *Bird of Paradise* - so they photographed me hanging off the back of a Vespa. You can imagine the looks I got flying down Bond Street in that.'

The boy said, 'Do you still have the photographs?'

'Do I heck,' she said.

'Why, what happened to all that stuff?' he said.

'What stuff?'

'All the photos from your modelling days?'

'Oh, I don't know,' she said. 'I threw them away I suppose.'

'Why?' he said.

'I don't know, love,' she replied. 'I just did.'

Sometimes their conversations could go on for half an hour and other times, they were brief and clipped, depending on Jamie's mood, depending on his mother's. Diego would give anything for half an hour with his mother now. Without her, the world was a like a house that was really only a facade and when you opened the front door and walked inside, there was nothing.

His father had sent him to a therapist the year after she passed away, and he'd confounded this therapist because no matter which angle she worked, she couldn't penetrate the wall he'd erected. Sometimes their sessions were more like mediations with a hostage-taker, that's how they felt to this woman, as though one false move could upend the entire negotiation.

Finally, nine months after they started, she sat back in her leather armchair and said, 'Diego, what are we doing here? What are *you* doing here?'

'Killing time,' he said.

'Until what?' she said.

He fixed his obsidian eyes on her. 'Until I can see my mother again.'

And just like that the woman understood everything she needed to understand about him.

*

It was when they were sitting in Diego's bed one afternoon that Jamie first asked him about his mother.

Diego looked at him briefly and then turned

away. 'She died,' he said. 'But before that she was the most wonderful woman in the world.'

The boy said, 'When did she-

'When I was sixteen. She was driving to the airport to pick up a friend and a truck hit her.'

The boy said, 'God.'

'How many people do you know who would stay up until two in the morning to go and collect someone from the airport?' Diego said. 'How many people do you know who would make you feel like you're the most important person in the world every single day of your life?'

He looked at the boy intently, waiting for an answer, but Jamie didn't say anything, not one solitary word.

'When she died, people came to my father, people we didn't even know saying, We loved Angelita, she was an amazing woman. They remembered her from when she was young. Three thousand people came to her funeral. You couldn't get in the church. They were on the street, that's how much people loved my mother.'

Diego could feel that thing rise up in him, that voltaic anger that had once spilled over into everything he did and now bubbled beneath the surface, like lava in the belly of a volcano.

Jamie kissed the side of his face and for a second Diego wanted to punch the boy, because what did he know about any of it? Even if his mother had been dead he wouldn't understand because his mother was just an ordinary woman. Diego's mother had been something else, an angel on earth.

How can you compare that with an ordinary woman? How is it that an angel can be taken from the world while all these millions of ordinary women are left behind? Where's the sense in that? That's what he'd been asking the last twenty years.

Jamie waited a few seconds and then he looked down into the creases of the strewn sheets and said, 'Do you still think about her?'

'Yes, of course,' Diego said. 'I think about her every day.'

'I think about my dad sometimes,' said the boy, his voice a whisper. 'But it's different because I never knew him.'

Diego said, 'Is he dead?'

'No. Him and my mum weren't together, he was married when they met.'

'But he knew about you?'

'Yeah.'

Diego nodded. 'So he knew about you but he didn't want to see you?'

'Basically. It's a weird feeling to know your

dad doesn't care about you, that he's been going around all these years knowing you exist and ignoring it or not giving a shit about it.'

Diego suddenly felt the urge to wrap his arm around the boy. 'Maybe he didn't know what to do. Maybe his wife found out or something.'

'Maybe,' said the boy. 'Mum told me she called him up to tell him about me after I was born, but he told her to leave him alone.'

Diego nodded. 'Sure, but he could have changed his mind.'

'But he didn't,' said Jamie, biting his nails. 'He's never tried to contact me.'

'Maybe he wanted to though,' he said, and he drummed his fingers off the boy's shoulder. 'Maybe he was scared.'

'Maybe. Anyway, it doesn't matter.'

'Of course it does,' Diego said. Suddenly he felt emboldened to bolster the boy, because he knew what it was to have something that followed you wherever you went, that sat permanently on your shoulder.

He thought about all the people who'd turned to him over the years and told him it was time to let his mother go now, it was over. All those people acting as though he could turn a page in a book and everything that had been written before would simply disappear, would seep away into the ether. He put his thick hand through the boy's hair. 'If it matters to you, then it matters,' he said.

'I guess,' Jamie said.

'Do you ever think about going to see him?'

'I don't know where he lives,' said the boy. 'I don't even know if he's still alive.'

'Sure. But you could find out.'

Jamie looked into his face. 'Really? How?'

'I don't know,' said Diego. 'You could ask your mother. You could search the telephone directory, there are things you could do.'

'Maybe.'

'The only way you'll ever be able to stop thinking about him is if you go and find him, go and talk to him.'

Jamie bit his lip and coiled a lock of hair around his finger. 'But what if he shuts the door in my face? What if he doesn't wanna know?'

'Then you tell him to go fuck himself. Simple.'

Diego reached for his cigarettes and lit one. He blew the smoke out and watched as it spiralled beneath a band of blue light. Jamie lay down on his chest and suddenly he felt the urge to push him away, to rush himself from the bed. The boy was awakening a feeling in him, one he'd set aside years earlier. It had remained frozen and still and now the sun was rising on it and a thaw was beginning.

*

He orchestrated things so his shifts started at two in the afternoon almost every day that summer. He could do this because he was the manager. He could do it because he didn't care if they fired him and because he had a deputy who didn't know how to say no. As Diego saw it, he was a person with nothing to lose.

Their mornings became a sort of ritual. Once his mother had gone to work, Jamie would pad across the landing, knock on Diego's door and when he told him to come in, he'd slip inside. In the beginning, Diego would say, 'Let's fuck,' but later the words grew thorny and caught in his throat, they no longer matched this act that had transcended the banal and become somehow beautiful.

Afterwards, when they'd made love or whatever it had become, Jamie would make them breakfast and they'd sit at the little pink table in the sunlight. They'd eat eggs and cereal and at intervals they'd lean into each other and kiss.

Sometimes, Diego would reveal a troubling detail about himself, admit he'd once conducted a sexual relationship with a man and the man's boyfriend simultaneously and had then blackmailed them both, for example. 'Fucking idiots,' he called them, after telling the boy about these men.

'That's so mean of you,' Jamie said.

'So?' he shrugged. 'They shouldn't have been fucking around.'

The boy lowered his spoon into his bowl. 'That doesn't mean it's okay to steal their money.'

'I didn't steal it.'

'You threatened to do something if they didn't pay you.'

Diego nodded and eyed the boy squarely. 'And it'll teach them a lesson on how to behave.'

'But what about your behaviour? Why do you think it's okay to do that?'

Diego bit into a bagel. He stared at Jamie, and like a switch being flicked, a current began to light up his senses. 'Because I don't give a fuck. Nobody gives a fuck about me, so why should I care?'

Jamie looked at him. 'What do you mean?'

Diego dismissed him with his hand. 'Nothing. Forget it.'

'Tell me. You can't just say that and then be like, *Oh nothing, forget it.*'

'You wouldn't understand,' said Diego, and he pushed his bagel to one side.

'Try me.'

He leaned forward. 'When the only person in the world who matters to you dies, your life becomes meaningless.'

The boy said, 'You mean your mother?'

'Of course I mean my mother.'

Jamie said, 'You talk about it like there's no point in anything now, as though your life ended the day she died.'

'It did.'

Jamie waited, and then he said, 'I'm sorry it feels like that.' He reached out and took Diego's hand.

Diego ground his teeth together and looked past the boy. He knew what was about to happen so he pulled his hand away and then he stood up and walked out of the kitchen. He went up to his room and closed the door. After a few seconds the tears came and he slid down the wall on to the floor.

'Are you okay?' the boy said when he appeared outside his room, and when there was no response he said, 'Can I come in?'

Diego didn't care what he did, he could go to hell or he could walk into his room, it didn't matter, so when he saw the boy crouching there in front of him, he didn't react or tell him to go. All he could do was wait for the fire in his chest to burn itself out.

When it was done he stood and blew his nose and then he went to the mirror and looked at his reflection. 'God,' he said. 'I look awful.'

Jamie came up behind him and said, 'Are you okay?'

'Yeah,' he said. 'Sorry, I don't know what happened.'

'It's okay.'

Diego turned to face the boy. He found himself reaching out and grabbing hold of him. This was followed by the quixotic urge to say three words, words he hadn't said since his mother. He didn't say them though, he wasn't stupid. What he did instead was to go to his dresser and fix himself a line.

He poured coke from the bag, cut it haphazardly and curled up a bank note. He pressed his index finger to one nostril and snorted through the other, and inside twenty seconds his anxiety had fallen away and been superseded by that familiar sense of peace, of immutable control.

If he could have had anything in the world besides his mother, he would have chosen always to feel the way he did immediately after that first line.

*

Diego thought about it obsessively afterwards, about how easily it could have been avoided if they'd been more vigilant, if they'd guarded themselves against complacency. But what did it matter now? It was over and done with, like so many things in his life.

It had been a thousand times easier for Jamie. He'd been made to choose so he'd chosen, and of course he'd chosen his cosy existence, his mother, his home. None of those options were available to Diego.

What he'd learned was that when you had no mother, your choices shrivelled like grapes ripped clean from the vine. Anyway, it wasn't important, everything had to end sometime. What could a person do with a seventeen year-old boy anyway? Beyond the obvious, what could a person really do?

He hadn't heard Jamie's mother leaving that morning, but that wasn't a cause for alarm, she often slipped out unnoticed. She could descend the stairs soundlessly, like a shadow. She could position herself in the corner of a room and sit so quietly, breathe such silent breaths that you wouldn't know she was there. To Diego, she was a person who occupied almost no space in the world, either literally or figuratively. That's why it didn't concern him that he never heard her leaving the flat.

He woke before Jamie and was too restless to hang around in bed, so he decided to surprise the boy. He slunk his way down the hall in his underwear and opened the bedroom door. When he saw Jamie was still asleep, he smiled his cobra smile and began across the room on the balls of his feet. When he reached the boy, he crouched down at his side and shouted, 'Boo!'

Jamie screamed and sat up suddenly. 'You fucking idiot,' he said.

Diego laughed and threw himself down on him. He began kissing the boy and that was the moment the door swung open, the moment a voice said, 'Jamie, what's going on, what are you shouting about?'

For a second she hung there in the doorway as though she was watching as her son peeled away his skin to reveal what had secretly been hiding beneath all along.

She stood and waited for thoughts to happen, for words to happen, for time to go backwards and walk her out of that room and back to the world she woke up to, the one that made sense. That's how it seemed to Diego anyway, watching her there in the doorway, like a nightmare that had escaped the parameters of sleep.

'Oh God,' she said.

'Mum, it's not what it looks like,' said Jamie.

To Diego's mind, that was something only people in telenovelas said. To hear an actual person say it made him want to laugh. *Of course it's what it looks like,* he thought. *It's two men kissing, it's exactly what it looks like.*

'Oh God,' she said. 'I don't believe this.'

Diego flipped himself over and stood up, and then the woman began yelling at him.

'How dare you come into my house and do this?' she said. 'Get out. Go on, get out.'

It was humiliating to be cast as the pervert, as the abuser. He hated this feeling he'd been made to feel all these years. Even his own mother, even she'd done it to him. She'd looked him in the eye and said, 'Guess what? Conchita's boy, Miguel, he's a faggot.' She'd shaken her head and said, 'Thank God I don't have to worry about that. Thank God I have you.'

This was when he was fifteen, the year before she was killed. That was the one good thing to come out of her death, that she never had to find out who he was.

Diego packed his things quickly. The boy didn't come to his room, he didn't say goodbye or slip him a note. His mother had probably told him to stay out of her sight, that she couldn't look at him, that she couldn't bear to think about what he'd been doing. Diego knew all about it, about what people said when they found out you were gay.

You'll get used to it, he thought.

As he folded his clothes and packed them away, the boy's mother waited outside his bedroom door. He could feel her disgust all over him, thick like oil. He didn't understand why she had to play chaperone, what did she think he was going to do?

He tried to pack with care, to be meticulous, but it was more than he could take knowing she was right there beyond the wall, waiting to eject him, to expunge him from their lives. That's why he left without his stereo or his bedding, it's why he left without his books. In truth they didn't matter to him, he didn't give a fuck about the books.

What was the point of them anyway, when there was television and sex and cocaine?

Appetite

The day Heidi Jenson's father packed his bags and walked out of the family home constituted a defining moment in her life.

He didn't disappear, he simply left her mother and started with another woman like a million middle-aged men before him. It was a perfunctory act, a predictably bourgeois move on the chessboard of middle-class convention. Heidi understood that divorce was a thing that happened to many children, so she didn't play on the fact or use it as an excuse for bad behaviour, and she wasn't bitter about it either.

When she was sixteen, something far more astonishing happened, which was that Mitchell King invited her to eat fried chicken with him after school. This she considered the second defining moment of her life.

He invited her during her lunch-break when she was sitting slack-shouldered in the sixth-form common room grazing on an apple and flicking through a copy of *Elle* magazine.

'Okay,' she said, and beneath that she thought, *I can't believe this is happening. Is it a trick? Is he going to burst out laughing in a second?*

But it wasn't a trick.

He'd broken up with Kim Miller – Tasha Cole had told her all about it, about him dumping the girl for being too clingy, for throwing her toys out of the pram every time he looked at someone else – and now he'd decided on her.

Heidi was amazed by this because she wasn't popular. She wasn't unpopular either, she had friends, but they weren't invited to parties and they never showed up for school in mini-skirts, in make-up they could have worn to a nightclub.

Sometimes this bothered Heidi, she wanted to turn to her friends with their sloppy hair and their matronly shoes and say, *Can't you make an effort?*, but she was too nice a person for that.

Most of the boys in her year looked like overblown children but Mitchell King was an exception. He was six feet tall and his chin was already bristling with black stubble. What impressed Heidi was that he could pass for a man in his early twenties even though he'd only just turned seventeen. She knew this because he was already going to clubs at the weekend, he was already partying with people two years his senior and french-kissing city PAs in fishnets on beer-soaked dance floors.

They ordered fillet burgers at a chicken shop on Shepherd's Bush Road and sat down in the window on swivel-stools that looked like they'd been pulled from an American diner.

Mitchell took a leopard's bite and with his mouth full told her she was *fit as*. Then he said his friends were all dying to have a go on her and laughed. There was something both thrilling and deflating about this, about being made to sound like a BMX, but she knew better than to question it.

Mitchell told her it was cute when she was thinking and she looked off into a corner and looped a sticky strand of VO5'd hair around her index finger. In one way this made her giddy and in another it filled her with anxiety because she realised it would look stagey and premeditated anytime she did it again now.

The first time she kissed Mitchell King, his mouth tasted like mayonnaise and charred chicken-skin, and no matter how many times she replayed the event in her head, it remained staggering, extraordinary.

Like everything in life though, what started out extraordinary was made ordinary by repetition. Soon enough it felt ordinary to be kissed by him or to feel the hard slant of his chest as he whispered typically juvenile sounding things like, 'Fuck, you're giving me such a boner,' in her ear. It even began to feel ordinary to sashay down school corridors with her hand in his, knowing absolutely everyone was drinking in her new and exalted status as his girlfriend.

Heidi was a virgin before Mitchell King came along, and the idea of sleeping with him terrified her.

What if I'm bad at it? What if there's something physically wrong with me and it won't go in? What if he's so big it tears something open?

These were the questions that flooded her brain.

She had the idea she couldn't keep him waiting either, he was a person with too many options to wait. So when he turned to her one morning, flashed a smile and said, 'My parents are out tomorrow night,' she acted out the naughty kitten part the way she thought he'd expect her to, recognising she had only one chance to get it right.

Heidi shaved her legs and armpits, she waxed herself, she washed and conditioned her hair, she cut her toe-nails, she even painted them with sky-blue nail polish, it was an evening's work.

On the Friday after school they walked back to his house together and on the way she told him she hadn't slept with anyone before. She knew there was no choice, her body would say it for her if she didn't. *Sexy virgin* was a thing anyway, she could play that part.

'I know,' said Mitchell, and then he smiled and

kissed her, and as he did she wondered how he knew. Was she a person who went around with *virgin* stamped on her forehead? Was she just like her friends with their clomping buckled shoes and their utilitarian bras?

His house was a semi-detached with the same pock-marked face as a thousand others on a bland suburban street like a thousand more. There was a white hatchback parked in the driveway and a mussy-looking hedge separating the tiny front garden from the tiny front garden of its conjoined twin. Inside, the rooms were compact and insipidly appointed in magnolias and lemons.

'Your house is nice,' she said, and Mitchell curled a lip and said, 'It's a shit-hole.' Then he pushed her against the wall and began kissing her. He kissed her softly to begin with, then aggressively, and Heidi found the transition jarring, like watching the shaggy buffers of a mechanical carwash humming momentarily before thrashing violently into life.

His room was as uninspiring as the rest of the house. The walls were an indeterminate off-white and the carpet was a threadbare sludge green affair speckled in detritus. There were the usual accoutrements; a desk, TV, drawers, wardrobe, a double-bed.

On the walls were posters of heroically-breasted women spilling out of bikinis and dark moustached footballers firing shots at goal mouths. Heidi wasn't sure if these were relics from earlier adolescence or if they represented Mitchell's current stage of development. Either way, they acted on her like anaesthesia, like a dull blow to the head.

He took her by the shoulders and sat her down on the edge of his lumpy mattress, then took off his t-shirt in one swift movement. It was the first time she'd seen Mitchell's chest and it was contoured and hairy, as she'd known it would be.

He kicked off his trainers and pulled down his jeans so that when he came and sat down beside her he was wearing only his boxers. He kissed her for a minute, and as he did, he eased her up on her two feet so he could unzip her dress and let it fall to the ground beneath her.

It felt surreal to hear his fingers unclipping her bra and even more surreal to watch him grow before her until his underwear couldn't contain him. She found the sight of his penis shocking, it scared her the way physical violence scared her.

He guided her hand and she took hold of it and did what she was supposed to do and he closed his eyes and panted and then after a minute he stopped her and said, 'Not yet'.

Then he placed her on her back and eased her out of her underwear whilst kissing her face, her neck. He pushed her legs apart and began to touch her. At first it felt procedural and coarse and then his fingers hit a spot and there was a flash through her body, a momentary shock lighting up her nerves.

What struck her about sex was how mystifying it was to have a naked boy on top of her and inside her, pounding away, as though this was a normal thing to be happening.

What the fuck, she thought. *What the fuck.*

It was happening, she could see it happening, she could feel it happening, yet somehow she'd disconnected herself and was watching it as though a screen separated her from the reality.

Towards the end he started to moan in lupine stabs and Heidi took it as a signal to make a few sounds of her own. Then the pitch of his voice dropped to a breathy growl and she understood he was climaxing. His chest convulsed and she wondered why nobody had ever warned her about this part, the part when the man's body starts making these sudden involuntary movements. She was bewildered that they continued after he'd come because how did she know he wasn't having a fit or something?

Even more bewildering was when he lay down on his back and began laughing.

'What's so funny?' she said.

'Nothing,' he said. 'I always laugh when I come.'

Mitchell carried on panting for a minute and then he reached out and began to squeeze her abdomen.

She looked at his hand for a moment, at that foreign entity pulping her flesh like pizza dough.

'What are you doing?' she said.

'Nothing,' he replied. 'Just feeling your belly.'

Heidi watched as he altered his rhythm, as he applied pressure more slowly and deliberately, a gardener mulching the soil. 'Do you think I'm fat?' she said.

Mitchell smiled up at her and said, 'Don't worry, it's fine.'

'What do you mean?' she said, and without knowing she would do it, she watched herself take his hand and remove it from her body.

He offered an avuncular smile.

'Seriously,' he said, 'I don't mind.'

'Don't mind what?' she said, drawing her legs up to shield her stomach. Her heart was banging.

'That you've got a belly.'

A lump formed in the back of Heidi's throat. She reached for her underwear and swung her legs over the edge of the bed.

'What are you doing?' he said.

For a second she thought she might pass out. She'd entered fight or flight or some other dead-brained state, she'd forgotten how to breathe.

'Nothing,' she said.

'You don't have to go, you know. They won't be back for ages.'

'I should go anyway,' she said, and she yanked her knickers up over her knees.

'Is this about your belly?' He reached out and took hold of her arm.

'No, it's fine.'

Heidi pulled away and began to climb into her bra. Behind her, she could hear him sigh.

'For fuck's sake,' he said. 'Why have you all gotta turn everything into a fucking drama?'

She didn't say anything to this. She didn't know what to say, she'd lost the ability to formulate original thoughts. As she pulled on her dress and scrambled around the floor panting, looking for her shoes, he said, 'Fine, go. But if you go now, that's it, you can fuck off.'

Heidi began to cry, but furtively, without making a sound, because she didn't want him to tell her she was being hysterical. She didn't want him to say anything.

*

When she got home that night, she stood in front of the mirror and surveyed her stomach. She stood side-on and looked at the curvature of it, the way a newly pregnant woman looks to see if the baby has made its mark yet, only instead of feeling exhilarated, she was horrified.

Heidi went to the bathroom, took off her dress and stood on the scales. She looked down at the reading, which was sixty-three kilos, and determined she would lose thirteen kilos by Christmas of 1986. She had six months, it was a doable thing.

The biggest issue was her mother. Heidi's mother had brought her up with the idea that food was more than just sustenance, it was a reward for being good, a consolation when things went wrong, and a sure way to make yourself feel instantly better when you felt bad about yourself. That's why she always had cake in the fridge, ice-cream in the freezer and biscuits in the cupboard. It's why she was fat.

'I want you to give me smaller portions from now on,' Heidi said the next day. 'And no dessert.'

She was standing in the doorway of the living room and her mother was sitting in her reclining armchair, a dead weight, glued to the television.

'And why's that?' she said.

Because I don't want to end up like you, Heidi wanted to say. 'Because I want to lose weight.'

Her mother turned to her and made a face. 'But you don't need to lose weight.'

'Yes I do. Look at me.' She held out her arms and looked down at her body.

Her mother said, 'I am looking.'

Heidi didn't have the energy to go into it. 'Please,' she said, 'I don't want any unhealthy stuff. From now on, I'm on a diet.'

The first thing she cut was breakfast. She stayed in bed an extra ten minutes and left the house without setting foot in the kitchen.

What she learned was that there was a mysterious thrill to seeing how long she could go without eating anything. It felt like an achievement to get to the end of her lunch-break without a single morsel passing her lips. There was a coruscating power to it, something far greater than the fleeting pleasure of biting into a sandwich.

Heidi re-arranged her existence so that her only meal of the day was dinner. Her mother would call up to her around six and she would come downstairs and sit at the table.

'Here you go,' the woman would say, and then she'd hand her a plate of cottage pie and baked beans and Heidi would think about all that potato sitting on the floor of her stomach like cement.

It was a curious thing to feel such resistance to this meal because she was also ravenously hungry, she was also cramping from the pain of ingesting nothing since dinner the previous evening. The animal part of her wanted to wolf it down, to lick the plate, to follow it up with chocolate.

That's what that part of her wanted, and the human, reasoning part wanted to consume the minimum amount necessary to remain alive, because her goal was to have total control over her body now, to look in the mirror and see someone skinny, someone powerful.

*

'Heidi, you've lost weight. You look amazing.'

Stacey Hack said this to her at the bus-stop one day in October. Stacey Hack was an important person because she was attractive and she was popular and she wasn't afraid to say what she meant. To have her turn around and say something like this was exceptional because she wasn't a person who complimented girls like Heidi, she was someone who called them on their bad decisions, who told them if they'd over-plucked their eyebrows or chosen shoes that looked like they'd been prescribed by a doctor.

'Thanks,' said Heidi.

'What is it, are you on some sort of diet?'

Heidi tilted her head and said, 'No, not really, it just sort of happened.'

'That's annoying,' Stacey replied.

It was an important lesson for Heidi. *Don't tell people it's easy to lose weight, tell them it's hard. Of course they don't want to hear that weight just falls off you.*

She didn't know why she'd said that it 'just sort of happened'. The truth was she spent entire days fantasising about fried chicken and vanilla milkshakes without attending to these cravings. Each morning she calculated how long she'd have to go to surpass her record for the longest period of time spent fasting. If she lasted all day it made her euphoric to know she hadn't taken a single bite, to know she was winning at a game almost everyone else was losing.

Starvation became an ally. It became a sovereign voice commanding her entire body, demanding she not eat any of the things that flashed up behind her eyes, reminding her that if she could continue to resist for another two hours, she'd have demonstrated she was in complete control of herself, like a person who'd mastered desire, mastered weakness.

Every time she thought she might crack, that she'd have to go to the fridge and pull out a block of cheese or a slab of cake, she floated herself back to Mitchell's bedroom, she relived the sensations that crashed her nervous system the moment he told her about her belly, and just like that she was reset.

Her mother was the first person to pass comment.

'Heidi, I don't think you're eating enough,' she announced one evening. 'You've lost an awful lot of weight.'

Heidi's body grew rigid. 'No I haven't,' she said.

They were stood in the kitchen and her mother was ironing clothes. Heidi looked at the woman's forearms, at the way the undersides of them sagged down. Then she looked at her mother's cushioned face with its white lips and its black eyes like two ink stains on a mile of paper.

'Heidi, you can't just stand there and say, No I haven't, I'm looking right at you.'

Heidi folded her arms and leant against the doorframe. 'What are you talking about?'

'You look ill. You look malnourished.' Her mother stopped what she was doing and placed her hands down on the surface of the ironing board.

'No I don't, I just haven't got any make-up on.'

'It's nothing to do with make-up,' the woman said. 'Your clothes are falling off you.'

'Yes, because they're all from when I was fat and you won't give me any money to buy new ones.'

'Heidi, you were never fat, don't talk rubbish.'

'It's not rubbish,' she said.

'It *is* rubbish. You were a perfectly healthy weight, I don't know why you decided you needed to go on a diet in the first place.'

'I've just told you. Because I was fat. And the only reason you can't see it is because you're fat.'

Her mother raised an arm and pointed a finger. 'Don't you dare speak to me like that.'

'Why?' she said. 'Because it's true? Just stay out of my business, it's nothing to do with you what I eat.'

Heidi said this and then she walked out of the house. What she realised as she walked along the road was that her mother didn't like that she'd lost weight because now she was being forced to look at herself and see what she'd become.

She decided that if the woman tried to engage her in an argument again, she'd refuse to rise to the bait. She'd read about this technique in *Cosmopolitan*. A girl in there had written an article about how she used to row with her father over the length of her skirts and the amount of cleavage she had on show, and then one day she accepted everything he threw at her and when he was finished she thanked him and gave him a hug, and then she went off in her short skirt with her breasts pushed forward and he didn't have a clue what had hit him.

There had been a time when her mother had been slim, it was when Heidi was six or seven years-old, before her parents' marriage collapsed. Her mother had started to put on weight before her father left, it wasn't that he walked out and then she consoled herself with cheeseburgers and banana splits. When Heidi really considered it, her mother's weight increase may have been the thing to seal the deal for her father.

After all, she thought, *what man would choose a fat woman when he could just as easily have a thin one?*

*

Heidi saw her father once a week, on a Saturday. When she was younger he used to take her to the cinema or the zoo or something, but now she was older she just stayed over at his house where he lived with his wife, Karen, and their son, Joshua. This was on a long luxurious road called Castelnau, which ran from Hammersmith Bridge to the corner of Church Road in Barnes.

The houses on this stretch were large and imposing, and the people who lived in them had been born rich and stayed rich. Her father wasn't one of these people, her father had made his own fortune, and when he moved to Castelnau he said the neighbours looked down their noses at him because to them he was just a commoner with a bank account.

Her father and Karen had been together for years, since the year he left home. Heidi's mother said she was on the scene before their marriage ended, but her father had always denied this, he said she was only his secretary and there had never been any funny business.

For a long time, Heidi believed her mother, but now she'd seen another side to her, now she wasn't so sure. In any case, she liked Karen. The woman was intelligent and she was kind and she was funny. She was the sort of person you could only dislike if you worked at it.

Heidi's father didn't like to pick fights. He'd rather sit back and let her mother discipline his daughter. That's what her mother said anyway.

I always have to play the bad cop.

So it seemed strange to her that the week after her mother told her she was too skinny, her father suddenly sat her down and said the same thing.

'Heidi, are you okay?' he asked. That was the first thing he said when she walked into his house, and then when she confirmed she was fine, he said, 'You're very thin.'

'No I'm not,' she said.

'I'm not having a go. I'm just concerned.'

'Well you don't need to be,' she said, and then she told him she was feeling tired and wanted to lie down for a while. It was true, she was feeling tired, she was exhausted.

There were side-effects that came with this diet, that's what she'd come to see. One was that sometimes she was exhausted, and another was that sometimes she grew dizzy and had to sit down. If she was already sitting, she would have to close her eyes and wait until it passed, and then she'd pour herself a glass of water.

Heidi wasn't worried, she'd read enough by now to know it was a fallacy that people needed food. What they needed was water, usually more than they realised. Food they did not need, except in very small quantities. All food did was age people and make them fat.

*

By the end of the year, Heidi had surpassed her target weight. When she stood on the scales on Christmas Eve, she weighed forty-one kilos. This was pleasing and it was also disappointing. It was disappointing because it wasn't forty flat. When she thought about it, forty flat would also be disappointing because that was still forty-something instead of thirty-something. That's why her new target became thirty-nine kilos.

If I'm thirty-nine kilos, I'll be in the thirties, I'll be ahead of everyone, she thought to herself.

Heidi stood in front of the mirror and surveyed her body in profile, just as she'd done six months earlier. She looked at her stomach and her breasts and her face. She could see her jutting hips and the protrusion of her ribs and the geometry of her skull. That's how she knew on some objective level she was looking at a person who was too thin. She knew this, and still she saw a person who was too fat, a person who was relaxing just at the point she needed to strengthen her resolve.

That's why she took off her top and her jeans and put on a tracksuit. It's why she did a hundred star-jumps in her room and then went downstairs on her tip-toes and put on her trainers. Heidi ran for half an hour, until black dots helicoptered around her eyeballs and shooting pains licked at her brain stem. *It's lack of water,* she thought, and she walked home and stuck her head under the kitchen tap.

On Christmas Day the whole thing blew up.

'You have to eat,' her mother said. 'I don't know what to do with you anymore.'

She said this and then she sat down at the table and cried and Heidi stood frozen in place in the doorway for a minute before walking away. The idea of sitting down at the dinner table in the middle of the afternoon and eating a three-course meal was inconceivable. Her mother knew if she sat down and ate that, all those months of effort would be for nothing. Heidi was stunned by the woman's selfishness, by the way she attempted to manipulate her, it was pathetic.

That evening, her mother came to her room and said this couldn't go on, they had to seek help. She sat down on the edge of Heidi's bed and told her she was scared she was going to die if she carried on, and Heidi had a strange urge to laugh.

Die of what? she wanted to say. *Health?*

Then her father appeared at the house and started having exactly the same conversation with her, as though the pair of them had marched themselves back through history to the point in their relationship where they remembered how to agree. Heidi couldn't recall the last time the three of them had been in that house together. They hadn't. Not since the day her father packed his bags and walked out when she was nine years-old.

*

The doctor concurred with Heidi.

If she was going to have an appointment, it was her right to have it in private. Her mother and father could sit in the waiting room like everyone else. Doctor Garvey was a tall bald-headed man with an equine jaw and a tapering chin. He'd been the family GP for many years.

When she sat down, he took off his reading glasses and let them hang from the silver chain around his neck. His expression was cool and focused, like a career interlocutor, and it made her nervous to look at him.

'Heidi,' he said, 'I can see this is a sensitive matter. And I know your parents have pressured you to come here. So I'm not going to push you. But what I'd like you to do is to stand on those scales.'

She looked over to where he was pointing, to the weighing scales that were on the floor next to a silver trolley containing a series of ignominious metallic implements.

'Now?' she said.

'Yes, if you would.'

She went over to the scales and took off her shoes.

'Take off your coat as well, Heidi.'

She stood still as a statue on the scale and Doctor Garvey came over and looked at the reading.

'That's fine,' he said. 'Put your shoes back on and come and sit down.'

Heidi put on her shoes and then she took her coat and carried it over to the chair. She sat down and looked into her lap. 'I suppose you're gonna tell me I'm too thin.'

'No, I think you're aware of that already. But here's the thing,' he said. 'If you lose any more weight, your organs are going to start shutting down and then you're going to go into cardiac arrest. Do you realise that?'

Heidi didn't realise that. What she realised was that as long as a person drank water regularly and occasionally ate some small thing, they would be fine.

'Are you trying to scare me?' she said. She couldn't think of any other reason a person would say something like this.

'No, I'm trying to help you. The human body is a machine, it needs fuel to survive. If you restrict its fuel intake enough, it will start to shut down. The problem is, when that happens you won't be able to do anything about it because you'll either be too disorientated to know what's happening or you'll be unconscious. So you'll be relying on someone finding you. And if there's nobody around, for example, if it's during the night and you're in bed, well that's it, you're just not going to wake up in the morning.'

'But it's not like I don't eat,' she said. 'I eat dinner. Besides, people have survived for weeks without food, on just water. I know they have, I've read about it.'

'Heidi, people can survive without food for several weeks. They can survive for months on very limited amounts of food. But eventually, they'll die.'

Doctor Garvey said this and then he put on his glasses and wrote something on a piece of paper.

'But I just told you I eat dinner. So what's the problem?'

Heidi could feel bubbles of emotion bursting in her chest as she spoke. It was overwhelming, like being plunged into a vat of iced water.

'The problem is, your mother tells me a different story. She tells me she finds your dinner in the bin. Or that she hears you in the toilet afterwards and she doesn't know if you're making yourself sick. Are you making yourself sick? Is that what's happening?'

Doctor Garvey took off his glasses again and looked at her. She could feel the blood moving through her face, slick and hot, like petrol through a cylinder.

'Look Heidi, all I have to go on is what I see before me. Your parents are very worried, and they're worried because you're killing yourself. Sixteen year-old girls of your height do not weigh forty kilos.'

Inside, she wanted to scream. She took a deep breath and let it out again slowly.

'Heidi,' he said. 'You have to start eating again.'

She thought about whether she would rather eat again and be fat or stay slim and die like Doctor Garvey was suggesting.

'Fine' she whispered, and then she stood up and put on her coat.

*

In January 1987, Heidi was waiting at the bus-stop on the first day back after the Christmas break when Stacey Hack came over to her and said, 'Are you okay?'

'Why?' she replied.

'Because you look ill,' Stacey said, looking her up and down. 'You look like you've just walked out of Auschwitz or something.'

Heidi told the girl she'd had a terrible bug and hadn't been able to keep any food down for days, it was the first thing she could think to say.

When she arrived at school, she went to the toilet and sat in the stall. She waited until classes had begun and then she sneaked out of the building. Twenty minutes later she walked into a bakery and bought a sausage roll, then stood on the street and pecked at it, even though it made her feel sick, even though it felt completely unnatural, like biting into human flesh.

How will I know when I've eaten enough? How will I stop from getting fat again? Where's the line between skinny and too skinny?

These were the questions that buzzed around her skull that morning as she stood trembling on the high street holding her grease-laden sausage roll. Up until then, Heidi had known not to eat, to simply keep going. But now the rules had changed and suddenly the game was too complex to make sense of.

When she got home she sat on the sofa and focused on the breaths she was taking – in, out, in, out – until she was calm enough to think. Then she went to the fridge and pulled out a bar of chocolate.

Later, when her mother arrived home, Heidi was sitting at the kitchen table with the chocolate wrapper torn into strips in front of her. She looked up at the woman and began to cry.

'What's wrong?' asked her mother.

Heidi dropped her head. 'I don't know what's happening to me,' she said.

*

She refused to say a word to the psychotherapist.

She kept this up until midway through their third session, but then the woman said, 'I know that voice is telling you I'm the enemy. But how do you know it's on your side? What if that voice is trying to ruin your relationship with your parents, to cut you off from your friends? What about that?'

Heidi had been determined not to fall into any traps, but it occurred to her that if she knew something was a trap and she chose to go into it anyway, she was still the one in control, which was all that really mattered.

Okay, she thought. *I'll talk.* And suddenly she was like a coconut that had been hacked open, and the juice began spilling out of her.

The psychotherapist's conclusion was that her problems stemmed from her parent's divorce and her mother's unresolved anger, that Heidi's refusal to eat was a way of taking control of her body, because up until then she'd had no control over anything else.

The woman told her she couldn't trust the voice in her head because it was the same voice that told the alcoholic to pour another drink and the intravenous drug user to push a needle into a vein. Heidi understood this, even if something about the explanation left her cold. She didn't really believe she was the same as people like that, people who shot up heroin and drank themselves to death.

The following year she decided to study psychology at university. She chose it because of her own experiences and because it fascinated her, the idea that people's actions could be analysed, that a set of causes could be extrapolated, that a way of re-directing their behaviour could be implemented.

Another thing that fascinated her was the notion that people were in some way self-sabotaging, that sometimes they chose to engage in activities they knew to be harmful. She knew it well, the desire to self-harm. Sometimes it was the thing she desired most.

*

'Sorry to bother you,' she said when he came to the door. 'It's just that someone told me you were the guy to speak to to buy hash.'

'Oh,' he replied.

'I'm Heidi by the way,' she said, and smiled. 'I'm in a room down the hall. Number sixteen.'

'Jamie,' he said, and they shook hands.

He was skinny and bandy-legged in his t-shirt and 501s. His hair was blonde and tangled and his eyes were blue like the ocean. She noticed that when he smiled his cheeks dimpled, and she knew immediately he was someone she would sleep with if he decided to initiate something.

'Come in,' he said, and she followed him into his dorm. He invited her to sit on a chair by the window. 'You want a coffee or something?'

'Are you having one?'

He shrugged. 'Maybe.'

This was in 1988, when Heidi and Jamie first began at university, when they moved into halls and occupied rooms at opposite ends of the same corridor. She looked around while he made the coffee. There were piles of books all stacked on the floor and a small TV on a stand, and all along the edge of the skirting board in plastic pots were little plants without flowers. On the walls he had posters of James Dean and Marlon Brando and Marilyn Monroe.

'How come all your posters are people from the fifties?' she said.

Jamie turned around and looked at her. 'I don't know, I just like old movie stars.'

'Do you like old films then?'

'I love them,' he said. 'I love the look of them; the colours, you know.'

She searched for the word. 'Technicolor.'

Jamie turned and walked towards her holding a coffee. 'Here you go.'

Heidi said, 'Have you seen *It Happened One Night*?'

She watched as he sat down on the bed and shook his head.

'It's good,' she said. 'It's black and white, it's

really old. But it's funny.'

'Who's in it?'

'Clark Gable. I can't remember the woman, but she's funny. I'll bring it for you, I have the video somewhere.'

She brought it for him the following day and when she did, Jamie asked her if she wanted to share a joint and a bottle of wine and watch it with him.

'Sure,' she said.

It was funnier than she remembered, although maybe that's because she was drunk and high, and all the way through the film she wondered if he would kiss her when it was over and if he would take her to bed after that.

Jamie didn't take her to bed though.

What he did when the film was over was to make another joint, and then just as he was about to light it, he dropped his head and said, 'I knew a guy that looked like Clark Gable once,' and then he looked briefly at Heidi, and after a few seconds he said, 'He was the first guy I ever slept with.'

Heidi felt something cut at her, somewhere in her abdomen, and for a moment she was too stunned to say anything, and then the feeling was overtaken by fascination. She'd never known a man who slept with men before. When she made no response he started to blush, he grew embarrassed.

'Sorry,' she said, 'I wasn't expecting that.'

He shook his head and blew out a line of smoke. 'I shouldn't have said anything.'

'No, I'm glad you did.'

Heidi was amazed to meet a man who went around in jeans and t-shirt, with scruffy blonde hair and a five-day beard, a man who appeared almost identical to any other, whilst simultaneously harbouring this secret life within himself. She found the whole idea thrilling somehow, as though she'd met someone exotic and rare, and it elevated him immediately in her mind above almost everyone else she knew.

'Did he really look like Clark Gable?' she said.

'Sort of. He was Spanish.'

Heidi smiled. 'That's hot. How old?'

'Mid-thirties.'

'Oh I'd love to fuck a guy in his mid-thirties. I hate having sex with children. All men are children until they're in their thirties.'

Jamie laughed and handed her the joint. 'How do you work that out?'

'It's true,' she said. 'You just have to talk to one.'

He shrugged. 'Well I must be a child too then.'

'No,' she said, 'you're okay. Gay guys are different.'

'Why?'

'I don't know, you just are. Do you spend your entire life thinking about football and tits?'

He laughed, and shadows swirled in the dimples of his cheeks. 'No.'

'Exactly,' she said. 'You're different.'

Heidi couldn't sleep that night.

She lay in bed and thought about Jamie, about what he thought about when he was lying in bed. She imagined him in front of a man, and then she tried to imagine the man kissing him. She found it almost impossible to imagine though, like an object imploding. A man kissing a woman was an explosion, it was easy to imagine that, but two men…

In the morning when she awoke, she got out of bed and threw on some clothes and as soon as she'd looked in the mirror and put a hand through her hair, she found herself on the corridor walking back to his room. She knocked on his door and when it swung back, he appeared before her wearing only his underwear, his hazy eyes squinting to see her.

'It's you,' he said, smiling. 'Fancy a joint?'

And that's how it began.

*

The third defining moment in Heidi Jenson's life happened on a dance-floor in an underground club near London Bridge when she was twenty-one. It was around four in the morning when Jamie pulled her to one side and said he was feeling hot, that he couldn't catch his breath.

'Do you want to get some air?' she said.

He didn't respond so she put her lips to his ear and asked again, only this time he dropped down beside her and lay on the floor. At first he lay still and then he began to jerk around and she knelt down and started saying his name. His eyes kept appearing and disappearing under the strobes and she could see that his pupils had rolled back in their sockets.

Heidi had never seen someone having a fit before.

When the paramedics arrived, they asked her what he'd taken and she told them he'd taken three ecstasy tablets, the same as her. She sat in the back of the ambulance while Jamie had another seizure and the paramedics held his arms down, and all she could think about was how suddenly the pills had worn off.

That's what she felt, riding in the back of that screaming ambulance, she felt sober and damp and cold and the only thing she could say was,

'Please don't die, please don't die.'

*

'What were you thinking?'

That's what Jamie's mother said to her when she arrived at the hospital. The woman looked gaunt and tired and she was wearing a cream raincoat that ran to her calves.

'I'm so sorry, Mrs Tierney.'

'Since when did you two go around taking drugs?' she said.

'It was just a night out, we were messing around.'

Heidi stood there trembling in her mini-skirt and her bomber jacket and Mrs Tierney took hold of her and started saying things she didn't know how to respond to. She said, 'Messing around? They don't know if he'll live for God's sake.'

But he did live.

He woke up the next day and remembered his name and recognised his mother and counted to ten, and pretty soon they knew he would be okay. But Heidi was not okay. She'd almost killed her best friend and she was traumatised by this in a way she couldn't articulate. At first she resumed her routine, she got up and attended lectures and went through the motions of pedestrian life, but pretty soon she had to give in to it, she had to begin starving herself again.

Heidi had no appetite.

She first noticed this on a Tuesday. She was sitting on a bus riding through Tavistock Square when she realised she hadn't eaten since the weekend. On the Sunday afternoon she'd heated beans in a pan and poured them on to a piece of toast, and that had been that.

On the Monday she hadn't even thought about food. She'd been to a lecture on the effects of parental separation in early childhood, and after that she went home and sat in her flat smoking joints. Then she'd taken herself to bed early and she'd stayed there until the following day, and now here she was riding along in this bus having eaten nothing in forty-eight hours. She didn't feel pleased with herself because of this, the same way she didn't feel disappointed about it. She merely noticed it and continued on with her day.

In the evening she walked into a shop and bought a prawn sandwich and when she got back to her flat she sat down and ate a few bites. She only ate a few bites because she wasn't hungry. This sandwich was like a pill she had to take to stay alive, that's how she thought of it. She ate a few bites and then she threw it away and picked up the phone.

She'd wanted to call Jamie the day before but she'd been too terrified of what his mother might say to her and Heidi knew she would cry if the woman yelled at her. But this isn't how Jamie's mother spoke when she answered the phone. Her voice was calm like unbroken water and she asked Heidi how she was feeling.

She said, 'I'm okay, thanks. I just wanted to see how Jamie is.'

'I'll let him tell you himself,' the woman said.

'Hey,' she said when Jamie came to the phone.

'Hey, how are you?' His voice was gravelly, as though he hadn't used it for a long time.

'I'm fine. How are you?' She was biting at her finger as she spoke.

'Yeah, I'm feeling a lot better.'

'That's good,' she said. 'Sorry I didn't call before.'

'It's alright.'

'I was scared of what your mum might say.'

'Don't worry,' Jamie said. 'She knows it wasn't your fault.'

'Okay,' she said without believing him. 'Are you up and about now then?'

'Yeah. Taking it easy but I'm okay.'

'That's good,' she said. 'What are you gonna do about uni? You gonna come back?'

Jamie sighed into the phone.

'No, I don't think so. I've missed too much work now.'

She felt something splinter inside her. 'Really? You can catch up.'

'I mean, I'd have to repeat the whole year.'

'I know, but you should come back. What about the future?'

'I dunno,' he said. 'I just have to sort myself out before I can think about any of that stuff. I nearly killed myself.'

Heidi didn't know what to say when he said that, it made her want to hang up the phone and walk away. 'Don't say that,' she said.

'It's true.'

She said, 'What am I gonna do if you don't come back?'

'What do you mean?'

'I dunno,' she said. 'Everything's different now. I feel so bad about it all.'

'Why?'

'I dunno. I shouldn't have let you get so wasted.'

'It's not your fault. I shouldn't have let myself get so wasted.'

Her body felt like it was folding into itself.

'It's gonna be weird if you don't live here any

more,' she said.

Heidi looked around at the drab living-room with its crumbling plaster walls and the posters Jamie had put up to cover the holes, posters of James Dean grinning next to his Porsche and a rippling Marlon Brando in a skinny white t-shirt.

'I know,' he said. 'Life was so fun before, wasn't it?'

'I know,' she said, and she thought back on it.

He was right, it had been fun, it had been like a party and now it was the day after the party and she was coming down, and the world was bleak and remote.

'I guess it had to end sometime,' she said.

'Not for you,' he said. 'You're still there, you can party whenever you like.'

Heidi sighed into the phone. 'No, it's different now, it isn't fun anymore. Now I just want the whole thing to end.'

'What do you mean?'

'I don't know,' she said. 'I just want uni to be over with I guess.'

'You only have six more months. Then you'll be a psychologist, then you'll be a fucking professor or something.'

She sighed. 'Yeah right. I'll be the same idiot I was three years ago.'

'No you won't.'

She picked up a pencil and tapped it against the wall.

'Jamie?'

'Yeah?'

'Will we stay in touch?'

'Of course,' he said. 'You're my best friend.'

A tear began to bud in the corner of her eye. 'Even after what I did?'

'You didn't do anything,' he said.

'I bought the pills, didn't I. I gave them to you.'

'Yeah, and how many times has it been the other way around?' he said. 'Seriously, it doesn't matter, it's fine. Okay?'

'Okay,' she said.

She said this without feeling it. What she felt was guilt. Guilt towards Jamie, towards his mother, towards her father. She felt as though she'd broken something sacred, something she couldn't repair. She told Jamie she'd call in a day or two and then she put down the phone and walked to her bedroom and when she closed the door, she lay down on her bed and tried to sleep.

*

Heidi continued on for several weeks like this, eating morsels every few days, turning up to classes, repeatedly composing opening paragraphs to essays and reading them back to herself.

She was like an automaton gliding robotically through the days, disturbing nothing and nobody, not even herself. And then one day she collapsed on the path outside the National Library and the next thing she knew she was laid out on a stretcher and a paramedic was loading her into the back of an ambulance.

'What's wrong with me?' she said.

The man said, 'I'm not sure yet, but you've got an irregular heartbeat. We're going to put you on an IV drip, okay?'

'Okay.'

'What's your name?' he asked.

'Heidi. What's yours?'

'Pete,' he said. 'Nice to meet you, Heidi.'

She looked at him. 'Hey,' she said. 'You're the same paramedic from the club.'

'Sorry?'

Heidi looked into his face, at his hazel eyes and his bent nose. 'It *is* you,' she said. 'My friend collapsed in a club the other week. At London Bridge. He had a seizure.'

The paramedic looked at her for a moment and nodded. 'Oh yeah, I remember. Is he okay?'

'Yeah, he's okay,' she said. 'He's back at home.'

'That's good.'

'Yeah. You probably saved his life, you know.'

The paramedic didn't say anything when she said this, he just put a line into her forearm and hooked her up to a drip. 'And how are you?' he said.

'Well I'm in the back of an ambulance with you, so, you know, can't complain.' Heidi smiled and the paramedic smiled back.

He said, 'Do you have a history of heart problems?'

'Not that I know of.'

'Anything unusual happen recently?' he said. 'Any drug use?'

'No,' she said. 'Not since that night in the club.'

'You look underweight, have you had any illnesses recently?'

She thought about this.

'No,' she said. 'But I haven't really eaten since the last time I saw you.'

The paramedic looked at her. 'What do you mean? That was three weeks ago.'

'I know,' she said. 'I just haven't been able to eat.'

'I see,' he said. 'Do you know why?'

'I just haven't been hungry.'

'Is that a new thing?'

'What do you mean?'

'Well, have you had any issues around eating before?'

'Yeah,' she said. 'I have spells when I don't eat.'

'And how long do these spells last?' he said.

'I don't know. A few months I guess.'

'I see. Have you ever been diagnosed with anything?'

'Like anorexia?'

'Yes?'

'Yes.'

'So when you say you haven't been eating, what do you mean? How much have you eaten today?'

'Nothing.'

'And yesterday?'

'I don't remember. Maybe an orange.'

'That's all?'

'I think so. I can't remember.'

'So essentially, what you're saying is that you've barely eaten at all in the last few days?'

'Yes.'

The paramedic nodded.

'Okay. That's probably why your heartbeat's down. It's probably an electrolyte imbalance.'

Heidi looked at him as he worked, as he prepared a solution and told her to sip it. She thought about how nice his arms were, about how nice it was that all the hairs moved in the same direction, and how neat that looked.

'Can I ask you something?' she said.

'Sure.'

She didn't know what possessed her to say it, it's not something she would usually have done, but right then and there she felt void of the sorts of anxieties that would ordinarily hold her back.

'Do you have a wife?'

'No,' he said.

'Girlfriend?'

'No.'

'You do like girls though, right?'

The paramedic looked at her and grinned. 'Yes.'

'Good,' she said.

'Why?'

'Do you like me?'

'What?'

'Would you go out with me?'

Heidi smiled and shook her head. 'Ignore me,' she said. 'Of course you don't want to go out with me.'

'I'll think about it,' he said. 'But for now just drink that.'

'What is it?'

'An electrolyte replacement.'

'Okay,' she said. Heidi drank the solution, and then she lay back on the gurney and closed her eyes.

*

The first time she went out on a date with Pete, they went to a backstreet curry house in Whitechapel. She ordered dhal and a Peshwari naan.

Heidi was hungry again by then, she was hungry enough to eat half the dhal, to tear strips from the edge of the naan and pull it through the sauce. He watched her as she ate and she let him do this, she let him do it even though she didn't like it, because she knew this is what you had to do at the beginning, you had to pretend to be somebody else, somebody better.

Pete ordered a chicken biryani and when he was finished with it, he asked her if she was done and then he ate what was left of her dhal and her naan. Heidi could see he liked this about her, that he got to eat what was hers as well as what was his own. She understood men liked this about women like her, this thing about them being slim and pretty and bird-like, this thing about them not taking up space, about them being in some way in need of protection.

Heidi wasn't proud of it, but she was a person who wanted to be protected, she craved it the way children crave sugar. She wanted to be protected from everything, from absolutely every last thing until there was nothing left to fear.

The first time she took off her clothes and stood in front of him, she wondered if he thought she was too skinny, and it thrilled her that she was wondering this. She'd never before wondered this because her body had never been this skinny in the presence of a man. Pete didn't seem to care, he kissed her and moved his hands over her small breasts, he did everything in a way that suggested he liked her.

When she opened her eyes in the morning, he kissed her again and pulled her into his chest. Heidi felt something move through her when he did this and already she knew she was falling in love with him, it was obvious to her. She wondered if this feeling was moving through him also and how long it would be before he felt he could say it.

When they got up, she was hungry again and she realised it had been a long time since she'd risen with this feeling. She decided she'd allow herself to feel it. She'd feel it and she'd eat, and then when she was done she'd go home and skip lunch and skip dinner, and the next time he unbuttoned her blouse, she'd once again be pretty.

Video

When Charlie Thomas's mother was dying, when she was in the hospital with an intravenous line plugged into her arm and a heart monitor by her head rising and falling like something from a physics class, he would sit by her side and read to her from *The Little Prince.*

It was the only thing she wanted to hear, it had taken on a great significance in her mind. She'd read this book to her son when he was a little boy, when he was learning what it meant to be a person in the world.

It was possible to see the whole of London stretched out like a scale-model from the window of his mother's hospital room. She was lying down the whole time though so the only things she could see were the high-rises, the skyscrapers, Big Ben. On a clear day the tower glistened like an enormous gold ornament as the sun passed over it, and what surprised her as she lay staring out into the day was how many birds there were flying around this city.

'A hawk came right past that window today,' she said. This was shortly before she passed away.

Charlie was sitting beside her and his mother spoke to him whilst looking out into the sky beyond the glass.

'Landed on the edge of that funny looking building over there,' she said.

'How do you know it was a hawk?'

She turned her head and smiled. 'See, sometimes I know more than you.'

'I know you do.'

'The council uses them to keep the pigeons away. There's a man.' She extended her hand.

'A man?'

'A handler. It's his job to handle the hawks, to look after them. For the council.'

Charlie raised his eyebrows. 'Interesting. I never knew that.'

'Well now you do,' she said. 'I wonder what he does when the hawks are all out working? The same as the rest of the council I suppose.'

'What's that?'

His mother looked at him for a moment. 'Sweet Fanny Adams,' she said.

She laughed and he remembered the way she used to laugh when she was younger, when he was a child.

Charlie's father had been the funny one. He was the joker and his mother was the one cleaning up after him, only sometimes when his father wasn't expecting it, his mother would smile to herself and Charlie would know she'd thought of something. She never came right out and said it, she delivered it to herself first, she tested the water and sometimes she might swallow it – he'd know if she was doing that because she'd shake her head and drop her eyes – and other times, she would let it out.

It was such a sweet pleasure when his mother said the thing that had come to her and such a sadness when she buried it, as though she didn't think it was good enough, because whatever she said was good enough for Charlie. He thought she was the most wonderful person in the world. It didn't matter that she was flawed.

Everyone was flawed.

*

Charlie's mother had been diagnosed in the January and now it was May of 2001. Now she was simply waiting to die, and he found this fact both banal – after all, she was eighty-four – and astounding.

It was *his* mother, she was supposed to just be there, quietly propping up some corner of his life. He'd worried about his mother dying, of course he had, but for some reason he'd always imagined she would go to sleep one night and that would be it. There wouldn't be tests and consultants and hospitals, and - most importantly - there wouldn't be *dying*. There would be alive, then dead. The *dying* part was what broke a person down, that's what he'd come to see.

Waiting for a person to die was like a pinprick to the heart followed by the long drawn-out process of all that heart contained being left to trickle free.

Charlie came into the room wearing his jeans and his red plaid shirt and sat down at his mother's side. His sandy hair was receding now and loose swirls of it circled his temples. He was as thin as he'd ever been – his appetite had dwindled since all this began – and the vertical creases cleaving his cheeks when he smiled ran deeper than they had at the beginning of the year.

'How are you feeling today?' he asked.

His mother was looking up at the ceiling.

'I'm fine,' she said, but Charlie recognised something in her tone.

'What is it?' he said.

'Nothing,' she said.

'Come on,' he said, 'I know you too well.'

'Honestly, I'm okay,' she said. 'But I worry

about you.'

Charlie waited a moment. 'Why? I'm fine.'

'No, I know.'

She fluttered her fingers.

'What are you worried about?'

'Well,' she said.

'Well?'

'I didn't want it to be like this, that's all.'

He could hear the sadness in her voice and somehow it caused that same sadness to cross over into his body, as though it was a virus transmitting itself between people.

'Like what?'

She sighed. 'I wanted you to have someone so that when I'm gone, I'll know you're alright.'

He reached over and took her hand.

'You don't have to worry about that. I'm fine, I promise.'

His mother nodded and waited. She waited a while and then she said, 'I just don't understand it. You're the nicest person I know.'

He was their only child – Marjorie and David were their names – and he'd come late to them, when they were forty-two and forty-five respectively.

It was a miracle actually, that's what the

doctor said when it happened. Before Charlie, they'd had six pregnancies and all six had ended in miscarriage. So it was easy to understand why they loved him so fiercely, why their lives were coloured by such joy, such terror, because here was this miracle, and what if?

'Charlie?' she said.

'Yes.'

'Can I ask you something?

'Sure,' he said. 'Anything you like.'

'Are you happy? You don't have to tell me. And you don't have to say yes just because I'm led in here like this. I wouldn't ask if I didn't want to know.'

Charlie hated lying to his mother.

That's why it was difficult when she asked these things. He wanted her load to be light because he knew she was heading somewhere that terrified her. There were also other considerations to be made, not just about how to word it, but about what was real and what wasn't. He understood that if you asked him a question like this one day, the answer that felt true might be different to the one that felt true the day following. *People are fickle, their minds are fickle.* His mother had taught him this.

'I'm sad, Mum. I don't want you to go.'

'I know. And if I could change it...'

She was becoming emotional, and she let it come and it moved through her and then it passed.

Charlie used a tissue to wipe the trails from her cheeks and his mother closed her eyes for a while. Her hair, which had once been blonde and was then made blonde in a salon, was silver now, almost white, and he drew it back behind her ear. She looked so delicate with the sun on her cheek, she was like a porcelain figurine under dappling light.

'Whatever happened to that boy?' she said. 'What was his name? The one with the problems.'

'What problems?' he said.

'The one with no father,' she said.

'Jamie,' said Charlie.

Saying his name made something shift inside him.

'That's it. Jamie. Do you ever hear from him?' His mother turned her head slowly and looked at him.

'No, I haven't spoken to him for a long time.'

'I wonder what he's doing,' she said.

His face was as clear as a photograph in a frame when Charlie thought of him. It was a nice face and he was happy to see it, because what was the point in wishing a thing hadn't happened? He'd been sad when it ended, he'd been heartbroken, but his heartbreak was a thing that sat halfway between himself and the horizon now, it wasn't pressed right up against him the whole time.

This was the moment the nurse came into the room – a nurse called Violet – and she was wearing her too-tight blue uniform, the one that made it impossible for her to bend more than a few inches.

'She must have had that uniform a while because she's grown since then, and I don't mean up.'

That's what his mother said about Violet when she first arrived at the hospital. She wouldn't say that about her now, she liked the woman too much. Charlie thought his mother might even deny she'd ever said such a thing if he were to ask her, because he knew her well, and knowing her as he did he understood she'd regret having said it.

She made her mistakes, this is what he knew. His mother made mistakes and she didn't always learn from them and she made the same mistakes again. But this wasn't important to him, it was fluff.

'Hello my lovely,' said the nurse, smiling at Charlie's mother. 'How are you?'

'I've been better,' she replied.

'I know, my love. Now we won't do any messing about, let's just take your temperature shall we?'

The nurse placed a thermometer under her tongue and asked if she'd had any movement. Violet was unfazed by bodily functions – she'd seen everything – but Charlie knew this would be too much for his mother, having him here listening to this.

'I'm going to get a sandwich or something,' he said. 'I'll be back soon.' He let go of her hand and stood up.

'You don't have to go on my account,' said Violet. She held up his mother's head and turned over the pillow.

'No, don't worry, I need to eat something.'

*

Charlie went to the hospital canteen, bought a sandwich and a coffee and sat down by the window. He didn't like the hospital canteen, it made him uncomfortable that such a disparate bunch of people were all crammed together like this.

In truth, this was really his mother's discomfort, but he felt it for her. Anytime he went anywhere he knew would make his mother uncomfortable he felt it for her, it was just a thing that happened. He gazed around at the people there and they looked sad or sick and what's more, weary of life, and he didn't want to keep seeing their faces so he stared out of the window instead.

What came to mind as he peered out over London and its slate-grey sky was that period of his life when he first realised who he was, when he was fourteen.

Charlie had been going along fine, he had friends and he was ordinary and there hadn't been any problem, but then out of nowhere a group of boys began to bully him for being gay. Charlie hadn't told anyone he was gay, it just wasn't a conversation he'd had, either explicitly or in a coded way. It wasn't a thing he was even in communication with himself about. These boys simply saw something in him. One of the boys saw it and then he turned and said to the others, 'Look, he's a queer.'

These boys would shout insults and mimic his manner of walking and blow kisses to him from the edge of the school yard. Charlie had to dart away and cry when they first started doing this, he couldn't control himself. They didn't hit him, there was never any physical harm, this bullying was purely with insults and derision and mimicry.

It continued for several months and then

quite suddenly, the boys stopped this behaviour. Afterwards, they never referenced it and neither did Charlie, but something in him had been profoundly altered by it, it was to do with shame. Later, when he met Jamie and they began dating, he found himself opening up about this period in his life.

There were two reasons for this, the first being that he found Jamie an unencumbered person in the sense that he didn't arrive in front of him bubbling with emotions and resentments and sensitivities, even if they existed somewhere underneath (and later he would see that yes, they existed underneath, of course they did).

The second was that Jamie was not typical of the men he'd dated, he didn't repress every last thing. He could say, 'When I was at school I was bullied, and it was bad. But I also bullied someone else. And that was even worse.'

He did say this. He said it very early on.

Charlie explained that the bullies hadn't laid a finger on him, that all they'd done was call him names and laugh at him, which he understood was really nothing at all. But Jamie put a hand on his arm and said, 'That's the worst kind of bullying,' and Charlie had to make an excuse and go to the bathroom to compose himself. He had no idea he'd been waiting twenty-five years for someone to say that to him.

If any of Charlie's friends had come to him and said they'd fallen in love with someone as quickly as he'd fallen in love with Jamie, he would have told told them that was wonderful and at the same time he'd have thought, *This is nothing to do with love, it's pure infatuation.* And knowing that, he'd look at himself in the mirror and say, 'You're an idiot,' but it didn't matter because they were only words, they slid right off him.

*

Charlie met Jamie in a video store.

People went to video stores all the time then, it was 1997, it was before anyone used the internet to watch films. At that time people still hoped the internet might disappear, that all these hard-to-imagine things they were reading about might never happen.

Back then, people watched TV and if there was nothing on, they might take a walk to the video store. Charlie was someone who did this. He was a lecturer, he taught English Literature at a university, and in the evening he wanted to sit with a glass of wine and push a VHS into an opening and forget himself.

The first time he met Jamie was the day he walked into that video store.

'What a day,' he said as he filled in his registration form.

He said this because of the wind and the teeming rain. That's why he stood there with sopping hair, with water streaking down his face.

The boy behind the counter smiled. 'Do you want a tissue for your glasses?'

'If you've got one that'd be great.'

He dried the lenses, put his glasses on again and looked at Jamie. He looked at this young man and then he turned around to see if anyone else was in the shop. Charlie never looked at a man he was attracted to without checking to see if some stranger wasn't watching him, waiting to let him know in some way that he knew all about him.

He filled out the registration form and then he walked out into the body of the shop and began to look around. He scanned the VHS boxes lined up, row after row like bricks in a wall. Almost immediately one of them caught his eye.

He'd wanted to watch this film for a long time but it was a woman's film, that's how people at the time categorised it. And Charlie's idea was that it was embarrassing for a man to take a woman's film to the counter, to put it down on the counter and have the video store worker look at the film and then at you and show you what he showed you with his eyes.

On the cover was a woman in a white wedding dress stood with confetti raining down over her.

She had a euphoric look on her face and in her hand she was holding a bouquet of flowers. He turned the case over but he didn't read the back. He simply thought about things and then he took the video to the counter. It made Charlie sweat to do this, he could feel it gathering above his brow.

'I love this film,' said the young man.

'Really?' said Charlie.

'Yeah, I've seen it, like, three times.'

Jamie smiled at him, and that was when Charlie understood he was also gay. Afterwards, he told his friends this was the moment it happened, but really he didn't know if that was true or if it was just the story people who'd fallen in love told, this thing about knowing the moment you met the person.

That night he went home and watched this film, which was called *Muriel's Wedding,* and saw that Jamie had been right.

I love this film, he thought to himself. He thought this even before he knew what would happen, when it had only been playing for ten minutes.

Charlie loved Muriel. He loved her because she was so overwhelmingly herself. Even when she tried to make herself into another person, her Muriel-ness spilled out of her. He thought this was a wonderful thing, even if she was made to feel ashamed about it.

One of the things Charlie came to love about Jamie was that he was also like this. His Jamieness spilled out of him. The first time they went on a date, when they sat down in a tapas restaurant off Tottenham Court Road, Jamie said to him, 'I'm only ordering stuff I don't know.'

'What do you mean? he said.

'I'm gonna use the Spanish menu and I'm only gonna order the ones with words I like the sound of.'

So he asked for *Pulpo a la Gallega* and *Boquerones* and *Pimientos de Padrón*. And when he'd tasted everything he smiled his squiffy smile and said, 'I can't believe it, I even like the weird green things.'

*

Charlie was the older man, a full decade older, but Jamie was the one to lead.

He was the one who asked Charlie for his number, he was the one who decided where they would go and what they would do. If somebody had looked at them stood side by side, they would have thought Charlie called the shots, that Jamie followed him around and nodded his head at the right moment, but it wasn't like that.

One thing Charlie noticed about Jamie was how many questions he asked. 'Are you seven or something?' he'd say to him.

That was Charlie's impression, that he was like a child, the way he was always asking things.

'What's it like being a lecturer?' was one thing Jamie asked. He asked this one day while they were sitting in the King's Arms on Poland Street.

'It's a good job. It's tiring sometimes, there's a lot of marking and planning, but I like it.'

Charlie was fiddling with the cuffs of his shirt, he was undoing the buttons and rolling the arms up past his elbows.

'Do you read a lot?'

Charlie shrugged. 'When I have time.'

Jamie said, 'Are you a writer as well then?'

'No, I haven't written for a long time. And it's a different skill, you need a certain type of mind.'

Charlie took a swig of his beer and licked his lips.

'Have you ever slept with any of your students?'

Charlie began to laugh. 'What?' he said. 'No, I've never slept with a student.'

'I bet you've wanted to though, right?'

Jamie wasn't laughing. He was eating peanuts from a little bowl and staring at Charlie.

'Well, occasionally I suppose. But I'm not that

sort of guy.'

'What sort of guy?'

'The sort of guy who sleeps with his students. It's a sackable offence for one thing. And it's not good, you know, ethically.' He motioned with his hand.

'But what if you fell in love?'

'Well that's never happened to me so I can't really say. But I don't think it would get to that point.'

'Why? Don't you think a person can just fall in love? Don't you think a person can meet someone and know, just like that? You know, you meet someone and talk to them and then suddenly it just hits you.'

'I don't know. That's never happened to me.'

Jamie looked at him wide-eyed. 'You've never been in love?'

Charlie said, 'No, not like that.'

He didn't have it in him to say, *Actually it's happening to me right now*. He didn't have it in him to say, *It happened the day I walked into the video store.*

'That's a shame. You're pretty old to have never been in love.' Jamie drank from his glass and looked out into the room.

'Well maybe I have. But I was never in love

the moment I set eyes on someone. I don't know if I believe in that.' He didn't know why he was saying these things, things that no longer felt true for him.

'I do.'

'Why, how many times have you been in love?'

'Well the first time I was about fifteen. It was dumb, he was my games teacher. He was called Mr Stokes, and he was this really hairy, macho guy. And then there was Diego, he was the first guy I ever slept with. He was a lodger at my house when I was seventeen.'

'And how old was he?'

'He was older, thirty-five or something. I've always liked older guys. Anyway, I thought I was in love with him but, you know, I was just stupid, the way you are when you're seventeen.'

Jamie put a finger in his mouth and bit at the skin.

'And what happened?'

'Nothing, we slept together for a while and then one day my mum found out and kicked him out.'

Charlie found it amazing that a boy of seventeen could find himself in this situation. It made him feel inadequate somehow, because nothing even resembling this had happened to him. No man had shown him the slightest interest when he was a teenager. 'How did she found out?' he said.

'She caught us in bed.'

Charlie laughed. 'Jesus, if my mum had caught me in bed with the lodger at seventeen she'd have dropped down dead.'

'We weren't having sex, we were just on the bed. Anyway, after that I never really fell in love again, except with straight guys. I fall in love with straight guys all the time, it's one of my hobbies.' Jamie laughed when he said this and began running a toothpick between his teeth.

'Why do you think that is?'

'I dunno. Because they're more natural I guess. Gay guys pay too much attention to what they look like, they try too hard. Straight guys don't give a fuck about what their hair is doing or if their shoes are clean. I like that, it's sexier.'

Charlie considered this. He pictured himself standing in front of the mirror each morning, teasing his hair with wax to set it just the way he liked it. 'I guess,' he said.

'It's sexier when someone doesn't try with you as well. Like, if you know someone really likes you and they're all over you, it sort of makes them less appealing. Don't you think?'

Charlie said, 'I suppose.'

'I know it's stupid because at the same time

you want someone to like you, but I'm like that. I'm stupid.'

'You're not stupid,' said Charlie. 'Actually, you seem pretty smart to me.'

Jamie looked down at the table and put his hand through his hair. 'Maybe. I'm pretty stupid as well though. Like, that guy Diego, he was a coke fiend. And he got me into it. I haven't told you about that, have I, about my drug issues.' He held the toothpick between his teeth and snapped it in two.

'Drug issues?'

'It's boring, I'm not gonna bore you with all that.'

He wasn't alarmed when Jamie said this. In a way he admired that he said things so bluntly, things other people were ashamed of, about drugs and bullying and sex. He was different, that was the point. He was different to any man he'd ever met.

*

Charlie sat in the window of the hospital canteen and thought back to the time he took Jamie to meet his parents. His mother had asked to meet him, she'd been standing in the kitchen running an iron over a shirt one afternoon and suddenly she'd said, 'Why don't you bring him over for dinner? How long has it been now? We still haven't met the boy.'

Charlie went through the whole thing with Jamie first. He wanted to prep him before he set him loose on his parents.

'I know you're an honest person,' he told him, 'and that's good. Just don't be too honest.'

'What do you mean?' he said.

They were sitting at Charlie's dining table eating a Hawaiian pizza from the takeaway down the street.

'I mean, they don't need to know about the drugs. Or about Diego. Things like that.'

'Why?'

'Because it won't sit well. My parents are conservative. And some things they just don't need to know.'

Jamie nodded. 'But how do I know what they need to know?'

'Use your discretion.'

'What discretion?'

Charlie didn't say anything to that, he just looked at Jamie, and Jamie looked back at him.

His mother wore cream trousers and a white silk blouse with a gold brooch in the shape of a peacock pinned to it. His father wore what he wore every day by that stage, his grey lounge pants with the elasticated waste and an old sweater. The man had given up on trousers and shirts, he was winding down.

'This is so good, Mrs Thomas.'

That's what Jamie said as he sat there eating her cream of asparagus soup.

'Call me Marjorie,' she said.

He shook his head. 'I genuinely can't believe it, Marjorie.'

'Can't believe what?' said Charlie.

'That your mum made this from scratch. It's amazing.'

Charlie watched his mother looking at Jamie, and inside he felt that nagging sensation, knowing the cogs were turning in her mind.

'What sort of things does your mother cook, Jamie?' she said.

'Oh, nothing really,' he said. 'My mum has a weird relationship with food.'

'Oh,' she said. 'Does your father not mind?'

'No idea,' Jamie said. 'He could be dead for all I know.' He laughed and Charlie's mother looked at him.

Charlie could feel the sweat on his lip, he could feel the blood moving through his face. 'Jamie's father was never really around,' he said.

Jamie nodded. 'Yeah, I think my parents only

met the once.'

Charlie's mother looked at him.

'She was a model,' Jamie said. 'And he was a photographer. That's how they met. He shot her for *Tatler* I think.'

Charlie's mother nodded. 'I see,' she said.

After that they carried on eating and nobody said anything for a long time, or maybe it wasn't a long time, but that's how Charlie remembered it. He could smile about it now, about that excruciating meal with his mother and father, wishing he'd been able to screen everything Jamie said before it came out of his mouth. He underestimated his mother that day though, he underestimated how lightly she'd taken the boy.

'I'm sorry,' she told him, when they split up. 'I liked Jamie, he made me laugh. And he was very kind when your father died.'

It was true, he'd arranged for a bouquet of white roses to be sent over to Charlie's mother the day after her husband died, and the card attached said, *So sorry for your loss.* He hadn't even asked Charlie for the address.

*

There was a time when a student made an accusation about Charlie which led to him being suspended. The girl said he'd sexually harassed her, that he'd propositioned her and tried to take her to bed. The staff knew it was a fiction, they knew he was homosexual, but his students didn't know this about him and there was a procedure that had to be followed, so the university went down the formal investigation route.

Almost as soon as the investigation began, the girl dropped the accusation. She admitted she'd tried to initiate something with Charlie and had been rejected, and now she said she was going to leave the university.

Charlie was upset when he heard this because he knew things about the girl. He knew her father had been killed in a sailing accident the year before and her mother had started a relationship with a new man, a man she didn't like. He expressed this concern to the Dean and it was made clear that he shouldn't try to contact her, that it would be perceived the wrong way.

Charlie said to Jamie, 'I don't know what to do.'

They were sitting at the dinner table and Jamie was eating a bowl of pasta. Charlie wasn't eating anything, his appetite had disappeared.

'What do you mean? Jamie said.

'Well I feel like I should make it clear that she's welcome back and that this isn't a problem, but I don't want to make it worse. The fact is she might not want to see me. And besides, the other students might not react well if they find out she's the one who made the accusation.' He pawed at his chin and looked over at the wall.

'So leave it.'

'But I want her to know I'm not angry. She has enough going on.'

Jamie put his fork down and placed a hand on Charlie's shoulder. 'Why don't you write to her? Then she doesn't have to see you but you can explain the situation and tell her you're not mad.'

Charlie did write to the girl, he wrote and told her it was all forgotten but she never replied and he never saw her again.

What came to him when he looked back at that time was how strong a support Jamie had been. The first evening after he returned to work, on the day he outed himself to his students, Jamie came over after his shift at the video store and brought flowers and a bottle of wine and as they were drinking it, he told Charlie, 'I love you.'

Charlie had been in love for many months by then, but to say it felt terrifying, like walking blindfolded into traffic. He'd been overwhelmed by the whole thing, that was the truth of it. He thought that to fall in love – to allow that, to lie back and let it break over him – was beyond terrifying, because if he let himself be swept up in those feelings and then the whole thing blew up in his face, well then what?

*

'Did you have something to eat?' his mother asked.

'I did,' he replied.

He sat down at her bedside and held her hand. Her skin was dry like paper.

'What did you have?'

'A sandwich,' he said. Charlie listened to the hypnotic bleep of the machines and his mother's shallow breaths. 'What did the nurse say?'

'Oh nothing. She took my temperature. The doctor's coming later.'

Charlie nodded. 'Mum?' he said.

'Yes?'

'What made you ask about Jamie before?'

'I don't know. He came into my mind I suppose.' His mother turned her head and looked at him. 'Why?'

'I just wondered. I was thinking about it.'

'About Jamie?'

'About everything,' he said.

*

Charlie had never been a confident person.

He alluded to confidence in the way he carried himself and the way he spoke, but always he'd been afraid of saying or doing something to demonstrate that he didn't have a clue how to live in the world. As a child he'd been afraid of his father, not because of anything he did but because he seemed like such an assured man, a man who understood how the world operated and how to exist within it. His mother was not like this, his mother was an anxious person, but his father had been assured, he'd been clear.

What Charlie realised when he learned he was gay was that he'd known for a long time there was something different about him, something *not right* in some way, only he hadn't known what it was. He'd known it was something that would be unpalatable to his father, and perhaps also to his mother, but especially to his father, because it was to do with his masculinity.

He would never have been able to articulate this as a child, but the understanding was there, it existed as a feeling deep inside of him. This feeling was like an animal that sat always in its burrow, and sometimes it would sleep and sometimes it would awaken, and when it awakened it might thrash at the walls.

What happened to Charlie is that one day, when he was already twenty-seven years old, his father invited him over and he sat with him on the small terrace facing the garden and they drank a beer together, and then after a long time the man said, 'Okay, here's the thing. I heard something and I want to ask you about it. If it's right you can tell me, and if it's wrong you can tell me.'

A chill ran down Charlie's back. He cleared his throat and told him okay, and his father nodded and looked out towards the fence beyond the cherry trees at the back of the garden.

'Well,' he said. 'Somebody told me they saw you with a man in a pub, a pub in Soho, and you were, you know, *with* this man.' His father turned and glanced at him and then he turned away again.

Charlie didn't move. He stayed right where he was with the adrenaline moving through him and he didn't say a thing. It was as though he was an electrical appliance that had blown its fuse. He couldn't move, he couldn't speak, it was paralysing. He simply hung there in space until finally his father leaned towards him and put a hand on his shoulder.

'Don't worry,' he said, 'I'll tell your mother. She'll be upset to begin with but she'll get over it. You know what she's like.'

That was the day Charlie felt he understood what it was to breathe, to really breathe. He couldn't believe he was sitting next to his father with the man finally knowing who he was without the ground crumbling beneath his feet.

'I'm sorry,' he said.

He said this because he *was* sorry, because he wanted to be the person his father wanted him to be. His father said it didn't matter, but Charlie knew this wasn't true. It was the summer of 1986 and the AIDS crisis was all around them, it wasn't a good time to learn your son was gay.

His father sat in his chair in silence for a while and then he said, 'Just be careful. The world's a different place now.'

His mother reacted exactly how he expected. His father called to say she wasn't coping well at the moment, that it'd be best not to come to the house for a week or two. It took her a long time to even mention it, for years she acted as though she knew nothing, but then when things settled down with AIDS and HIV, when the media started to talk about accepting gay people, during the mid-nineties, then she started asking him if he had 'a friend.'

Charlie found this intensely awkward, this talk of a friend, but he couldn't bring himself to correct her. In the beginning there was Joseph; tall, bow-legged Joseph with his crooked nose and his neatly cropped hair, with his little teeth and his obsession with model aeroplanes. Charlie's mother called him 'a nice boy'. It impressed her that he'd learned the clarinet as a child, it didn't matter that he hadn't played in fifteen years.

His mother had always had ideas about who was and wasn't good enough for her son. Years before, when she'd imagined he'd bring a girl home, she'd had ideas about that, and now it was a man coming through the door, it was no different.

Jamie was the third boyfriend he brought home to his parents. By then his mother had come to realise she liked the men she'd been introduced to; she liked that she could talk to them and they understood things in a way her husband didn't. But a person like Jamie was not what she had in mind for her son.

His father was a different story, he didn't care who Charlie went out with. He just wanted the man to be good to him. That was his idea, that two people should be good to each other. 'Life's hard enough,' he'd say.

Each man he introduced to his father was given a firm handshake and the man was always told, 'Look after him, won't you,' at the close of the meeting. Charlie loved his father for this, he could so easily have said nothing.

The day he brought Jamie to meet his parents, his father said, 'So what is it you want to do with your life, Jamie?'

'I'm not sure,' he replied. 'I'm trying to work it out at the moment. I just want to make something of myself.'

'Well that's a good start. What did you study?'

'English Literature.'

Charlie's father skewered a roast potato and slid it through a pool of gravy. He held it in front of his lips for a second. 'Right,' he said. 'So you'll have plenty to talk about with Charlie then.'

'Not really,' he said, 'he's way cleverer than me. And I never completed my degree.'

Charlie's father waited a few moments, until he'd swallowed his food. 'Oh. Why's that?'

'I got ill,' he said. 'I missed a lot of work and in the end I decided to stop.'

'That's a shame,' the man said. 'Would you like to go back to it?'

'I don't know. Maybe. I'd like to write a novel, that's what I really want to do.'

'I see. And what have you written so far?'

'Mostly shit. I mean, mostly rubbish. Poems and stories and stuff.'

Charlie winced, because he knew something inside his mother would have recoiled when he said the word *shit*.

'I see. So you're going to tackle the novel next?'

'Yeah, maybe. I'm not really good enough yet but maybe.'

'You know, the only way to get good at

something is to keep doing it. Before you can be good, you have to be bad. Remember that.' Charlie's father made his eyes wide and leaned in to Jamie when he said this, and Jamie nodded in a way that suggested he was learning something.

'Your dad's really nice,' he said to Charlie that evening, as they took off their clothes and lay down in bed. 'I wish I had a dad who said these things.'

That was the first time he said anything about being fatherless and Charlie didn't know how to respond, so he put his arms around him and kissed his forehead and said nothing at all.

What he wished now is that he'd found the words, that he'd attempted them at least. He wished this because it was the avoidance of difficult conversations that had hurt their relationship the most. That's how he saw it now.

What Charlie learned about Jamie was that he used sex as a vehicle to discharge tension, to short-circuit pain. He learned that he also used sex this way, it was something they did to each other. He learned these things after they broke up, when he was sat in a therapist's office with a glass of water at one side of him and a pot-plant in a pale blue vase at the other.

In the beginning, they might have sex three times in a day, they might get out of bed and shower and dress, go through all the motions of getting on with life only to retreat back to where they started.

At the time, Charlie thought their voracity was a sign of their compatibility, proof they were meant to be, but later he saw it was the thing they used to avoid communicating. If they had a fight or some resentment arose, they would use sex to override it.

What he could never have predicted was that the physical side of their relationship would disintegrate. It was so sudden that it took him by surprise, it took both of them by surprise. It happened around the time Charlie's father died, and that made sense – he was grieving, he was in pain – but what was mystifying about it was that this part of their life never resurrected itself.

Without sex they were suddenly made to stand there looking right at each other the whole time. Then all those accumulated resentments and hurts rose up like bubbles to the surface.

For one thing, Charlie hated that Jamie used drugs. Especially when he did it in front of him, when he was right there in the room. But he'd spent their entire relationship telling him he didn't mind, that he could do whatever he wanted. So Jamie would rack up lines on the coffee table and Charlie would sit there and sometimes he'd have a line himself, but the truth was he hated cocaine. He hated the way it made him jumpy and sleepless. All he wanted was to have a Scotch and go to bed.

For a while they went on like this without addressing anything, then finally an alarming thing happened. Jamie turned up one night in a bad state, he'd been drinking and taking drugs, Charlie didn't know what. All he knew was he was a mess, he was incoherent. So he sat him down on the sofa and went off to get him some water, only when he came back, Jamie was on his knees taking a line of white powder from the coffee table.

At first Charlie thought it was cocaine but when he saw the way it affected him, he knew it was something else. When he asked, Jamie looked at him with rolling eyes and told him it was ketamine.

The drug did something to the boy's face, something that made him look like a person who'd suffered a brain injury. He was groaning and a line of drool was hanging from the corner of his mouth. There was something so repellent to Charlie about this that he felt he'd never be able to see him the same way again. It was as though a switch had been flicked and his heart had shut down.

The following morning, Jamie came into the kitchen and said, 'God, I feel rough.' He wandered aimlessly for a few seconds before taking a glass from the drainer and turning on the tap. 'What happened last night?'

Charlie could barely look at him. 'What happened?'

'Yeah?' said Jamie. He poured out a glass of water and sat down at the table. His eyes were bleary and pink.

'What happened is you started snorting ketamine off my coffee table at one in the morning. Which is apparently what you're doing now.'

Charlie stood up and went to the sink. He placed his hands on the edge of the counter and looked out of the window.

'You're mad at me.'

'Yes, I'm mad. I must be. I must be insane to put up with this.'

Jamie said, 'What's that supposed to mean?'

Charlie turned around and looked at him. 'I'm thirty-eight, Jamie. I want a simple life. I want to have a drink on a Saturday night and go to bed, not play nurse-maid to you. You were so fucked you couldn't speak.'

'I wasn't so fucked I couldn't-

'You were sat on the floor dribbling for fuck's sake. You couldn't even stand up.' Charlie walked over to table and sat down again. He took in a breath and let it out. 'I'm tired of pretending like this isn't a problem, like this is normal.'

'Fine, I'll stop.'

Charlie shook his head. 'Don't you think I realise what's going on when you disappear into the bathroom every half hour?'

'What are you talking about? You said it was fine.'

'Well it's not.'

Jamie began biting his nails. He said, 'Why are we doing this now?'

'Because I've had enough. I loved you and I wanted to make this work, but what's the point? You don't love me, you love drugs.'

'Of course I love you. I only do it because I thought you were okay with it.'

'You thought I'd be okay with the bullshit I had to put up with last night? Cleaning puke off the stairs, carrying you upstairs like a fucking baby, undressing you.'

'I'm sorry. Look I'll stop, okay?' Jamie reached over and put his hand over Charlie's.

'I'm sorry, I can't do this.' He pulled his hand away and folded his arms in front of him.

'Meaning what?'

'Meaning I don't want this anymore.'

'Don't want what?'

'The way you looked last night, it was, I don't even know how to describe it. Your face was like something out of a horror film. I can't look at you the same way now.'

Jamie waited a while, then stood up and walked away.

*

The first day it felt like a relief that it was done with, but on the second Charlie felt terrible remorse. He suddenly wished he'd never said any of those things, that he'd given himself time to cool off, to reflect on what had happened. His love wasn't something that could be peeled away and discarded, it had roots.

Those thoughts about never being able to see Jamie the same way again seemed to wilt before him now. All he wanted was to kiss him and feel his body pressed up against him.

Charlie turned up at his flat the next day and told him he wanted to work it out, that he was sorry, but Jamie wouldn't hear it.

'No, you were right,' he said. 'Everything's different now.' He walked back inside and sat down on the sofa and looked at the wall.

'But I love you,' Charlie told him.

'Is that what you do to someone you love?'

'I was angry. I made a mistake.'

'So did I. And you left me for it.' Jamie held his knees up to his chin and hugged them.

'Look, I admit I handled it wrong. I'm sorry.'

'You told me you'd never be able to see me the same way again. And now you want me to carry on like nothing's happened?'

Charlie went down on his haunches in front of him. He said, 'You know I think you're beautiful.'

'But I'm not beautiful,' Jamie said.

Charlie reached out and placed a hand on his arm. Jamie allowed him to do this for a few seconds and then he unfurled himself and stood up.

'Please,' Charlie said.

Jamie shook his head. 'I think you should go.'

Charlie was stunned by this, he was devastated. He had expected Jamie to accept his apology, he'd been sure of it. For weeks afterwards he walked himself through the memory of that conversation, he relived it from every angle, and each time the ending remained the same.

He'd never in his life felt like he was losing his mind on account of a man, and here it was, happening.

*

'Don't feel bad, love.'

That's what his mother said.

He was honest with her, he told her about the drugs and about the argument that followed.

'You can't have a relationship with someone with all that going on,' she said. 'It's bigger than you are.'

His mother had been sitting at her white-topped kitchen table eating a yoghurt while listening to all this. She finished the yoghurt and then she put her spoon in the pot and pushed it to one side.

'You did your best, love,' she said, and then she came over to Charlie and put her arms around him, which was a thing she never did.

Even now he could barely believe she'd done that.

*

It was just after ten in the morning on the last Sunday in May when Charlie's mother died. She'd been unconscious for a long time and she didn't wake up to say goodbye or offer any final thoughts. The woman drifted out so gradually it was almost imperceptible.

Violet was in the room and she whispered, 'She's gone, sweetheart,' and then she put a hand on his shoulder and he kept on holding his mother's hand and looking into her face and not saying a thing.

It was hard to believe that his parents were dead. Three years ago they'd both been alive, they hadn't even been ill, they'd been wandering around their house without any problem. Anyway, that's how life is, that's what he'd learned.

Everything felt strange to Charlie because he was middle-aged and his time had passed, or that's how it felt to him. To his mind, the world was for the young and everyone else was falling away, as though they were all standing on a giant plate that was slowly being turned on its edge. He sat beside his mother, waited until the right moment, then placed a kiss on her forehead, stood up and walked out.

When he arrived home, he was desperate to talk to someone, but the only person he wanted to talk to had gone, so he pulled out the whiskey bottle and sat down at the table.

In the evening, he picked up his phone and placed a call. His heart began drumming in his chest as he waited with the tone sounding in his ear.

'Hello?' said a familiar voice.

'Hi,' he said. 'It's me. Charlie.'

Car

Jamie's earliest memory was the day he and his mother landed in Angel.

It was a cold, dazzlingly sunny morning in the spring of 1973 when they pulled up outside a row of white-fronted Georgian terraces on Noel Road, and the first thing he noticed was the sky blue Ford Consul parked outside the house. It belonged to the husband of the couple who lived in the ground floor flat. His name was Adam Everlast, and he was returning with his morning paper as the removals man unloaded their boxes from the van.

'Are you moving in upstairs?' he said.

Jamie's mother nodded and he reached out and shook her hand.

'I'm Adam,' he said, 'I'll give you a hand.'

He was inhumanly tall and strong, like something from a comic strip, and he wore a t-shirt that clung to his back like a pelt. Jamie was mesmerised by him, by the leonine way he moved and the dark blur of a voice that came out of him. Next to this man, his mother looked flimsy and ephemeral, like a thing that could be picked up with one hand and tossed in a box.

The flat was bare except for a bed in each bedroom, two easy-chairs in the lounge and a couple of chests of drawers the previous inhabitants had abandoned.

Jamie's mother hadn't been able to afford a bigger removal vehicle so she'd had to leave behind anything that wouldn't fit in the van; the sofa, a wardrobe, a pine cabinet. Another thing she left behind was Jamie's clockwork teddy, the one that played a lullaby when you wound the silver turn-key on its back.

Adam heard about that, he and his wife heard all about it, everyone in earshot did.

'What's wrong with him?' they asked.

'It's his bear,' she said, and Jamie's mother put her head in her hand.

The couple were very kind, they showed up again a few hours later with a new bear, a gleaming thing with soft golden fur and a ribbon around its neck. Jamie loved them for that, but it wasn't as simple as replacing one teddy with another.

What about my bear sleeping outside or being thrown in the garbage? Who is going to protect him now?

Those were the questions running through his

head.

*

He first understood they were poor when he started school. A boy said to him, 'There's a hole in your jumper,' and he said, 'I know,' and this didn't seem strange to him until he looked around at the other kids and saw he was the only one.

Another thing he remembered from this period of his life was telling his mother his shoes were too small, and her saying, 'I've no money, Jamie, you'll have to wait.'

For a long time, or what seemed like a long time, he went around like that, with his toes curling under themselves in his shoes. In class he would take them off under the table to relieve the ache, and more than once his teacher said, 'Jamie, what are you doing? Put those back on.'

Then the other children would laugh and he would sit there with his face burning, unmoored from every last word the woman was saying.

There were other things with his mother when he was young. Sometimes, breakfast was a piece of bread with jam slathered over its face and other times it was an apple, an orange. Whatever it was, it was never enough. That's why he began stealing food. He used to wait for the other children to go out at break-time and go through their bags.

The day he was caught was the day everything changed for him. After that, the other kids didn't want to play with him, he'd become a person who couldn't be trusted.

The social worker first called around when he was six. Evelyn was a sinuous black woman with gleaming skin and long braided hair, and when she smiled her teeth flashed white. Jamie knew about social workers by then so he told her his mother *did* clean the house, she *did* cook, she *did* make sure he had all the food he needed. It's just that he lost things sometimes, and sometimes he was bad and he did things he knew were wrong, it was nothing to do with anyone else.

'Why do I do that? I don't know, just to see.' That's what he'd say. 'I won't do it again, I promise, but don't put me in a home.'

And Evelyn would shake her head and say, 'Don't worry darling, nobody's putting you anywhere.'

For the next two years, this social worker would appear sporadically and sit in the living-room and Jamie's mother would bring her a cup of tea and jaffa cakes, and always she ate two and left one. Jamie liked her because he could feel she meant it when she smiled. He could feel it like a dancing sprite inside his belly.

Each time she came she would talk with his mother and then she'd talk with him. She wanted to be alone with him when she did this, so his mother would go and sit in her room and wait.

'How many friends have you got at the moment?' she would ask and he might say, 'Three', and then he'd give her the names of three boys who didn't like him, boys who called him *scab* and *tramp*.

When Evelyn left, his mother would ask, 'What did she say?' and he'd tell her, and then she'd lie down on the sofa and he'd say, 'Shall we play a game?'

'Not tonight, love,' she'd reply.

He knew one time she might change her mind though. He knew because once she asked him if he wanted to play a game, she asked him right out of nowhere, and then she brought out *Connect 4* and they played it until she was exhausted, until her eyes watered. But now he'd play it on his own or else he'd carry it downstairs and play it with Inez.

Jamie loved Inez.

She gave him cake and biscuits, she read with him, she told him stories about the past.

'What was it like in the olden days?' he'd ask and she'd laugh and say, 'How old do you think I am?' and then she'd tell him about the war, about the German bomber that came down in the wheat field behind her house.

After school he would knock on her door, it was the first thing he did after changing out of his uniform. Sometimes his mother would let him do this and other times she'd say, 'No, not tonight, give the poor woman some peace.'

When his mother wasn't well, she never stopped Jamie doing anything, she just lay on the couch saying nothing at all. Inez would run him a bath and wash his clothes and cook him something to eat, she loved making pies and cakes and things. Then she would take food up to his mother on a tray, and if it was still early she'd open the blinds so the light poured in. She and his mother would sit and talk but Jamie didn't hear what they said because they spoke very quietly, and he understood their talking was pitched so he couldn't hear.

Adam and Inez's flat was totally different to the one Jamie lived in with his mother. Their flat was filled with exotic things like a gold cherub the size of a baby that had a clock-face carved into its belly, and corniced, gilt-edged mirrors.

There were endless framed portraits too, and when Jamie would say, 'Who's that?' Inez would look at the picture and say, 'Oh, that's my sister,' or, 'That's my husband's mother.'

The finest items in Inez's flat were the chandeliers. To Jamie they looked like appendages from a story-book palace.

'Wow', he said when he first looked up at one, and then he pointed and Inez crouched down to him and said, 'It's beautiful isn't it, but don't say anything in front of Adam, he had to pay for it'. Then she laughed, and Jamie laughed along, though he didn't see what was funny.

*

When he was eight years-old, his mother began taking him to the leisure centre to learn to swim. He'd go off with the other kids and she'd get a coffee and sit in the cafe reading a beauty magazine.

Jamie loved swimming, it came naturally to him. He loved the feeling of cutting through the water with his arms and the chlorinated smell of the pool, it set off a warm throb of adrenaline each time he picked up the scent. He loved also the freedom of being underwater, with the sound all muffled and the world beyond rendered blue and slippery.

One day, his swimming teacher announced he was leaving and that another man would replace him. The new coach, whose name was Mr Flood, singled Jamie out for praise after just a few weeks because in his opinion he had a natural aptitude for swimming.

'He's a real talent, Mrs Tierney,' Mr Flood told his mother.

Jamie felt special in a way he never had before because of that. He lay on his bed staring up at the ceiling the day his new swimming coach told him this, and every time he thought about it, he could feel a smile stealing up over his lips.

It wasn't long after this that Mr Flood told Jamie he wanted to work with him one on one.

'I need to coach you on your own. We can't get the best out of you with all these other kids in the way,' he said, sticking out an arm in the direction of the busy pool. They talked it through, and Mr Flood told Jamie to ask his mother about it. 'You speak to your mother,' he said, 'and next week I'll chat to her myself.'

When Jamie told her she said there was no way, they didn't have the money for private coaching, and he recognised straight away it was hopeless. But he needn't have worried, it was all a misunderstanding, the coach didn't want money.

'God no,' he said to the woman when she brought her son to the swimming class. 'I don't want any money. I just want to see him reach his potential.'

So one cold April morning, Jamie rose early and took the bus to the leisure centre to meet his coach for their first session. This time Mr Flood's techniques were different. For one thing, he got in the pool and swam himself. He used his hands to demonstrate how Jamie's arms should slice through the water. Then he said, 'Climb on my back, I'll show you how it's done.'

So Jamie climbed on his back and the coach swam from one end of the pool to the other. Then he had Jamie swim lengths and at the end of each length he would tell him what had been good and what had not.

Jamie didn't think it was unusual when Mr Flood joined him in the shower afterwards, or when he said, 'Here, let's wash your hair, close your eyes.' But when the man started rubbing soap into his back, the sensation was like ice falling through his chest. And when he spun him around and said, 'That's it,' when he crouched down and began washing between Jamie's legs, a terror he'd never known bloomed in his chest. 'You like that, don't you,' he said, and then Mr Flood took the boy's hand, drew it towards him and closed it around his penis.

Afterwards, the man showered and then he shut the water off and began whistling and towelling himself down. Jamie was frozen in place the whole time this was going on, he didn't move until a stranger appeared in the changing room and reminded him that life was still happening, that the world hadn't stopped rotating.

He didn't cry as he dressed, or as Mr Flood

appeared at his side and whispered, 'Don't worry, I won't tell anyone how bad you've been,' but later, when he was in the safety of his bedroom, he did cry, he cried with his face pressed into his pillow so his mother wouldn't hear.

Jamie didn't plan to tell her anything about what had happened, but all that day and the day following he felt too sick to eat, and when she lost her temper and said she was tired of asking what was wrong it exploded out of him, and he began sobbing in a way that made it difficult to breathe.

His mother contacted the police and made a report, but it was 1978 and it turned out the police didn't trust a child with a mother who didn't work, a mother with a list of problems as long as your arm. Not over the word of a man who sat on the board of a private equity firm and drove a Mercedes. That's not how this thing went.

Jamie was afraid of swimming pools and communal showers and he was afraid of men and of what they might do to him if he wasn't vigilant, of what they were really thinking when they looked at him, when they smiled at him as though a smile meant only that. He had to put measures in place after Mr Flood and life became a lot more complicated because suddenly there were a series of rules he had to follow to protect himself, it wasn't a case of doing whatever he wanted anymore.

Another thing that changed was his mother, his mother whose actions had been rooted in the predictable and who now began to behave in startling ways.

The first thing she did was to cut off her hair. She'd always had long hair, long ash-blonde hair she raked her hands through and drew back behind her ears, only one day, he arrived home from school and she was kneeling on the floor in the kitchen and she was holding a small round mirror in one hand and scissors in the other, and her hair was strewn around her in dark nests, and from a distance those nests looked like little animals, like sleeping mice on the floor.

'I just can't manage it anymore,' she said.

She looked at him for a moment and then began again on the strands that were still in place, and Jamie said nothing. Once again arose the sensation of being paralysed, of dark shoots breaking through the floor of his stomach and coiling up into his chest, tendrils unfurling themselves along the walls of his oesophagus, their black flowers budding in his throat to shut out the air.

When he finally made it down the stairs and Inez asked him what was wrong, he didn't speak, and after she soothed him with her steady heartbeat to his ear and her hand through his hair he explained that his mother was on the kitchen floor with the scissors.

Inez poured him out chocolate milk and told him to wait and then she went upstairs, and when she came back down again she said, 'Mummy's very tired, she said it might be nice for you to have a sleepover with us.'

The doctor came to see her that night, Inez arranged it. She made a call and conveyed to him the facts, and then when he arrived she led him upstairs. Adam was already home from work by then, he was teaching Jamie how to make a paper aeroplane. Jamie didn't interrupt him or demand to know what was going on with his mother, he just let him make the thing, and then he sat down and ate with him and Adam said, 'Later I'll take you out in the car if you like,' and that was the first time he got to ride in his sky blue Ford Consul.

They drove to the top of a multi-storey carpark, and when they arrived Adam let him sit on his knee and hold the wheel while he worked the pedals.

Jamie loved him for that, for letting him drive his car. He had always been intimidated by the physicality of the man, but after this he began to imagine him into the role of his father, and in his mind he played out humdrum conversations in which Adam would ask him to pass him the television remote or the newspaper and he would nod and say, 'Okay, Dad.'

After the doctor saw his mother that night, she began taking pills and after a few weeks, she emerged from her sadness, from her lassitude.

She no longer lay on the sofa staring at the television or in bed with her face pointed at the ceiling all day. Now he'd come home and find her running a vacuum over the carpet or cooking some small thing. Sometimes she'd be sitting in the kitchen doing a crossword puzzle in the *Evening Standard* and he'd be pleased because he'd know that she'd been outside. She could do this, she could sit in the kitchen because she'd bought a little table and two chairs, a tiny thing with a shocking pink formica top, barely big enough for two people to eat a meal.

It was so bright that when he came down for breakfast the following morning he wore sunglasses and held his hands in front of his eyes, and when his mother said, 'Very funny,' he said 'I'm blind, I'm blind,' and they laughed.

Jamie's mother remained this way for a while, and then, like the sky when the sun drops down beneath the horizon at the end of the day, the light went out of her again. This was when he was ten, and it was during this period that he began to wake in the night and hear her crying beyond the wall. It made him freeze to hear this, he was like an oyster snapping shut, and he wouldn't be able to move until she was quiet again.

Usually he couldn't sleep afterwards, and then he was unable to concentrate at school and there were times when he fell asleep at his desk and was sent out of the room. When that happened he stood outside in the empty corridor and pictured himself walking out of there, walking out of his whole existence and arriving at his real life, the one he was meant to be living, the one in which he was already a man, a man with money and a sports car and a house with a swimming pool bathed in bright sunlight.

*

One day, Jamie came home from school and his mother wasn't to be found in any of the rooms of their flat. He stood outside her bedroom and called for her but she didn't respond, and the feeling of this was like his insides being rearranged by a cold hand.

Finally he opened the door and went inside to find only the circumstantial evidence that she'd been there - her hairbrush, her tweezers, a tattered magazine - as though she'd redacted herself from the framework of her own existence. It wasn't until he saw a slippered foot poking out from the wardrobe that he realised.

'Mummy,' he said.

But she didn't reply.

His breathing was so gnarled and thin that he had to hang back for a few seconds. He had to inch towards the wardrobe door with his heart licking at his ribs, and even when he put out a hand and took hold of the little brass handle, he couldn't pull it open in one spontaneous snap. It had to be drawn back slowly, as though it was a decaying thing about to come off its hinges.

His mother was sitting with her head pressed way back in the corner so it was hidden behind the hems of her dresses. Jamie didn't need to see her face anyway. He could tell from her hands, from the way they were limp and curling into themselves there in the bowl of her lap.

This is how dead people look, he thought. *But mummy isn't dead.*

Two thoughts, one after the next.

When he pulled back the dresses, her face was dark and cloistered like a plaster bust that had been covered with a sheet and hidden away to preserve it. Her eyes were closed and there was a loose strand of hair bisecting one eye. Jamie moved this strand of hair. If she was going to be unconscious and he was going to call an ambulance and strangers were going to see her, he knew she'd want to be presented in the right way.

He put a hand on her shoulder. 'Mummy,' he

said.

He waited a second and then he ran out of there and down to Inez's flat. He had to do this because they didn't have a telephone. Anytime she wanted to make a call, his mother would go down the stairs and knock on Inez's door because Inez had insisted she do this. 'Anytime you want to make a call, you just come down,' she'd said.

Inez didn't waste time asking him what was wrong and going to check for herself, she let him make the call. She let him make the call and at the same time she went upstairs.

The man on the other end of the phone asked which emergency service he wanted and when he said, 'Ambulance', the man asked what had happened. Then he asked if his mother was breathing and if there was anything obstructing her airway.

Inez had already pulled her out of the wardrobe when Jamie went back upstairs. His mother was lying on her back on the floor and Inez was on her knees beside her and she had the back of his mother's head in her hand.

'Are they coming?' she said.

Jamie nodded and then he asked what had happened to her and Inez told him she was in a deep sleep. He asked if she'd taken too many pills and Inez said she didn't know. She was shaking his mother lightly and telling her to wake up.

She told Jamie to go downstairs and take the whiskey bottle from her drinks cabinet. So he ran downstairs and found the whiskey bottle and brought it back up with him, and Inez poured a measure of it into the cap and put it under his mother's nose. Then she put his mother's head in her lap and used a finger to open her mouth a little. She poured the whiskey from the cap over his mother's lips but still she did not move.

Inez said, 'Come on, Marie. Please.'

The ambulance men put his mother on a stretcher and placed a mask over her mouth. They did other things too but Jamie didn't know what because he was taken out of the room.

Inez took him in the Ford Consul and they drove behind the ambulance to the hospital. When they stopped at a red light, that's when it hit him. He couldn't see the ambulance anymore, it had disappeared into the mirage of traffic. Something about this made him feel like he was going to be sick, like he was stuffed with poison.

'Is she going to die?' he said, and Inez held his hand and told him no, she wasn't going to die.

Jamie believed her, he trusted Inez. She was the most trustworthy person he knew.

They didn't have to wait long in the hospital. They sat in a room with strip-lighting and cream walls and after a few minutes a doctor came and said his mother was going to be fine, they could go and see her now. What had happened was they'd pumped out her stomach and this had reset her whole body, it had rendered her instantly well again.

'Hi sweetheart,' she said when he first saw her in the hospital bed. As though he'd just come home from school and she was sitting at the kitchen table. He went around the bed and stood next to her and she kissed his cheek.

'Are you okay?' he asked.

'Yes, I'm okay,' she said, and at the same time she began to cry.

After a while Inez came and took him away and he stayed with her and Adam in a bed she made up for him in the spare room. The next day he didn't go to school and Inez made him chicken nuggets and in the afternoon they went to collect his mother.

For a while he had a recurring dream about finding her in the wardrobe again, but the dream passed. It passed along with the fear that every time his mother receded from sight she might be dying somewhere.

In the beginning, he didn't want to leave her alone and go to school and he didn't want to open the front door when he came home in case she wasn't sitting at their little pink table or reading an article on the sofa, but this also passed.

Somehow the whole thing with the wardrobe altered her, as though she'd been sleepwalking all those years and had finally woken up, only instead of waking up and assuming the characteristics she'd exhibited before, she woke up and took Jamie for adventures that cost barely anything, like deer-stalking walks across Richmond Park and trips to the swimming ponds at Hampstead Heath. Now she made spaghetti and threw it at the ceiling and when it didn't fall, she jabbed at it with the handle of a broom and giggled.

The best thing was when she said, 'I can't sit around here anymore,' when she marched down Upper Street and went into every cafe and restaurant she could find until someone gave her a job.

After that, Jamie would go to *Ffe's Cafe* after school and she'd sit him down and bring him orange squash and iced buns while she finished her shift, while she cleared plates and wiped down tables and picked up sodden chips from the floor.

'Put it there, big man.'

That's what Mr Antoniou would say when he saw Jamie, and then he'd hold up his palm for him to high-five. Mr Antoniou was his mother's boss, only secretly she called him Kojak because of his shiny bald head.

'Try telling Kojak that,' she'd say, when she was chatting on the stairs.

This always made Inez laugh. 'Oh Marie,' she'd say. 'You're awful.'

But she wasn't awful. She was the mother Jamie had been waiting for all these years, unlocked by a deep sleep and a wardrobe.

It was like something from a fairytale.

*

Towards the end of Jamie's first year at high school he submitted a composition for his English class and when his teacher handed him back his work, in the top right hand corner was the letter *A*. It was drawn in red ink, and Jamie was so staggered by it that for a few seconds it seemed to swim up from the page and attach itself to his retina. He'd never been given an A for anything.

After the class ended, Mr Fletcher asked to see him, and when Jamie stood before him he said, 'Jamie, this is excellent,' and tapped his finger off the page. 'If you carry on producing work like this, you're going to be a very good writer.' Then in a different sort of voice he said, 'Is everything alright at home?'

The last thing Jamie wanted was to get his mother in trouble, they'd already sent another social worker after she'd been in the hospital, and this routine was only now beginning to wind down. That's why he told Mr Fletcher everything was fine. He said, 'It's just a story. It's not real.'

After that, Jamie made a deal with himself not to write about anything personal again, and after this he found his compositions wouldn't write themselves. The process became laborious and his sentences sat like warped of Lego that wouldn't connect to each other and he never received another A, at least not until he was sixteen.

That's when he was overtaken by a secret hand, when he wrote a story about a boy who looked at another boy as though he was a girl and afterwards was unable to look at girls at all anymore. Then he did receive an A, and Mr Fletcher held him back after class and told him, 'You're a talented writer, you write from truth.'

*

Jamie knew that if you were popular, you could do many things, you could experiment with girls when you were thirteen or fourteen and you could learn something about yourself. Jamie wasn't a popular boy though, he wasn't a boy any girl wanted to kiss.

In his first three years of high school he was bullied by a classmate called Darren and this boy's friends. Sometimes this was bullying with words and sometimes it was bullying with actions.

At first it left him stunned when he was humiliated in front of the whole class but after a while he stopped feeling anything about it. He could pick himself up or walk to the toilet to fix his tie and wash his face and it was like he was watching the whole thing from outside himself.

When he was fourteen, a boy came to the school whose family had moved from another part of the country and settled in London because the boy's father, who was in the forces, had been deployed there. His name was Jacob and he was thick-set and mildly theatrical in a way that made him a target for the same boys who made things difficult for Jamie.

What he noticed was that Jacob didn't react when they threw a book at him or tripped him in the corridor, and that's how Jamie understood he was accustomed to being treated this way.

It was Jacob who approached him, he came to him and said, 'We live in the same direction, don't we?' and after this they began to walk home together.

Jacob explained that his family moved every two years, and that each time, he had to attend a new school. Jamie asked how this felt and he said, 'I'm used to it,' but after a few weeks, when they knew each other better, Jacob returned to this point only now he said, 'Actually I hate it, but my dad doesn't care.'

Jacob said that when he was older he wanted to be an actor and Jamie thought about this and then he said, 'I can imagine you doing that.' He could imagine it too, it was obvious that's what Jacob should do. It seemed strange to Jamie, meeting this person who knew so clearly how to direct his life.

He didn't have any idea what to do when he grew up, and when he told Jacob this, the boy said, 'Don't worry, hardly anyone does.'

As the weeks passed, Jamie understood something unusual was happening between them, though he had no way of articulating it, and when they were up in Jacob's room one day, the boy came to the end of what he was saying, looked at him briefly, then kissed him.

Jamie let it happen, it felt natural to be kissed by this boy, even if a voice in his head said it was the opposite of natural.

For the rest of that term, he would go to Jacob's house and they would kiss and lie on the bed and place their hands, and Jamie felt like a part of him had come alive, and he understood then that in some way he had not been alive before, that merely being a person in a body with a beating heart and a brain had not made him a living thing.

This routine continued until Jacob's mother walked into his bedroom without either of the boys noticing one afternoon. She didn't see them kiss because they weren't kissing, but from the way they were lying on the bed she understood there was a level of intimacy between them that she hadn't expected to see.

That evening Jamie thought a lot about the look on Jacob's mother's face when she walked in on them, he thought about what that look said about him. He wondered whether this was the way all people would look at him once they knew who he was. Something inside him seemed to split, and afterwards it was as though there were two parts of him, and one part couldn't stand to look at the other.

He didn't go over to Jacob's house again after that, and when the boy approached him before classes started the following week and asked him what was wrong he said, 'Just leave me alone.'

At first he couldn't talk to Jacob, and later he couldn't stop himself talking to him. Only this time he was calling him a fat bastard, he was scrawling pictures of him on scraps of paper torn from notepads. These were pictures in which Jacob was huge, much heavier than he really was. In speech bubbles he wrote, *I'm Jacob, I'm a fat queer.*

Jamie continued to abuse Jacob until the

summer holidays came around. The boy never retaliated, he absorbed everything silently, he let it happen.

In the evenings Jamie felt a terrible remorse and promised himself he'd be kind to Jacob the next day, that he'd apologise and start over. But when the next day came around he found himself saying something else, doing something else, he couldn't seem to stop himself. At that time in his life, the shame in him was like a river bursting free of its banks, and he couldn't find a way to contain it.

Jacob didn't return to school that September, and the teacher announced that his family had moved again. Jamie was so stunned by this news that he had to walk himself to the bathroom and lock himself in the stall. It was devastating to him that he'd never be able to apologise, that he'd never be able to undo any of what he'd done to this boy. It was as though a full-stop had been placed in the middle of his adolescence and now it was finished.

*

When his mother announced she was going to take a lodger when he was seventeen, he said, 'Why not put a sign on the front door saying *Murderer Wanted* and be done with it?'

To his mind, taking in a lodger was something only dysfunctional families did, families who'd rather live with strangers than each other.

'Don't be ridiculous,' his mother said, 'plenty of people do it.' And then she placed an ad in the newspaper.

Nothing about Diego gave Jamie any indication he was gay, so when the man seduced him and took him to bed, it felt completely unreal, like watching a person walking calmly in front of a train.

When the man began snorting cocaine in front of him, that also seemed unreal, but when he tried it for himself, the situation seemed to crystallise and afterwards he understood all of life had been a dress rehearsal to this point, and now the performance was beginning.

Like everything else, their relationship came to an end.

When Diego had gone and his mother would no longer speak to him, his loneliness was like a blister over his whole body, and everything that touched him hurt. It was in the midst of this sadness that he began to think about his father, about this man who existed somewhere, or who'd once existed somewhere.

Is he still alive? he wondered. *Does he ever think about me?*

These were the questions that arose in him. They were like pockets of air rising to the surface of a stagnant lake.

It wasn't hard to track the man down because he'd been a successful portrait photographer. He'd photographed Julie Christie and Michael Caine and Twiggy, he'd photographed other icons of the sixties. He'd exhibited at the Tate.

This amazed Jamie, to know his father was successful and wealthy, to know he had the phone numbers of movie stars in his address book. Another thing that amazed him was the fact he shared the man's DNA. It made him feel special somehow, as though he'd discovered he had royal blood.

As it turned out, he couldn't see any of himself in his father. That was the first thing he realised when the man opened the door and stood looking at him circumspectly, as though he was a con-artist trying to cajole money.

He thought the man must be in his mid-sixties, seventy even, which made sense, his mother had explained he was older. Somehow, he'd put the knowledge to one side though, he'd imagined his father would be athletic and vital, and here he was, grey-faced and stooping, an old man like any other old man.

His father lived in a detached house in Highgate, and inside it was filled with portraits and the rooms were cavernous and high-ceilinged and the walls were painted in oceanic blues and claret reds. Jamie thought it was a beautiful house, beyond any house he'd ever set foot in. Even the messiness of the man's studio was perfect, as though a set designer had laboured for hours to create the chaotic aesthetic.

His father's voice was low and scabrous and when Jamie asked if he'd ever thought about him, he waited a long time before replying.

'Sometimes,' he said. 'Usually when I was drinking. That's what you do when you're drinking, you think of the all things you regret.'

Jamie folded into himself. 'Did you ever try to find me?' he said.

'No.'

'Are you mad that I came?'

His father sighed and stared at the birds on the feeder outside the window. 'Is it money you want? Do you want me to write you a cheque?'

'No,' said Jamie. 'I didn't come for that. I came to find out who you are.'

The man wouldn't look at him. He said, 'I think you should go home, Jamie. Tell your mother I'm sorry. Tell her she was a good model. She *was* a good model, she was a damn good model.'

Jamie didn't know what to say. It felt jarring that this stranger was talking about his mother as though he was the one who knew her.

His father was talking about a different person altogether though, a person who'd existed before he was born and had sacrificed her own life for his. Suddenly all he could think about was what it would be doing to her that he was here, giving this man the time of day.

'She hates you,' he said. 'We both do.'

*

One night during Jamie's final year at university, he collapsed on a dance floor.

In the ambulance he had a series of seizures and a coma was induced. The doctors didn't know if he'd survive, it was new territory for them. They didn't know if he'd wake up and if he did they didn't know if he'd be brain damaged. They didn't know because the effects of ecstasy were not well understood at that time. The doctors were learning from Jamie, he was like a textbook opening itself up at a crucial chapter.

His mother sat by his side and held his hand. He didn't look like her son. His face was swollen and the capillaries in his cheeks had burst open, she could see them under his skin like microscopic lightning forks. He was surrounded by machines and tubes like a character in a hospital drama, only this was real and it was unclear if he'd recover or if his life would be reduced to a defamatory tabloid article.

On the second day the doctors came to his

mother and told her there was an improvement in Jamie's condition, the swelling had reduced, his brain activity looked promising. Shortly afterwards, he was brought out of his coma. He didn't remember seeing her upon waking, or playing the game of naming the animal cards that a consultant held up in front of him as though he was a little boy. He didn't remember anything from that first day.

After twenty-four hours he was taken out of intensive care and two days after that he was discharged. He didn't go back to his student home, he went to his mother's house, and he lay on his childhood bed and allowed slow tears to trickle past his temples and into his hair.

After he'd slept a while, his mother sat him at the little pink table in her kitchen and gave him tomato soup and glasses of pulpy orange juice.

For a long time she was quiet and then she said, 'I can't help feeling this is all me.'

'What's all you?' he said.

'When I think back,' she said. 'All that time with me in bed and you looking after yourself.'

'What are you talking about?'

'Coming home from school and I wasn't even dressed. All those years taking pills.' Jamie's mother was staring at the wall. 'I'm just sorry it's come to this.'

'It's fine,' he said. 'I'm fine, mum.'

His mother turned and looked at him and he understood she didn't believe this.

For a while he thought about returning to university, but in the end he took a job in a video store instead. English Literature seemed like such a pointless thing now. What use was literature in the real world, in the world of mortgages and direct debits and insurance policies? This was something he asked himself when the party was over.

That's how it was for him. There had been a party and now it was over.

*

It was his mother who persuaded him to speak to their GP after he came home.

He told Dr Parker the truth, that he'd been using ecstasy and cocaine and valium and codeine, which wasn't something he'd admitted to his mother. He said he'd been using these drugs in a loop, to bring himself up and drop himself down, to induce pleasure and subdue pain. He felt he could be open because of the man's objectivity, his lack of judgement.

Dr Parker was fascinated by the scope of human experience, it was clear from the level of attention he paid to his patients. It was clear because if a person said, as Jamie had done at seventeen, 'I think I'm gay,' he would reply, 'That's a perfectly natural impulse. You aren't the first.'

And then he would recount the numerous occasions patients had confided in him that they had homosexual feelings throughout his life, and how un-extraordinary this was.

Jamie had found this a deeply touching thing, to be assured by a man who wasn't gay, who belonged to a generation that castigated gay people, that there was nothing to feel ashamed about.

'I think I need some help,' he admitted, sat there with the peak of his baseball cap pulled down so the man couldn't see his face. 'To stay clean.'

'Of course,' said Doctor Parker. 'I understand.'

He asked Jamie if he'd heard of Narcotics Anonymous, and then he said he was lucky he lived in London because there were NA groups here, which was unlike virtually any other place in the country. He explained that NA followed the same principles as AA, that the group was formed of other people who struggled with addiction.

'This is the best thing I know of for what you're dealing with,' he said, and then he opened a drawer and pulled out a pamphlet with details about what NA was and who it was for and where to find a meeting. 'Is there anything else you want to talk about?'

Jamie was quiet for a while, he had to talk himself into releasing it.

'There is one thing.'

'Go ahead.'

'Is it normal to want to die sometimes?'

Dr Parker tilted his head again and narrowed his eyes.

'It's just, I dunno, sometimes I think about it. I don't know if it's because my brain is recovering or what it is. I'm not suicidal. I mean, I'm not seriously thinking of doing something. It's more just this desire for everything to stop. To just go to sleep and that be it.'

Dr Parker nodded.

'It's something that happens to people sometimes,' he said. 'In your case, it could be to do with chemical depletions in the brain. Everything needs to be in harmony, chemically speaking. But there could also be a depression there, you could be what my father called *a melancholic*. The best thing to do is to keep an eye on it. If it persists, come back. And in the meantime, I'm going to refer you to speak to someone. A therapist. Would that be okay?'

'Okay,' Jamie said.

He trusted the man, he trusted that he knew the best thing and he would have done pretty much anything he suggested. Dr Parker made a note and told him someone would be in touch.

*

Jamie was twenty-one when he went to his first Narcotics Anonymous meeting.

He walked into a church hall in Marylebone wearing a denim shirt and a baseball cap, sat down in the circle of grey plastic chairs and listened as people read aloud the twelve steps to recovery.

The man leading the meeting invited newcomers to raise their hands and offer their names. It made Jamie anxious to speak with all those eyes on him, it was as though he was admitting to a crime, but the people nodded sympathetically and welcomed him.

Then a person read something from a book about surrendering and when the reading was finished, people took turns to talk about what had been happening in their lives over the past week and how they felt about those things.

A woman called Joss said she'd been to a work event on the Friday evening, she'd taken a glass of champagne, and this had been a mistake because later she went to the toilets with a male colleague and began snorting cocaine, and then the two of them took a taxi to his house and had sex and continued taking drugs until it was light outside and people were already driving to the supermarket and walking their dogs.

Joss said she didn't like this man, that she would never have had sex with him sober, and that made her hate herself. Then she began crying and waved a hand, and after a moment the next person began talking.

Jamie thought the people in the room were brilliant in their honesty.

One man stood up and said this was the one year anniversary of him taking drugs for the last time. He'd cut ties with his friends and ended his relationship with his girlfriend because he couldn't be around them and stay sober. He'd also left his career and was now a courier living in a room in a shared house. The man said it didn't matter though, what mattered was his life wasn't about lying and running away from himself anymore.

When he finished talking, the people clapped.

Close to the end, the man who was leading the group said that if the newcomer would like to speak, this time was reserved for him to do so.

Jamie felt a cold sweat breaking out across his palms. He was scared that when he spoke, his voice would crack or that he wouldn't be able to breathe.

'I'm Jamie,' he said. 'I came here because I was using too many drugs and one night it caught up with me and I ended up in a coma. That was about six or seven weeks ago and I haven't done any drugs since. Anyway, I don't want to go back to all that and my doctor said this was the place I should come.'

Some of the people in the circle had their heads down and others looked at him when he spoke, and when he was done they said, 'Thank you, Jamie.'

At the end of the meeting, the people stood up and held hands and recited something called *The Serenity Prayer*.

After they were finished the man to his right let go of his hand and told him well done, and Jamie felt suddenly uncomfortable, it was to do with the way the man looked at him. He could tell he was about to engage him in conversation and he didn't want to talk so he picked up his jacket and walked out of there, and in the cool of the night he knew he would never go back.

*

The following week he received a referral from Dr Parker to meet with a therapist for an introductory appointment. The therapist's office was in a red-brick building off Rosebery Avenue, near Exmouth market.

When Jamie arrived he pushed a buzzer and

almost immediately a voice said, 'Come up to the second floor. The door on your right.'

The therapist's name was Marina and she was a small woman with dark hair and large probing eyes, like a nocturnal animal. The room she kept had a bay window with venetian blinds and was painted white. In the corner sat a yucca plant with sloping fronds. She invited Jamie to sit down and told him there was a glass of water on the coffee table by his side.

'Why don't you tell me a bit about why you're here,' she said.

In the beginning he didn't know what she would think of him if he told her the unadulterated truth of his life, but he did tell her, both because he didn't have the energy to censor himself and because he knew it was the only way to make things work.

That's how he found himself saying things he'd never said, about how silent his mother had been when he was young and how he'd assumed this was in some way his fault.

'How did it make you feel to believe that?' said Marina.

'I guess it made me feel like I wasn't what she wanted.'

Marina nodded and said, 'And how do you think that informed the way you behaved around her?'

'It just made me not want to ever make a mistake. And every time I did something wrong I'd get really mad at myself. Then eventually I just gave up I guess.'

She tilted her head.

'What do you mean? In what sense did you give up?'

'I just stopped trying, I just thought, *you're useless.*'

'And this feeling of being useless, is that something you still have?'

'I don't know. Sometimes.'

'Did your mother ever say you were useless?'

'No. She once said to me, "When I picture you as a grown-up, I see you wandering around in old clothes, not having any money, but not caring." That always stuck with me, this thing about her seeing me as a dropout.'

'How did you want her to see you? How old were you at this point?'

'I don't know, maybe fourteen or fifteen or something. I don't know, I guess if she'd expected me to be super successful then that would have been hard too, you know, like too much pressure. I just wanted her to think I could do whatever I wanted, that if I put my mind to it, I could do anything.'

Marina nodded.

'And you don't think she felt that way?'

'I don't know, she never said stuff like that. My mum doesn't talk like that.'

'Are you angry with her for that?'

'No, I'm angry at myself because she was right. I work in a video store and I have nothing, you know. I mean, I have a job. But I have no degree, no money, no prospects.'

Marina adjusted her positioning and folded her hands in her lap. She said, 'Is that true?'

'Yes.'

'I mean, is it true that those things are fixed?'

Jamie began biting his lower lip. He said, 'What do you mean?'

'Well, is it possible you could get a different job, or that you could go back to university, or that you could one day have savings?'

'It's possible. I don't know how I would do any of that stuff now, but I guess it's possible.'

'Maybe now isn't the time to worry about it. I'm just pointing out that so much of life is down to perspective. What do you want for your life, Jamie? Do you know?'

He looked at her, at this diminutive woman

in her blue suit with her sharp eyes and her questions.

'I'm not sure,' he said. 'I want her to be proud of me.'

'So you don't think she's proud of you now?'

'How can she be? I just came out of a coma from drugs, I'm gay, I dropped out of uni. I'm basically everything a parent doesn't want their kid to be.'

'Jamie,' she said, tilting her head. 'Two things. Firstly, I think your mother would be heartbroken if she knew you felt this way, because the chances are she *is* proud of you. Mothers aren't proud of their sons because they have jobs in the city and drive expensive cars. They're proud of them because they're decent people, because they're kind, because they take care of their mothers. And secondly, there's nothing wrong with being gay. Do you think you're less of a person because of your sexuality?'

He could feel a familiar and uncomfortable emotion rising up in him. He began to bite the skin around his fingernails.

'I don't know.'

'What did your mother say when she found out you were gay?'

'She stopped talking to me. She didn't shout or get angry or anything, she just acted as though I wasn't there.'

Marina offered a consolatory nod. 'I see. And how did that feel?'

'It was hard. I thought I was in love with this guy and then my mum found out and the whole thing ended. It was like I lost both of them overnight.'

'And how old were you when this happened?'

'Seventeen.'

'That's a lot to take at seventeen.'

Jamie nodded. He found it difficult to get his head around the fact he was having this conversation with a woman he didn't know at all.

'How did you resolve things with her?'

'After a month or so she started talking to me again, she apologised. I don't wanna make her sound like a bad person, she's not a bad person. It was just hard when all that happened.'

'Of course. Do you feel like that part of your life is something you can talk to her about now?'

Jamie blew out some air, drummed on his knees with his palms.

'Yeah, she always asked when I was at university, you know, if I had a boyfriend or whatever. It's not like, off-limits, it's just different. Your mum doesn't want you to have a boyfriend like she wants you to have a girlfriend. If you're a guy I mean.'

'Well if she loves you, she does. If she really loves you, I mean. What a mother wants most for her child is his happiness. Sometimes it might take her a while to see that what she thinks will make him happy and what will actually make him happy are different things, but once she's worked it out, that's all she wants.'

Jamie looked at Marina. To his mind, this was an impossible sentence that had come out of her. It was something he had to play back to himself in his head.

'Maybe,' he said.

Marina said, 'Have you ever asked your mother what she wants for you?'

'No.'

'What do you think she'd say?'

Jamie shrugged. 'I don't know. Probably for me to be happy.'

She nodded and he wondered if a therapist was supposed to talk like this, if this was how therapy really worked.

He came to love this woman for the things she said to him. Even after that first session he loved her. He loved her for listening to him without making judgements and for telling him he was good.

She told him there was nothing wrong or deficient about him, and somehow he knew she meant it. To Jamie's mind, there was no greater gift a person could give another person, and he felt also that this wasn't her professional mouth talking, that she was giving him the truth as she saw it. That's why he loved her. It didn't matter to him if this was how therapy was supposed to be, he didn't care.

After twelve weeks it ended, that was how many sessions were provided by the health service. Jamie didn't want to stop talking to her though, he told her this. Marina understood, she didn't think twelve sessions was sufficient.

'Nobody can unpick a lifetime of confusion in twelve hours,' she said.

Marina was kind, she would see him at a reduced rate, she knew he had limited means. Sometimes he would bring her something besides money, usually flowers, because these she couldn't refuse. When he first gave her flowers and she said she couldn't accept gifts he told her they weren't for her, they were for the room, for all the people who sat in this room and sifted through all the things that ate away at them.

It was a small gesture he was making. His mother had taught him to pay attention to the small things, she'd taught him it was the small things that made up a life.

For three years, Jamie saw Marina every week, he sat with her and talked about the things that had hurt him by happening, about the things that had hurt him by failing to happen. Then, one blustery afternoon in 1994, she turned to him and told him she was going to leave London, she was going to move to Cornwall with her family and start again.

'Why?' he said.

'It's just the right time. My children are young, they'll adapt better if we do it now.'

'But why Cornwall? Is that where you're from?'

Words were coming out of him but his mind wasn't connected to them, he was in shock.

She nodded. 'Yes, I came here years ago, but my intention was always to go back. It just took longer than I expected.'

'Oh,' he said.

He was suddenly aware of how little he knew about this woman, this woman who knew everything about him. He needed her and she didn't need him, that was the difference.

Their sessions continued for three more months, and the focus shifted from Jamie's internal world to how he would transition to a life without Marina in it. She said it was the right time for him to stop seeing her, that there comes a point at which therapy can become indulgent, a point at which it can become a crutch.

'So you think I'm done?'

Marina tilted her head. 'I think you know yourself better now. I think you're resilient and capable, absolutely I do.'

'But how do you know when someone's finished with therapy?'

'Jamie, I'm not saying that's it. There may be other times in your life when you need to talk to someone. And you should absolutely do that. But I don't think you need me. You don't need me. That's a fact.'

He found himself nodding, and later when he was lying on his bed, he thought about why it would be good for him to move on, about how nothing can last forever. He thought about that and then he turned on the radio because he didn't want to think about it. The future was like a black hole carved into the earth, and he didn't want to look at it.

The last time he saw Marina was on a balmy day in July. He gave her an orchid and a card. She also handed a card to him but told him not to read it until later, until he'd gone home.

During the session, she asked him what he was going to do next and he replied that he didn't know, that he'd probably look for a new job or think about studying again. She asked him whether he felt ready for a relationship and he said he did, or he thought he did.

He would like to have had better answers, to have already achieved something that would evidence his progress, even if proving these things didn't mean anything to her. At the close of the session she hugged him goodbye and it was then that it hit him that he would never see her again.

When he got home, he opened the card. Inside she had written, *To Jamie, Thank you for your kindness, honesty and courage, M.*

Jamie watched the words move around his mind and tried to connect them to himself. He'd never thought of himself as courageous. This wasn't something that came naturally – the word *courage* couldn't hold all this virtue contained, it couldn't touch it – but it pointed towards something and Jamie could sit with that and see it for himself, he'd learned how to do that. It was down to Marina, to this woman who for three years had been the most important person in his orbit.

*

At first he thought Charlie was just a man off the street coming to rent a video like anyone else, but when he appeared at the counter and looked into his eyes, Jamie felt something passing between them, something ineffable, something he hadn't experienced before.

'I know this sounds lame,' he said, 'but I feel like I knew you before we even met. The moment I saw you that day it was like I recognised you.'

Jamie said this the night they first slept together, as they lay in Charlie's bed with the white sheets strewn about them and their bodies bathed in pearlescent light from the bedside lamp.

'It doesn't sound lame,' said Charlie. 'I felt the same thing.'

'About me?'

'No, about the postman,' he said, and knocked on Jamie's forehead. 'Yes, about you.'

Jamie smiled and Charlie leant in and kissed him.

Jamie said, 'Does it scare you?'

'What?'

'You know, wanting to get it right and being scared you're gonna screw it up.'

'It does.'

'Really?'

Charlie nodded.

Jamie said, 'Does it bother you when I talk like this?'

'Like what?'

'I don't know,' Jamie said. 'I know I can be intense.'

Charlie put a hand through his hair. 'No. I like that about you.'

'That's weird,' said Jamie, biting his lip. 'People don't usually like it.'

Sometimes, when Charlie left for work, Jamie imagined him being hit by a car or something. This was before everyone had a mobile phone, so he'd reason with himself for a while and then in the end he'd call the university.

'Can you ask Mr Thomas to call me?' he'd say. 'My name's Jamie, he has my number.'

Then he'd pace around behind the counter at work and when Charlie's class had ended he would call and tell him, 'Baby, I'm fine. Nothing's going to happen.'

This is how being in love was for Jamie.

One moment he was flooded with joy, the next he was consumed by the fear it could be taken away any second. He didn't know how to manage this, how to direct his brain or arrest these emotions when they arose. It made him want to take a scalpel and dissect himself, to remove the part that had to feel, because how was a person supposed to withstand all this and live a normal life?

When he told his mother about Charlie, she said, 'And what's so special about this one?'

'Everything,' he said.

She gave him a look. 'Like that, is it?'

He didn't see the point in waiting around, he brought Charlie to meet her within a few months. His mother still didn't own a dining table big enough for more than two people so she and Charlie ate at the little pink table and Jamie sat on the counter by the sink with his plate in his hand. She hadn't wanted to do it this way, she'd wanted the men to sit down, but Jamie insisted.

'I'm sorry,' she said, looking over at Charlie. 'I'm sure you're used to nicer than this.' She scanned the room with her eyes.

'Not at all,' he said, smiling. 'I like it.'

'Well you must be due at the opticians,' she said, and Charlie laughed.

Jamie saw right away they liked each other. He'd known they would, but the confirmation of it was like a warm tide breaking in his chest.

After this, he would take Charlie to his mother's every Sunday and they'd eat breakfast together. Usually this was bacon and eggs and the men would sit at the table and Jamie's mother would talk to them as she cooked or as she scoured the frying pan in the sink.

'Aren't you going to eat?' Charlie would ask.

'No,' she'd reply, 'I had a bit of toast earlier.'

One wonderful thing Charlie did for Jamie was to encourage him to write. Ever since dropping out of university he'd toyed with writing, carrying notebooks around with him, sketching out ideas, fleshing out conversations.

He'd started writing short stories, sometimes no more than a couple of pages long, stories about people's lives coming together, coming apart. Jamie had shown these to nobody, he hadn't even told anyone he'd written them. But one day he looked at Charlie and said, 'Would you look at something I wrote? I know it's bad, just tell me what to do to make it better.' Then he handed over a notepad and Charlie read it.

'This isn't bad, Jamie,' he said, and then he added, 'but there's a bit too much exposition. Remember; show, don't tell.'

Jamie didn't understand. 'What do you mean?'

'Just write as though you're writing for the most intelligent person you know, someone who doesn't need anything explaining.'

So from then on Jamie wrote everything as though his audience was only Charlie, and the next time Charlie read his work he said, 'This is good.'

Towards the end of the summer, Charlie took

him to Cannes for the weekend, because he'd once driven the coast highway from Ventimiglia to Antibes and the impression it had left was still with him.

The weather was terrible, but it didn't matter. They walked down La Croisette with the mizzling rain skirting their faces, talking, laughing. Jamie had never been abroad before this and everything about it was unreal to him; the strange aspect the foreign registration plates gave to cars, the profusion of people with skin like caramel, the distinctive smell of indigenous fauna and the incessant wail of horns as the vehicles clattered through the streets.

He loved the impossibly tall palm trees lining the boulevards and the softly crashing Mediterranean sea as it broke on the shoreline, these things were amazing to him, they made him feel like he was in a movie.

Charlie booked two rooms, a single and a double. Jamie didn't know if this was because two men couldn't share a room here or because he didn't want to explain himself at the reception desk. He thought about how much easier it would be to have a girlfriend instead of a boyfriend, he thought about why any person was gay in the first place.

On the Saturday evening, they walked into the old town and found a seafood restaurant. Jamie ordered rigatoni and Charlie ordered swordfish.

In the soft candle-light, Charlie looked handsome and tan and Jamie wondered how any of this had happened. It had been handed to him on a plate, and it made him feel like he'd been mistaken for someone else and given what should have been theirs.

'Look at that couple over there,' he said.

Charlie turned and looked at a man and a woman who were attractive and middle-aged, who wore expensive clothes and sat in silence.

'What about them?'

Jamie said, 'They haven't spoken to each other in ten minutes.'

Charlie leaned in and raised his eyebrows. 'Maybe he's in trouble.'

Jamie bit his lip and said, 'Do you think that's what happens to people when they've been together too long?'

Charlie shrugged and smiled. 'Why, are you worried that'll be us in ten years?'

'I'm serious,' he said. 'Do you think all couples end up like that?'

Charlie shook his head. 'No, I don't think so.'

'It seems like people always get bored of each other or start hating each other in the end.'

Charlie poured wine from a carafe. 'Not

always,' he said. 'Sometimes they fall more deeply in love.'

'How do you know that? Is that what happened to your parents?'

Charlie sat back in his chair and considered it. He said, 'I don't know. Maybe. The nature of a relationship changes as time goes on.'

'Do you think people stay together out of fear?' Jamie said. 'Because they're scared of being alone?'

'Sometimes. I think sometimes people should probably break up, it would be better for them. Maybe these two behind me should break up. Or maybe they're just so comfortable with each other they don't have to talk anymore.'

'Maybe,' said Jamie. 'But they both look so miserable. Imagine going for dinner and sitting there like that.'

'Well it's not something we have to worry about.' Charlie reached under the table and put a hand on Jamie's knee. He said, 'I love you, you know.'

*

Jamie expected the intensity of his feelings to subside as time went on, but instead he was plagued by fear, by thoughts of Charlie coming to his senses and leaving him, and the anxiety made it difficult to navigate daily existence. He felt in a way like he was losing his mind, like he was walking through the happiest period in his life with a grenade stitched into his side.

Around that time a student started working at the video store whose name was Ali. He was a bad employee, he was late and he couldn't work the till, he put the wrong videos into the rental boxes so that ageing housewives went off with slasher movies and soft porn, he placed the new confectionary in front of the old confectionary instead of rotating the stock. Worst of all he handed people the wrong change so that sometimes they left with more money in their hands than they came in with. Jamie liked him all the same though, this droll, sardonic boy with a hairline that began an inch above his eyebrows.

The only reason Ali assented to having a job at all was to service a lifestyle he'd constructed around clubbing, something he did week in and week out, first loading himself up on drugs, then dancing from dusk til dawn. Sometimes he travelled great distances to do this, to Manchester and Leeds and Sheffield, or to warehouses in industrial estates on the outskirts of the city.

To begin with Jamie said no when Ali invited him to party with him, he made his excuses and brushed him off. But then one day Ali gave him a friendly push and said, 'Come on, stop being a loser all your life, it'll be fun. Just try it once. For me.'

Ali tilted his head and grinned.

'I'm out with work people on Friday night,' he told Charlie over dinner that evening.

'That's nice,' said Charlie. 'Where are you going?'

'I'm not sure. Some club or other.'

'A club? I didn't know you went to clubs.'

'I don't. It's just a one-off.'

Charlie smiled at him. 'You should, it'll be fun.'

That was the night Ali introduced him to ketamine. Jamie hadn't tried this drug before, he'd never even thought about it, but afterwards it felt like something that had been waiting for him all along. He did this drug once and after that life without it seemed like a pale still photograph by comparison.

'How was your night out?' Charlie asked the next time they saw each other.

'It was fun,' he said. 'More fun than I expected.'

'That's good,' Charlie said. 'You should do it more often.'

So once every couple of weeks, he went out and partied and then he returned to normality, and the two worlds remained distinct from each other.

But like everything in life, it didn't last.

Pretty soon things started to overtake him so that the desire to be with Charlie was replaced by the desire for a hit, for thoughts to be replaced by silence and feelings to be replaced by a warm umbilical throb, like the heartbeat of the universe.

In the black shimmering sea of bodies and dry-ice he recalled those nights with Heidi when they used to position themselves in front of the amps and let the roar of the bass catch in their throats and reverberate along their bones. This was the thing he'd been longing for, the thing he'd been hungering for all those years. Suddenly he felt like a person who'd discovered himself anew.

Somehow he managed to deceive Charlie into thinking nothing had changed, he managed to live two lives and run them concurrently, like a man who was married and kept a mistress on the side. From Monday to Friday, he went to work and played the dutiful boyfriend, and then at the weekend he adopted another persona and went out until seven in the morning and did things to himself that kept him in darkened rooms for the entirety of the day following.

Jamie was wrong about Charlie though. Of course he'd seen a change in him, he just didn't name it because he didn't want any trouble between them.

'This weekend, why don't you stay with me?' he said one day, as they sat on the couch watching the television.

'What do you mean?' Jamie said.

'Well, instead of going out. I feel like I never see you at the weekend anymore.'

Jamie didn't turn to look at him, he didn't want to see his face. 'I can't this weekend,' he said. 'I already said I'd go out with Ali.'

Charlie didn't say anything to that, but after a while he stood up and went upstairs.

Jamie felt a strange anxiety move through him, and when he turned off the TV and went up to the bedroom, he didn't know if he should speak to Charlie or kiss him goodnight or what he should do. He hated this part of being in a relationship, the part that required you to gauge the other person's feelings, the part that required you to sit in the discomfort of not knowing what the other person was thinking, the part that required you to say you were sorry.

'Next weekend, I'll keep the whole thing free,' he said as he lay down on the bed. 'We can spend the whole time together.'

'Okay,' said Charlie.

But it turned out that spending the whole time together wasn't a good thing. All Jamie could think about was how much he wanted to be lost in a strobe-lit fog with his mind locked down and the heavy bass cocooning his skull.

'You seem distracted,' Charlie said.

'No, I'm fine,' Jamie said, and he drank his wine.

Charlie kissed him, he kissed him the way he did when he was initiating something, but the last thing Jamie wanted to do was that, so he pulled back and when Charlie asked him what was wrong he said, 'Nothing.'

Charlie sighed and sat back in his seat.

After a long time he said, 'I love you. But you don't love me, you love drugs.'

'You know that isn't true,' Jamie replied.

But Charlie wouldn't say anything else, and he stood up and walked away.

*

'I don't believe it,' his mother said. 'I thought you two were happy.'

She was sitting at her little pink table with a cigarette in her hand, she was waiting for her son to say something. Jamie didn't know what to say though, there were no words so far as he could see.

He moved back in with her towards the end of 1999. He was thirty years-old.

One reason he did this was because he could

no longer afford the rent on his flat. His landlord had increased it at the beginning of the year and Charlie had been helping him cover the shortfall. That wasn't the main thing though. The main thing was that he wasn't going to fall any deeper into any hole. It was safer for him to be at his mother's, she'd keep an eye on him. Besides, she wouldn't worry the same if she knew where he was. That's the way he saw it.

Immediately after coming home, he started seeing another therapist. The therapist's name was Nathan and he was also gay, it was a thing he stated plainly to market himself. Jamie felt this was important, he needed to talk to someone who understood his position in life, who understood what it meant to be a gay man in this city.

'Shame,' Nathan told him, his pallid face sombre, a lock of dark hair falling over one eye. 'All of this is shame. That's what we grow up with, that's the hand we're dealt.'

He wasn't surprised to hear the things Nathan told him, that gay men had more sex and used more drugs because they were escaping their feelings or trying to short-circuit intimacy. What surprised him was the way he could know a thing and still continue living as though he didn't know it, as though it was beneath his awareness. 'I know all this,' he said, 'so why do I still want to get wasted all the time?'

Jamie stopped hanging out with Ali after he started his sessions with Nathan. He switched the rota so they wouldn't be on shift together, he talked to him about his dependency issues and Ali was fine about it, he shrugged and said, 'C'est la vie.'

After this, Jamie found his existence lonely and narrow and he became despondent both about what had happened with Charlie and about what his life looked like on the other side of that.

His mother was kind to him, she cooked for him and asked him nothing other than how he was feeling and if she could do anything. She was wonderful at that time, she was like an anchor ploughing the seabed to bring him to rest, though sometimes he snapped at her anyway, simply because she was the person in front of him.

He started to write short stories again, sometimes one after the next, it was the only thing he could do to quell the sadness, the boredom. That was the thing that really struck him during this period when he was thirty; how dull life was. Get up, go to work, come home, do chores, watch TV, eat, sleep, repeat.

He thought about this, about how it wasn't surprising he wanted to alter his consciousness with drugs; why wouldn't he when most of life was drudgery, when he'd grown up imagining all these superlative experiences going hand in hand with adulthood, only to discover the reality was the polar opposite.

'The fact is, life is painful.' Nathan said this to him during one of their sessions. 'Sometimes it's unbearably painful.'

To Jamie, hearing someone say that was like being presented with a piece of himself that had been hacked off years before. He thought about this, he took some time and thought about it and then he said, 'You know, sometimes I say to God, or whatever it is out there, I don't know what, but I say, *Please don't make this go on too long*. Like, I don't want to be an old man. I already feel like an old man.'

Nathan drew a finger along the line of his chin and nodded. 'Why do you feel like that?'

'Because my life's been hard, you know. I know lots of people have it worse than I do, I know that. But being gay is hard. I find it *so* hard. I don't want it to define my life, but it does. Like, every time you meet someone you're thinking, *Do I tell them, will they hate me if they know who I am?*, it makes you so scared all the time.

'So many times I just don't attempt things, just because I can't face having to come out to people. And I know this probably sounds crazy but honestly, I'm so scared of straight men, I never know how to be with them, if I should just pretend to be straight, or how they'll react if they find out I'm gay. The thing is, I'm so tired of being scared all the time.'

It was hard to hear himself say these things, to hold that mirror up to himself. It was overwhelming, like somebody stripping back his skin and pressing down on the tissue beneath.

Nathan acknowledged what he said, he gave it credence and encouraged him to allow himself to feel this pain, to see that it was natural given the world he'd been born into.

He also challenged Jamie to bring into focus all the people who had shown him kindness and love, all the people who had cared for him in his life, and what he saw was that these people outnumbered those who had not. There had been wonderful people in his life. This was also true.

Jamie didn't use drugs again, not ever.

There were times when he wanted to use them, when he wanted them more than he wanted life itself, but he didn't follow through.

Anytime he had the urge he reminded of himself of the aftermath, of the despair and the terror of a bad come-down, of the physical ache in his chest from knowing he'd fallen back into that hole. Sometimes reminding himself of this wasn't enough and he wanted to buy drugs anyway and then he made himself sit down and write, even if what he laid down was terrible, even if the sentences sounded like they'd come out of a child.

Eventually he began submitting stories to literary magazines, he made it a focus to try to get something published somehow. Usually he received cursory rejections or no response at all, but one day after many months he received a letter from a magazine telling him his submission had been accepted for publication. It was March of 2001.

The letter said his story - about a taciturn gay man who lived his whole life alone, only to fall in love in his seventies - would appear in the next issue. He couldn't believe it when he read that letter. It was the first time in his adult life he felt he'd achieved something. When he told his mother about it, she said, 'Jamie, that's fantastic,' and opened a bottle of wine to celebrate.

He lived so frugally at that time that by April he'd set enough aside to do what he'd wanted to do since the day Adam Everlast took him to the top of a multi-storey carpark in his Ford Consul all those years ago.

He learned to drive in little over three months, passed his test at his second attempt and bought an electric blue Ford Orion. An old man had owned it since it rolled off the production line, he'd clocked twenty-four thousand miles in ten years.

Jamie didn't tell his mother about it. He simply walked through the front door one day with a smile on his face and stood in front of her.

'What are you so happy about?' she said, looking up from her newspaper.

Her hair was piled on her head in a loose bun and she was wearing her gold earrings, the ones he gave her for her birthday the year she turned fifty.

'Come downstairs,' he said. 'There's something I want to show you.'

'I don't believe it,' she said when she saw the car parked in front of the house, and she raised a hand to her mouth.

Jamie told her to jump in so she opened the door and sat down in the passenger seat and he drove her along Upper Street and Holloway Road and up the hill towards Highgate Village with its pretty stone buildings and its voluptuous trees and the blue sky unravelling itself before them like a band of bright silk.

*

Towards the end of May, Charlie called. He said his mother had died and he didn't know what to do.

They spoke on the phone and then Jamie

suggested talking in person, so they met the following day in Regents Park and walked down the pretty tree-lined colonnade in the direction of Primrose Hill. A light rain was falling and Charlie looked pale and tired. He was wearing shorts and a vest and his hair had grown so long he could draw it back behind his ears.

'Thanks for meeting me,' he said.

'No worries,' Jamie said. 'How are you feeling?'

Charlie nodded. 'I'm okay.'

'Do you know when the funeral will be?'

'No, I still have to sort all that out.'

Jamie put a hand on his shoulder. He said, 'If you need any help with anything, let me know.'

'Will you come?' Charlie asked. 'The thing is, she doesn't really have any family now, they're all dead except me. I don't want there to be nobody there. I was thinking about it, and I thought, *God, I don't know who to tell*. She didn't see many people.'

'Yeah, of course,' Jamie said. 'I would have come anyway, I always liked your mum.'

'She liked you too,' Charlie said. 'She was sad when we broke up.'

'Really?'

'Yeah. When she first met you I don't think she knew what to make of you, but you won her over.'

Jamie smiled. 'Do you remember the first time I met your parents, and I was on my best behaviour but then I swore, I said *shit* or *bullshit* or something by accident?'

'God, it was awful, that night.'

Jamie gave him a little push. 'It wasn't that bad.'

Charlie smiled. 'It was.'

'I was nervous. I thought you'd finish with me if they didn't like me.'

Charlie stopped and looked at him.

'You didn't really think that, did you?'

'Yeah,' Jamie said.

'I had no idea you felt that way.'

Jamie shrugged. 'It doesn't matter.'

The leaves of the trees were unmoving and at intervals, squirrels leapt out on to the path before them and rose up on their hind legs to see who was coming. The birds were cutting across the sky and calling to each other, and these were the only sounds except for the children in the fields.

Jamie pulled a hand through his hair. 'We're gonna be soaked by the time we're done, you know.'

'I know,' said Charlie. 'I don't mind. Do you?'

'No, it's warm anyway.'

'I was soaked the day we met. Remember?'

Jamie smiled. 'Yeah, I gave you a tissue to wipe your glasses with.'

'That's right.'

They were both quiet for a moment.

'Even now I think that's amazing,' Charlie said, 'to just walk into a video store one day and fall in love with the boy at the counter. Don't you think that's amazing?'

It made something inside Jamie light up to hear this. He said, 'Yeah, I guess it is.'

Charlie said, 'How's your mum these days?'

'She's okay. I'm living with her again now. I've been there since we broke up.'

Charlie said, 'And how's that going?'

Jamie bit his lip. 'We have our ups and downs, but it's been good, she's been good to me.'

It was right at that moment, as they were halfway up Primrose Hill with no place to hide, that the rain became suddenly torrential. Turning to each other, they began to laugh, then ran back down the bank until they reached the bottom. They took shelter under a tree and for some reason they began to hug, it was a spontaneous thing.

Jamie attended Charlie's mother's funeral the following week, and when the guests had gone Charlie asked him if he'd come home with him, he didn't want to be alone. They slept in the same bed and nothing happened, but in the morning when they woke up Charlie reached over and kissed him.

It felt unbelievable to Jamie that this was happening. He'd imagined his relationship with Charlie was grist for the mill and nothing more. To watch it come alive again was like watching a tree that had stood naked and barren for a generation suddenly bearing fruit.

*

In July, Charlie invited him to spend the weekend with him in Oxford. He was presenting at a conference during the week and had booked a hotel for them for the Friday and Saturday.

Jamie had never driven on the motorway before but he wasn't nervous. If anything he was calmer than on a standard road. To begin with he stuck to the inside lane and let it all unfold around him and then after a while, when he'd acclimatised, he flicked the indicator and put his foot on the gas pedal.

At first he didn't have a clue what had happened, it sounded like a heavy balloon bursting beneath the chassis. Then the front end shifted and when he grazed the brake, the car switched course.

What he learned in that moment was that time is elastic, it has the capacity to expand or contract according to the nature of the event inhabiting it. Sometimes it slows enough that the whole of life turns into a show, a choreographed dance. That's how his car spun when the tyre blew out, like a figure-skater at the top of an Olympic routine.

As the central reservation rose to meet him he saw the long sweep of pasture in the valley and the finely scattered clouds above, as though a celestial gardener was pulling a rake across the face of the sky.

He saw everything in that moment, and in the next he saw nothing at all.

Son

It was a bitter Friday morning in February and Marie was sitting in the consultant's office with one leg crossed over the other.

She was suddenly aware of her perfume, it had announced itself from some hidden place, from the inside edge of her collar or the skin beneath that. Soon it would fold into nothing and she'd forget it once more. In her hand she held the small plastic cup she'd taken from the water-cooler and was gazing at the long luxuriant leaves of a plant by the window.

'It's called devil's ivy,' said Mr Nahal.

'It's lovely,' she said.

She meant this, she thought it was a beautiful plant.

The consultant smiled briefly from his place on the other side of the desk. He was wearing a navy suit, delicate round-framed spectacles and a tie with polka dots in baby pink. His cuff-links were sculpted in the shape of tiger heads.

Marie admired his attention to detail, he reminded her of a man she'd once known who cut suits on Saville Row. She could imagine Mr Nahal cutting suits had he not gone into medicine, he had that air about him.

'Marie, it's not good news,' he said.

'Oh, don't worry,' she said, 'I told you that, didn't I? Didn't I say it was back?'

She could feel the tension in her throat as the words passed over her tongue.

'You did. In any case, the preliminary test results are here. So we know a little more about what we're dealing with.'

Mr Nahal raised his chin and Marie wondered if he was waiting for a signal to continue. She placed her cup down on his desk. 'Go on,' she said.

'Unfortunately, it's not localised to the breast. We've found secondary cancer in the lymph nodes. We need to do some more tests in order to get a fuller picture. I'd like to do these as soon as possible so we can work out a treatment plan.'

She tilted her head back and took in the air through her nose. She couldn't think for a moment - it was all a blur - and then when she could, she imagined the inside of her body, she pictured tumours hanging off her organs like fruit. She ran both hands over her scalp, following the curvature of her skull until she was holding the hair at the back of her neck.

'I don't want any treatment,' she said. 'Not now.'

'I understand this is a lot to take in. And I'm not sure what the treatment plan will be yet. It's likely we'll have to operate. That's why I want to get the tests done as soon as we can. The sooner we know what we're dealing with, the sooner we can work out the best way to attack it.'

'I don't want to attack it,' she said. 'I'm tired. The last thing I want is radiotherapy, let alone getting my chest cut open or whatever you're suggesting.'

Mr Nahal lowered his head and lay one hand on top of the other. He'd been doing this work for thirty years. He knew by now when to pause, when to push, when to lean back. For a count of five the room was silent.

'I understand it's frightening,' he said. 'Of course you're tired. And I'm not going to pressure you to do anything.'

'Do you mean that?'

'That I'm not going to pressure you?'

'Yes,' she said.

'Yes, of course.'

'Good. Because I don't want to fight you. I don't want to fight anyone. I'm seventy-three years old,' she said. 'I don't care about making eighty-three.'

Mr Nahal looked into her eyes.

'What are you saying, Marie?'

She shifted in her seat so that she was upright, so that her posture was good. She wanted to do things the right way. 'I'm saying I don't want any treatment. My mother had the right idea. She always said, *If I get past seventy and they try to cut me open, tell them no. Tell them enough's enough.*'

'Marie, how about we at least do the tests and see what we're dealing with? If you still feel the same when we have the results, then fine. The fact is you'll need medical intervention. Even if it's non-invasive. You'll need pain management, you'll need nurses, palliative care if it comes to it. This isn't something you can do on your own.'

'I know,' she said, 'but that's further down the road. We're not there yet.'

He looked at her and she could see he was searching for something in her eyes, that's how it felt, as though he was trying to see beyond them into her thoughts.

'Maybe it would help to go away and think about things.'

'Maybe,' she said.

Marie looked over Mr Nahal's shoulder and out of the window to the car-park. A mother was walking hand in hand with her child. She watched their meandering progress and the little boy as he pointed into the sky and as he bent down to pick something up off the gravel. She used to hold Jamie's hand like that, she used to crouch down beside him to see all those fascinating things on the tarmac.

'What's that, Mummy?' he'd once said, reaching for a white spherical object on the ground.

'It's a sweet,' she told him. 'Don't touch it.'

'Why?' he said.

'Because it's on the floor, it's dirty.'

'Why is it on the floor?'

'I don't know, love. Someone must have dropped it.'

'Why?'

'I don't know, love. By accident I suppose.'

'Who dropped it?'

'You ask so many questions,' she'd said.

She had no idea why this memory should have grafted itself in place when so many others had been washed clean from her mind, no idea why it had grown legs and walked into her consciousness again. It was a mystery, like everything else.

She found herself thinking about the day she swallowed a handful of sleeping pills and sat down in her wardrobe, behind all those old dresses where the light couldn't reach her. She recalled the absolute conviction she'd had that it was the only thing left to do. She'd had to do it because she wanted somebody to notice her, to see what was happening inside her, to grasp that she was a person in the world and not just a superfluous thing, a breathing ghost that had once had friendships and held down jobs and been of some use.

Her mind had been so far gone that she hadn't considered what it would do to her son to find her like that. She'd known it would be him, who else was about to come waltzing into her bedroom?

She remembered how she'd managed to convince herself that in some way he was complicit in the whole thing, that he was a willing participant in this plan, that he endorsed her decision. How else could she have made herself go through with it?

She recalled sitting in that hospital bed and the horror that came over her when the reality set in. It was that horror that jolted her back into the world. She'd known then that things had to change, it wasn't her son's job to parent her, to press her to eat and post her letters and do the food shopping while she hid away in darkened rooms. She had value, she had someone who needed her, she had the most precious thing of all.

What in hell had she been thinking, what world had she been living in that she'd failed to notice her own child there in front of her? That's what she wound up asking, sat there in that hospital bed.

Mr Nahal was smiling when she looked back at him.

His was a gentle smile, a smile that had been refined through many thousands of consultations and many moments of heartbreak and terror and confusion. Marie knew he must be waiting for her to go now. The next poor soul would be waiting outside, going over it all in his or her head, bargaining with God. That's how this thing was, she knew all about it.

She stood and thanked him for his time, shook his hand and walked out of his consulting room.

*

It had been many years since she'd spoken to him, seventeen in fact, but the instinct to contact him was overwhelming.

His face appeared to her one night, just after she turned off the kitchen light. She suddenly felt such sorrow at having closed him out. 'Oh Marie,' she said. 'Whatever did you do that for?' And then she thought, *Please don't be dead*. He was older than her after all.

She couldn't sleep that night. She lay in bed

thinking back to the day he came to see her at her flat. This was immediately after her son's death, it could even have been the same day. She'd wanted to see him then. She'd wanted to talk to him because she'd wanted him to say something, to do something to stifle the agony. She'd wanted him to perform a miracle. She'd wanted him to bring back her child and if he couldn't do that she'd wanted him to obliterate her.

Father Gannon had waited on the doorstep to begin with.

'Marie,' he said, 'I hope I'm not disturbing you. Do you have family in there?'

'No, Father.'

'I know you must be devastated,' he said. 'I wanted you to know you don't have to sit in this alone.'

Her eyelids were swollen from crying, from pulling the backs of her hands across them. The whites of her eyes were pink. He reached out and took her wet fingers and squeezed them, and she pulled away because this devotional thing only made her worse.

'Can I get you a tea, Father?' she said.

'No, don't trouble yourself. I just wanted to come and sit with you, Marie. I know there are no words so I'm not going to say anything. I'm just going to sit here, and if you want to talk then we can, and if you want to cry then you can. And if you want to pray, we can do that.'

'Pray?' she said. 'What is there to pray for now?'

For a while she sat in her chair weeping, for a while she was hysterical. Father Gannon sat with her through this, he didn't move a muscle. Then when she grew calm he went away and came back with tissues and a glass of water. He watched over her as she drank, as she set her hair back in position, and then he took her hand.

'Father,' she said, 'why is this happening? What did I do to deserve this? What did Jamie do?'

'You did nothing to deserve it,' he said. 'Jamie did nothing to deserve it either. But what I can tell you for certain is that his death is not in vain. It could be that it takes a long time to see the meaning behind it, but one day you will. And I know it demands an incredible faith, perhaps more than you think you have, but it's there.'

She didn't take any of this in. It didn't matter.

'What am I going to do now?' she said.

'I don't know, Marie. I'd be a liar to answer any other way. But God knows. God won't forsake you.'

'He already did,' she said.

She wept again then, and it went on for a long

time, until she was dizzy with it, until she felt sick. After that Father Gannon helped her up to her room and she lay down. Then he called for the doctor to come and give her something to put her to sleep.

So the doctor came and administered a sedative.

When he left, Marie turned to the priest and said, 'Father, will you stay with me until I fall asleep? I don't want to be alone.'

'Of course I will, Marie,' he said. 'I'm here.'

She closed her eyes, but after a minute she opened them again and reached for his hand.

'Yes, I'm here, Marie.'

'Father,' she said. 'There's something I want to ask.'

'Yes?'

'Did you know Jamie was gay, Father?'

'No, Marie,' he said. 'I didn't.'

'Well he was. Do you think he was sinful for being gay?'

The priest drew breath. 'I think God loves him.'

'But do you think it's wrong? Do you think he was committing a sin?'

She wouldn't take her eyes from him.

'No, Marie,' he said. 'I think God loves him.'

'Is that true?' she said.

Father Gannon nodded his head. 'Yes, it's true.'

'Do you promise?'

She wanted to know this man was on her son's side. Before God, before anything.

'I do.'

'And is that what you believe?'

'It is,' he said.

That he said all this without hesitation was such a comfort to her. It was as though he was cutting through shackles that were pinning her to the ground.

'Thank you,' she said.

*

Lying in her bed, she thought back to the time she caught Jamie with the lodger; that man who she'd secretly desired herself, that man she'd imagined taking to bed, and then she'd found him on top of her seventeen year-old son.

God, that had been a shock.

Mothers know these things about their sons, that's what people said. But she didn't know. She didn't have a clue. She obsessed over that afterwards. *Why didn't I know? What's wrong with me?* This had gone on for weeks, and then finally she thought to herself, *Marie, why do you have to make it about you? It's not about you.*

The thing that had been hardest was the worry about what would happen to him. Would he be beaten in the street for holding a man's hand? Would he start wearing make-up and high-heeled shoes? Would he be diagnosed with AIDS? Would he waste away and die a leper like all those other young men? Marie was terrified for him, and in the beginning her only defence was to pretend it wasn't happening.

If she saw him in the kitchen she'd say 'Good morning,' just the same, but she'd make sure her tone was a little frostier, so he'd know he'd broken something between them, because this was the only thing she could think to do.

Shaming him was the only thing she could think of to stop him being gay. It was a sacred thing that had been passed down through the generations, like a wedding band. Her mother had done the same thing to her when she found out she'd had an illegitimate child.

At that time, Marie had really believed that if he saw how sad the whole thing was making her, if he realised how terribly all this was affecting her, he'd stop. He'd always been a good boy, the last thing he'd want to do was hurt her. She knew this about him. But as the days went on, it became more and more painful to have these curt exchanges with the person she loved the most. It started to cut at her insides, and soon she was lying etiolated in her bed with the curtains drawn against the day.

That's when she knew she couldn't keep on doing this to him, to herself, it was a form of torture she was enacting. So one day she went to his room and knocked on the door and when he answered, she looked into his face and said, 'Can I talk to you for a minute?'

He looked terrified when she asked him that. *I've made him scared just to look at me,* she thought.

It was so long ago, but even now it hurt to know what she'd done to him. *Why on earth did I do that?* she wondered. Anyway, he nodded and she went into his room and sat on the edge of his bed with her hands on her knees.

'I'm sorry I haven't been in a good mood recently,' she said. 'I just, well, I haven't found this easy.'

Jamie looked at her briefly. He was leaning back against the wall.

She said, 'If I ask you something, will you promise to tell me the truth?'

'Okay,' he said.

She had to steel herself just to say it. The word *gay* had so many connotations back then. It meant *pervert*, it meant *sickness,* it meant *death*; not to her but to people out in the world, people with power, like the clergy and the police and the gangs of shaven headed boys. Just thinking about it all terrified her, it made her nauseous.

'I think I know the answer to this already, but I want to be sure. Are you gay?'

To begin with he said nothing, he just stared at the floor.

'You can tell me,' she said. 'It's okay. I'm not going to be angry.'

'Yes,' he said.

'Yes, you're gay?'

'Yes.'

'Okay love,' she said, and that was it.

She went over to him and held him and they were both silent for a moment and then he said, 'I'm sorry,' and she told him, 'Don't be sorry, we'll get through it together.' She said that and then she told him, 'It'll be fine, I promise,' and at the same time she thought about how she had no idea if that was true. It didn't matter. She was his mother, she had to say this.

Anyway, it was fine.

She educated herself about gay men and safe sex and risky behaviours and she made him talk to her about things – to do with sex and drugs and all the rest of it – and together they beat a path through it. That was what mattered. She loved him and he knew it. All that silent treatment was just a blip. She was allowed that. She was allowed one mistake.

Please tell me I'm allowed that, she thought.

She'd done everything she could think of to make up for it afterwards, she really had. She'd even told him she was glad he was gay, that it endowed him with sensitivities he'd never have known otherwise. Besides, he wouldn't have been Jamie if he wasn't gay.

'I want you exactly as you are,' she used to say to him. She said that to him all the time.

I did, she thought. *All the time.*

*

She pulled herself up and sat in the pool of soft yellow light from her bedside lamp.

She was looking up at the picture-hook nailed into the wall opposite her bed. Jamie had once hung a portrait of the Virgin there. She'd seen this painting in an antiques shop window while they'd been out walking together one day. This was three or four months before he died.

'What are you looking at?' he'd said.

'Look at that,' she replied, pointing to the painting. 'Isn't it beautiful?'

'Just look at her face,' she said.

Jamie leaned in to the window. 'It's nice,' he said.

This painting had done something to her, something she couldn't articulate. It was hard for her to make words of this portrait, it was beyond words.

'Should we go inside?' he asked.

'Don't be silly, this shop's expensive.'

Jamie put a hand around her arm. 'So? We might as well check.'

'No, come on, love. It's nice just to look.'

And just like that, they'd walked away. But the next day Jamie appeared in the doorway of the kitchen with his hands behind his back.

'What are you smiling at?' she said. 'What's that behind your back?'

'Close your eyes,' he told her.

'What?'

'Close your eyes.'

'Oh Jamie, come on. I'm too old to be playing silly beggars.' She said this, but inside she felt like a child.

'Just close them.'

So she closed her eyes. And then when she opened them he was holding the portrait up.

'You didn't?' she said. 'Jamie, you didn't?'

He began to laugh.

'Oh Jamie,' she said. 'How can you afford this?'

'It wasn't so expensive.'

'I bet it was,' she said, 'I know that shop.'

'Don't worry about that,' he said. 'Do you like it?'

'Of course I do. Oh it's lovely. Jamie, you're naughty. You can't afford this.'

'Yes I can,' he said.

'Oh, it's beautiful.'

He propped the painting on the kitchen table and she studied the Virgin's face, her open hands, the light pouring from her chest. To Marie, it looked like the sort of painting a person might see in a gallery.

'Where shall I put it?' she asked.

'Why don't you put it in your room? You don't have anything in there.'

'But what about in the living room so everyone can see it?'

'Forget about everyone else,' he said. 'This is just for you.'

Her son hammered nails into her bedroom wall and hung the painting opposite her bed, so it'd be the first thing she saw when she woke up. And that's how all of her mornings began; with an outpouring of love from the Virgin. And each morning, the gift was her son.

The day after he died Marie took the chair

from her dresser, stood on it and took the painting down. In the beginning it went behind the wardrobe and then when she was ready she called down to Inez.

'Inez,' she said, 'I can't have this painting in here, will you take it?'

'Of course I will,' the woman said. 'What do you want me to do with it?'

'You can do whatever you like, it's worth money. You can take it to the antiques shop if you want.'

So Inez took the painting, but she didn't take it to the antiques shop. She was a good friend, she knew that eventually Marie may change her mind.

Now the moment Inez had foreseen all those years ago had arrived. Marie wanted the painting back, just as she wanted Father Gannon back.

What's happening to me? she thought.

Those things she'd thrown out, she wanted them back. She wanted to go to the phone and call Inez right then and there. She wanted to say, What did you do with that painting, the one I asked you to take all those years ago? Please tell me you know where it is.

But she couldn't do that, it was the middle of the night.

Everything was crumbling now. The painting

was just the start. Right then and there, sat on the edge of her bed in the nadir of the night, she wanted her son back; the son she'd put into a chest tied with ropes and chains; the son she'd sent away; the son she'd buried all those years before. She wanted to wrap herself in him. She wanted him to cut open her heart and crawl inside.

Marie stood up and walked over to the wardrobe. There was a shelf at the top that had all of her old sweaters folded and piled upon it. Behind them, underneath an even older pile of clothes was a large tin. She hadn't touched that tin in years.

She took the sweaters and put them on the bed and then she stood on a chair and pulled the tin out. It said *Rover Assorted Biscuits* on the front. Marie sat down on the bed and ran her hand over the square metal lid. She could feel her fingers trembling, she was frightened to open it.

The first thing she found was a birthday card. The picture on the front was of a yellow breasted bird wearing a red bobble hat. The bird said, *Tweeting you a Happy Birthday!*

She opened the card.

To the best mummy in the world. Love Jamie.

Marie felt herself not breathing and gulped down the air deliberately. She sniffed at the card. It smelt of dankness and her son. She could smell Jamie all over it. *Is that even possible?* she wondered.

There were drawings he'd made when was very young. Some were just scrawl, crayoned lines in spasm. In others she could make out a small person and a larger person. She knew one represented her son and the other represented her. Then there were the ones with a small person and two larger people. She'd asked him about that.

'Who's this?' she'd said.

'That's Daddy.'

'Daddy? Who's that?'

But he hadn't been able to answer.

Marie had cried about that afterwards. He'd wanted a father, he'd wanted to be like the other children. She'd felt such guilt about that.

'Your father was a photographer,' she told him when the time came. 'We met when I was modelling.'

'Does he know about me?' Jamie said.

She found this part difficult. She knew children needed to feel wanted.

'Yes, I told him,' she said. 'But he had his own family and he didn't want to know.'

Marie was shocked by how much anger she still felt towards this man.

'Do you know where he is?' Jamie asked later, when he turned eighteen.

They were in the kitchen when he asked this. She was sitting on one side of the little pink table and he was sitting on the other.

'No,' she said. 'I don't even know if he's alive. Why? Do you want to find him?'

She felt the terror moving through her as she said this. The questions stacked up inside her. *What if he loves this man? What if he's absorbed into his family? What if he decides he wants his father more than he wants me?* She knew her fear was irrational but it made no difference.

'You'll tell me, won't you, love?' she said.

'Tell you what?'

'If you decide to go looking for your father,' she said. 'You'll tell me?'

'Yes.'

She knew just by looking at him.

'You're going to try and find him aren't you?'

Jamie turned away from her when she said this. He turned and looked out of the window into the neon haze of the city.

'Do you mind?' he said.

Of course I mind, she wanted to scream.

'No love,' she said. 'I don't mind.'

Later, after he'd found his father and had been to visit him, after he'd talked with him, he came home and said, 'He's just like you said.'

He was heartbroken about this, it was obvious to her, but he wouldn't talk about it. She tried to comfort him, to find out what was happening inside him, but he closed up like a clam whenever she raised the topic.

How can you have lived and died and been dead so long and I'm still here? she wondered.

She held her son's drawings against her chest. She brought them up to her face and smelled them. His fingers had once touched all these things.

I can smell him, she thought.

After a while she put everything back in the biscuit tin and closed the lid, but she didn't put the tin back on the shelf in the wardrobe. She lay it down by the side of her bed, in the soft lamplight, where she could reach for it whenever she wanted.

*

Marie sat down in one of the pews near the back of the church. She looked at the stone pillars and the arched ceiling and the slanting columns of light coming in through the stained-glass windows. She hadn't been in here since Jamie's funeral.

She looked at the altar and the tabernacle beyond it, at Jesus on the cross, at the blood trickling from the holes in his feet. She looked at the statue of Mary, at her blue and white robes, at her open hands and lachrymose face. She didn't know the name of this priest, the one who was appearing right at this second, the one who was crossing himself and looking out over his thin congregation.

When it was time to say the *Hail Mary*, she realised she hadn't recited that prayer in seventeen years.

Blessed art thou among women. Blessed is the fruit of thy womb, Jesus.

It made her feel strange to say the words. She really only mouthed them but it made no difference. She hadn't intended to take communion but something led her from the pew and down the aisle. Butterflies drifted along the terrain of her stomach.

The woman in front of her was wearing a chiffon blouse. She'd known this woman once. Her name was Judith and she'd worked in the supermarket, in the section with the cold cuts. One day she'd come out from there and said, 'How are you?' and then she'd said, 'If you want anything, you must let me know.' And just like that she'd returned to her glass counter without pressing Marie for a response. This was a long time ago. She was probably retired now. Marie didn't know, she hadn't been in that supermarket for years.

After the service, she sat down and waited for the congregation to file out and then she hung back a little longer, and this was when the priest came to her and asked if she was alright.

'You don't know me,' she said. 'I used to come to this church many years ago.'

'Oh,' said the man. 'Did you leave the area?'

'No, I lost my faith.'

She could see his expression shift.

'I see,' he said, and he sat down beside her. 'Is this the first time you've been back?'

'Yes.'

'Well I'm glad you've come,' said the priest.

'I had to,' she said. 'I had a vision.'

'A vision?'

'Yes. Or an instinct. I had an instinct to speak to Father Gannon.'

'Father Gannon?'

'Yes.'

The priest said, 'I'm afraid he isn't at this parish now.'

'Oh, I know,' she said. 'He's been gone years. I just wanted to know if you could help me find him.'

The priest looked at her.

'Well I can try,' he said. 'But is there anything I can help with? Perhaps you could talk to me first.'

She smiled.

'I don't think so. You see, my son died and Father Gannon tried to help me at the time, only I was very angry and I shut him out. And now I'd like to see him.'

The priest nodded.

'I see,' he said.

*

For a while she sat there at the kitchen table, staring at the number on a slip of paper. Then she pushed the digits and held the phone to her ear. It rang for a long time and finally a voice said, 'Hello?'

'Hello,' she said. 'Could I speak to Father Gannon?'

'This is Father Gannon. Who's calling please?'

'It's Marie,' she said. 'Marie Tierney.'

For a moment, the line was silent.

'Marie? I don't believe it. How are you?'

His voice hadn't changed.

'Father,' she said.

'Marie, I'm so pleased to hear from you. I've been praying for you all this time, you know.'

He could hear her sobbing.

'It's alright,' he said, 'just take your time, don't worry.' He waited, breathing softly into the mouthpiece.

'I'm sorry, Father.'

'Oh, you've no cause to be sorry.'

'Father, are you in London?' she said. 'It's a London area code.'

'Yes, I'm back in the city.'

'Since when?'

'Oh, three years now. I was up in Cumbria for eight years and now I'm back. This is my final assignation, as it were.'

'Father,' she said, 'can I see you?'

'Of course.'

'Can I come tomorrow?'

'Tomorrow?' he said. 'I don't see any reason why not. I have a service in the morning and house-calls until two or so. Could you come at three?'

'Yes, that's fine,' she said.

*

I'll have to do something with myself, she thought. *I can't turn up to Father Gannon like this.*

She walked into the hall and looked in the mirror. 'Look at the state of you,' she said. 'You'll have to shape yourself, Marie.'

She went to her room, sat down at her dresser and opened the drawer containing her make-up. She started with the foundation and next she applied bronzing powder. When she was done, she stood up and went to the mirror in the hallway. She looked herself up and down and let out a sigh.

'It'll have to do,' she said.

Marie sat on the tube in the black suit she'd bought in the seventies and the pixie boots she'd bought the following decade and twirled a thread of long grey hair around her finger. It was hot in the carriage.

How can people bear this day in and day out? she wondered.

Next to her was a man with large black discs in the lobes of his ears. He had a phone in his hand and on the screen were many different coloured balls or symbols and he was doing something to them with his fingers and they were exploding. She wanted to ask him about it, but he had his earphones in, he wouldn't hear her.

The church was set back off the street behind a row of trees. It was an old church, a church with a spire that had pointed up to the clouds for well over a hundred years. Marie liked this church immediately because it reminded her of the church in Eccleston with its lancet windows and its sloping slate roof.

She walked down the pathway and around the side of the building to the entrance. A squirrel was on the grass there.

'Hello,' she said, and the animal peered at her and worked its nose. The sky was softly white and a gauzy rain was beginning to fall.

Father Gannon was thinner and more drawn in the face. That was her impression when he pulled back the door. He was wearing silver-rimmed glasses that sat on the bridge of his nose and the lenses magnified his eyes slightly.

'Marie,' he said.

'Hello Father.'

He smiled and ushered her inside. Once he'd closed the door, he reached out and embraced her. She could smell scent on his neck, and she remembered instantly that he always wore cologne, which was one thing that marked him out. She'd never known any priest to smell of cologne besides Father Gannon.

'Come in,' he said. 'Sit down over here. Would you like some tea?'

Marie sat down on a wooden chair. 'Oh no,' she said, 'don't worry about that.'

'It's no worry of mine. Besides, I'm making

some for myself.'

'Oh, well okay then.'

'Will you have milk and sugar?' he said.

'Just milk,' she said.

She looked up at the stained-glass windows and the delicate carvings in the eaves. The stone walls were white and adorned with paintings in elaborate gilt frames, of Jesus Carrying the Cross and The Resurrection of Lazarus and Mary Magdalene.

'It's a beautiful church,' she said.

'It is,' said Father Gannon. 'Do you know, my mother used to come to this church as a child.'

'Really?'

'Yes, she used to come every Sunday. I often think about her when I'm leading a service. I look out over the seats and think, *Which one was yours?* Although I expect she went wherever there was space.'

'I expect she did,' said Marie. 'How's your health, Father?'

Father Gannon carried on making the tea as he spoke.

'Oh, I have a few aches and pains and I can't kneel anymore, but my mind's still good. Or nobody's told me if it isn't. How's yours?'

'Oh, fine,' she said.

She felt embarrassed for what she was about to say but she began anyway, it was something she wanted him to know.

'Father, I had the strangest experience. I walked out of my kitchen the other night and your face appeared right in front of me, clear as day. You'll think I'm mad I know, but it was so vivid. Anyway, that's when I knew to come and see you.'

He handed Marie her tea and sat down opposite her, behind a small ancient-looking table in dark wood. He focused his gaze on her and smiled.

'I don't think you're mad, Marie. I'm glad you've come, I really am.'

'Do you think I sound silly?'

'Not at all. Mysterious are the ways of God.'

'Yes,' she said. She hesitated for a moment. 'Father, I'm sorry. I shouldn't have stopped speaking to you, it was wrong of me.'

He flicked his hand.

'You were in pain. The most important person in your life was taken away, that's a hell of a thing to deal with. Nobody could hold anything against you. Certainly not me.'

'Father, I haven't been to church in eighteen years. I haven't said a prayer, I haven't done a thing. And now I feel like I don't know how. Will you help me?'

'Of course,' he said. He leant forward and reached for her hand. 'Would you like to pray now? Would you like to pray together?'

'I don't know,' she said. 'I don't know how to begin.'

Her hand was trembling.

'Would you like me to start?' he said.

'Would you, Father?'

'Of course.'

He closed his eyes and raised his head up.

'God,' he said, 'Thank you for bringing Marie here today. Thank you for opening our hearts enough that we can let you in even when we have no proof you're here. Thank you for allowing us to believe in that which we cannot see. Let us see that our suffering is not in vain. Let us see that our suffering exists to show us that who we are is not to be found in the things of the world, but in you.'

Marie found it remarkable that a man could speak like this, in a way that was in no way logical or scientific, with total compassion and devotion, it was a thing that men had been disallowed.

Her eyes were closed and the room was still. She could hear the breath moving through her nostrils, she could hear the traffic, the sirens of the police cars, the birds in the trees. Father Gannon's words seemed to trail off and there was a moment when something in her awareness shifted. For a long time she sat in the bliss of whatever this was, with the light all around her like the Virgin in the painting.

Finally, he let go of her hand and waited and the room was bathed in silence. When she was ready she opened her eyes again and looked at him.

'God never left me, did He?' she said.

He shook his head and smiled.

She smiled back at him and turned things over in her mind. Marie understood that nothing had changed, she could say anything at all to this man, there was nothing he couldn't hold.

'Father,' she said.

'Yes?'

'I'm not well,' she said. 'I have cancer.'

He nodded slowly and took a breath.

'I'm sorry, Marie.'

'Can I ask you something?' she said.

'Yes, of course.'

'What'll happen to me when I die?'

'Only the body can die, Marie. Death of the

body can't touch you.'

She thought about this.

'Do you really believe that?'

'I do,' he replied. 'I do.'

*

When she arrived home she sat down at her kitchen table and made a call.

'Inez,' she said, 'how are you?'

'I'm fine,' came the reply.

'Good. I was wondering about something. Do you remember that painting I gave you after Jamie died? The one of Mary.'

'I do,' said Inez. 'It's in the spare room.'

'Is it?'

'Yes,' she said. 'It's been waiting for you since the day I took it.'

'Oh, you're such a good friend,' Marie said.

'Don't be silly. What did you think, that I'd sold it to the highest bidder?'

'Ha,' she said. 'I wouldn't have blamed you.'

'Now listen, do you want me to get it down for you?'

'Would you?'

'Of course I will,' Inez said. 'When do you want it? You can come now if you want.'

'Can I?'

'Yes, of course.'

'Oh thanks, Inez,' she said. 'I just need to do a few bits and then I'll pop down.'

Marie looked into the vacant space opposite her on the other side of that little pink table; the space that Jamie had filled, first as a boy with his child's body and then with his awkward teenage body and finally with a man's body. How beautiful he'd been.

She held him up in her mind then, and the feeling that arose alongside this image of him wasn't sadness or anger or desolation, it was something she'd never expected to feel again.

She pulled a crisp white card from her purse and picked up the phone. Then she dialled the number printed on the front.

'Mr Nahal,' she said, 'it's Marie Tierney.'

'Hello, Marie.'

'Hello,' she said. 'I'm sorry about the other day, it was a lot to take in. Anyway, I've thought about it. Let's do the tests, let's see what we're dealing with.'

'Really?'

'Yes,' she said.

'I'm so pleased, Marie. You'll feel much better for knowing what's going on.'

'Yes, I'm sure you're right.'

'Can you come in on Wednesday?'

'Yes,' she said.

'Good. Can you come first thing? Nine o'clock?'

'Yes,' she said. 'That's fine.'

Printed in Great Britain
by Amazon